I0763143

BODY COUNT

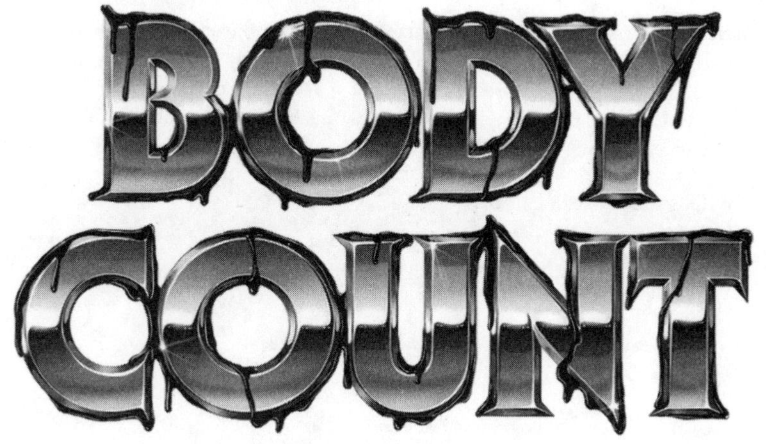

CODIE CROWLEY

HYPERION
Los Angeles New York

Text copyright © 2026 Codie Crowley

All rights reserved. Published by Hyperion, an imprint of Buena Vista Books, Inc. No part of this book may be reproduced or transmitted in any form or by any means, electronic or mechanical, including photocopying, recording, or by any information storage and retrieval system, without written permission from the publisher. For information address Hyperion, 7 Hudson Square, New York, New York 10013.

First Edition, May 2026
10 9 8 7 6 5 4 3 2 1
FAC-004510-26050
Printed in the United States of America

This book is set in Horley Old Style MT Pro/Monotype
Designed by Zareen Johnson

Library of Congress Cataloging-in-Publication Data
Names: Crowley, Codie, author
Title: Body count / by Codie Crowley.
Description: First edition. • Los Angeles : Hyperion, 2026. • Audience: Ages 14+ • Audience: Grades 10–12 • Summary: "When Sundae Valentine arrives in Wildwood, NJ, for a killer prom weekend, she comes face-to-face with a monster who is determined to make her pay her debts"—Provided by publisher.
Identifiers: LCCN 2025015602 • ISBN 9781368101424 hardcover • ISBN 9781368115513 ebook
Subjects: CYAC: Monsters—Fiction • Wishes—Fiction • Murder—Fiction • Lesbians—Fiction • Horror stories • LCGFT: Horror fiction • Lesbian fiction • Novels
Classification: LCC PZ7.1.C7725 Bo 2026 • DDC [Fic]—dc23/eng/20250320
LC record available at https://lccn.loc.gov/2025015602

Reinforced binding

The authorized representative in the EU for product safety and compliance is Disney Trading B.V., Asterweg 15S, 1031 HL, Amsterdam, The Netherlands
email: DCP.DL-EU.bookscontact@disney.com

Visit www.HyperionTeens.com

Logo Applies to Text Stock Only

For the monsters who have tried to
make me small enough to swallow.

Now I'm everything you were afraid I could be.

ONE

JULY 2019

The first time Sundae saw the man who lives in the pool, she was afraid of him.

It wasn't totally his fault. She was afraid to begin with.

It was her ninth night at the Coral Cove Motel, and Sundae *couldn't* sleep. She stared at the stripe of light on the ceiling, the way it perfectly lined up with a crack in the plaster to form an upside-down P when she closed her left eye. She thrashed her sunburned legs until she'd kicked that weird Styrofoam blanket down to the foot of the bed. She even covered her face with a pillow, but she couldn't smother herself to sleep.

Because every time she closed her eyes, she couldn't help feeling like she might wake up back in her room at home. In the house where her father lived, the house she and her mother had run from with only the bags they could carry, all the way to this little motel on this little island that seemed as far away from her father's fists as possible.

Nobody knew their real names. When she was waiting tables at the Coral Cabana, the greasy motel bar facing the boardwalk, Mom wore a name tag that said *Liv* on her pink uniform, even though her name was actually Danielle. And everyone thought Sundae was named Aquamarine, like the mermaid in her favorite movie, because her mom had let her pick any name she wanted.

Mom promised he wouldn't find them here.

But the fact that they'd really *gotten away* was settling on Sundae like a healing wound, and on that ninth night at the Coral Cove Motel, it was a searingly itchy scab that kept her writhing and sweating and wide awake in bed.

Her mom had no such trouble. Exhausted from yet another double shift, Mom was dead asleep with the TV blaring, open-mouth snoring to the rhythm of "Gonna Make You Sweat (Everybody Dance Now)." Her mom, like, literally always did that and nobody ever believed Sundae about it.

So just to prove to herself that things really were different now, Sundae slid out of bed and shuffled across the stained pink carpet. Carefully, quietly, she unlocked the door and twisted the handle.

Back in the house where her father lived, Sundae never would have left her bedroom at night, no matter how thirsty or hungry she was, not even if her bladder was so full she could scream. But when she stepped out onto the motel's second-floor balcony, nothing met her except the cool night breeze blowing off the ocean. She propped the door open with the loop of the latch and listened to her mom's snores through the crack in the door, making sure she was still asleep.

Then she wandered down the balcony, to the ice machine, because if there was no one around to yell at her for leaving her room, then there was no one around to call her greedy for treating herself to a midnight snack.

One of Sundae's favorite things about the motel was the ice machine. Nestled into a dark alcove conveniently located just six doors down from their room, the humming steel hull was filled with some of the best ice Sundae had ever munched in her life. It made the kind of ice with a hole in the center, like a little empty ice cannoli, and Sundae could have as much as she wanted *for free*.

Sundae wasn't sure what time it was when she left the room, but it must have been pretty late because the balcony that wrapped around the motel's second floor—usually bustling with sunbaked vacationers—was totally empty. So was the courtyard below, and the pool that gleamed in the center like a bright blue crown jewel.

And as much as she liked the ice, the pool was definitely her *most* favorite thing about Coral Cove.

Back home, Sundae had been the fastest on her swim team and one of the strongest swimmers in her division. When she and her mom ran away, she'd had to leave behind all the ribbons and trophies that proved it. (She wondered if her dad had already thrown them all in the trash. He always said it was vain and stupid to clutter her room with them, said they give out awards to anyone these days.) But back home, she could only swim at practice, or on the days when her mom got off work early enough to take her to the pool.

Here, she could swim *whenever she wanted.*

And every day since she'd come to Coral Cove, Sundae had spent as much time as she could in the pool. She rarely even changed out of her bathing suit, which annoyed her mom a little, but not enough that she stopped Sundae from wearing it to bed.

That night, as she stood on the balcony, crunching on an ice cannoli while she looked out at the motel courtyard, a breeze blew in that was strong enough to make the pool gate bounce and clang. It drew

Sundae's attention to the swinging gate—and to the hand-painted sign posted there.

CORAL COVE POOL RULES
No diving.
No running.
No glass.
DO NOT OPEN YOUR EYES UNDERWATER.

Before that moment, she'd never noticed it—but once she did, she couldn't stop looking at it.

That last rule.

It just didn't make any sense. Like, sure, chlorine burns, but why was that rule down at the bottom of the sign in bright red brush-strokes, screaming loud in all caps like it was the most important of them all?

And why did she feel like that rule was made to be broken?

Little drip-drips from the ice in her hand made a trail down the pink steel staircase as she descended to the courtyard. She stopped in front of the pool gate and stared at the sign while she popped another ice cannoli into her mouth. It wasn't a *new* sign—the wood was weather-worn and the paint feathered with cracks—so it seemed like this arbitrary eyes-closed rule had really stood the test of time.

She bumped the gate open and stepped through.

She brushed some beach sand off a wobbly side table and deposited her handful of ice on the frosted-glass top. She snapped the scrunchie off her wrist and twisted her blond hair into a topknot. She tapped her toe against the glittering surface of the water, testing the pool's temperature.

And then she jumped in.

Cool turquoise swallowed her, and she sank into the deep end. When her toes scraped the slick tiles at the bottom of the pool, Sundae floated there like a music box ballerina.

She opened her eyes.

Marbled light snaked across the pool floor, the courtyard lamps refracted by the rippling water. Bubbles swirled around her like pearls. The water pressed against her ears, filling them with muffled swishes, gurgles, and glug-glugs as she bobbed in the undulating blue.

She looked out at the length of the pool before her, inclining gently all the way to the staircase at the shallow end. Without all the splashing kids and swimming vacationers, the pool seemed huge and hollow. Her toes poked at the aqua mosaic below, the ground slowly slipping away as she floated back toward the surface.

Maybe that rule really was there for no reason. Maybe the worst that would happen if you opened your eyes inside the pool at the Coral Cove Motel was a case of conjunctivitis.

But as the breath held in her chest began to thin, she heard something else in the muted murmur of splishes and glugs.

Something like . . . a growl.

And she realized: Ever since she'd opened her eyes, she'd just been suspended there, staring out at the length of pool ahead of her.

She never turned around to see what might be behind her.

Sundae kicked her legs and twisted in the water. At this end of the pool, the courtyard lights were just a distant glimmer. Sky blue faded to darkest night. And as she floated there, lungs burning, she saw something in the shadowy deep.

It was his eyes that she noticed first. The way they shone like two silver coins, glinting in the murky dark. Shrouded by shadow, he crouched perfectly still in the corner of the deep end, like a spider in an eave. Between the ripples of water, she could make out his shape. The suit he wore, brown as tree bark. A crown of holly on his head, berries red as rubies.

And his mouth, when he smiled, full of pointed black teeth.

Everything that came after was a blur. Sundae screamed. She swallowed a bunch of pool water. She smashed her knee on the concrete pavers climbing out of the pool. She ran so fast across the courtyard and up the pink steel stairs that her feet hardly touched the ground, and when she made it back to room 257, she leapt into bed and yanked the musty comforter over her head.

She woke up the next morning to a damp chlorine-scented bed, the sheets streaked with bloodstains from her busted knee. Mom didn't notice as she sleepwalked out the door in her pink Cabana miniskirt, and Sundae swiped fresh sheets off a housekeeping cart so she'd never find out.

For the next few nights, Sundae avoided the courtyard after dark, and whenever she passed the pool gate with its hand-painted sign—DO NOT OPEN YOUR EYES UNDERWATER—his sawtooth smile flashed inside her mind.

And, even during the day, when the sunlight would shine through the water like sea glass, Sundae refused to swim in the pool.

Instead, Sundae sat in the shady motel room, watching TV and filling in the pages of the marine-life coloring book her mom got her on the boardwalk, giving all the fish multicolored scales and glittery fins with her big box of crayons.

But after a few days of this, Sundae had colored every page of her book, and her mom had started to notice something was wrong.

Again and again, she asked Sundae why she wasn't leaving the room, but no matter how many times her mom questioned her, Sundae didn't tell her the truth. It wasn't because she thought her mom wouldn't believe her; it was because she didn't want to be the reason they had to run again.

So, when her mom forced her to come to work with her instead of sitting in the room all day again, Sundae saw the man from the pool for a second time.

She didn't notice him at first. Her mom sat her at the bar, and Sundae perched on the edge of the pink vinyl stool, smacking her flip-flop on its bamboo leg while she stared out at the pool through the window. She only turned around to face the bar when her mom brought her a plate of French toast and an icy strawberry milkshake.

She opened her mouth to say thanks, but her jaw dropped open instead.

There, over her mom's shoulder, was the man from the pool.

Well, not *physically*, but his picture was hanging there inside an old wooden frame. He looked different because his teeth weren't sharp and serrated and his eyes didn't glow like mirror glass, but it was *him*. He was smiling in black-and-white, striking a merry pose with a guitar in his arms and a sprig of holly pinned to the lapel of his suit jacket.

And in big, looping script, the photo was signed with black ink: *Holly Jolly*.

"Baby? What's wrong?" Sundae's mom asked, glancing over her shoulder like she expected to see a different monster looming behind her. Seeing the fear in her mother's eyes reminded Sundae why she'd never mentioned what she saw in the pool that night.

She shook her head quickly and reached for the frosty pink shake topped with a mountain of melting whipped cream.

"How'd you know I wanted strawberry?" she said, like the shock was just on account of a delightful surprise.

"You always want strawberry." Her mom laughed, rolling her eyes and scrubbing her fingers against the top of Sundae's head.

Then she wandered off to refill someone's coffee, and Sundae went back to staring at the photo on the wall.

Behind the counter, Tony the bartender was polishing a glass with a rag and humming along to the old song playing over the speakers above the bar. Like Sundae and her mom, Tony lived at the motel, but he'd been there way longer—Sundae had no idea *how* long, but she thought if anyone might be able to explain what she'd seen, it was him.

She speared a bite of syrupy battered toast on her fork, glanced over her shoulder to make sure her mom wasn't nearby, and then said, "Hey, Mr. Tony?"

"Yes, Little Mermaid?" he said, using the nickname he'd given her the first week at the motel, when he noticed how much time she spent in the water.

Sundae chomped on the French toast in her mouth and pointed her fork at the photo behind the bar. "Who is he?"

Tony looked surprised by the question, but then he laughed and leaned a hip against the bar between them. "He's one of Wildwood's best-kept secrets. Another bit of history they try to keep buried so it doesn't scare off the tourists." With a heavy thud, Tony set the shining glass down on the bar top and continued: "He went by the name Holly Jolly, and in the sixties he lived here at this very motel. See, back in the day, Wildwood was the doo-wop capital, and Holly Jolly was here looking for his big break. He got real close to it, too. He got a manager. He got a record deal. He got booked to headline at the

Riptide. That gig should have been the start of his career. Instead, it was the end of his *life*."

Sundae didn't know what doo-wop was, but she was afraid if she asked too many questions Tony might realize she was too little to hear this story. She got the feeling that whatever was coming next was something she'd have to appear grown-up enough to hear. She nodded, swirling her straw through the pink slush in her glass as she listened.

"See, the Riptide was *the* place for doo-wop. It was like the Grand Ole Opry for crooners. And the night of Holly Jolly's show there, his first record was hot off the press, and he was ready for stardom. But shortly after he took the stage, the whole place caught fire and the Riptide *burned to the ground*. Afterward, they could never figure out what started the fire, or why the whole place went up so quickly. But that wasn't even the weirdest part. The weirdest thing was nobody tried to get out. They all just stood there and burned alive on the dance floor."

With chills crawling up her spine, Sundae glanced at her mom across the Cabana, but she had her back to Sundae as she delivered an armful of hot plates stacked with pork-roll-egg-and-cheeses to the table nearest the boardwalk. And though she longed to meet her mom's eyes, to find comfort in the steady blue of her gaze, she also desperately wanted to hear the end of Tony's story.

Because when she looked back to him, it was clear he wasn't done telling the tale of Holly Jolly.

Tony leaned in closer to Sundae over the bar and dropped his voice as he said, "All of them except for Holly Jolly. Somehow, he survived the fire at Riptide. There were folks that saw him walking along the boardwalk in his singed suit, looking like he'd just crawled out of hell. Then he came back here, to the Coral Cove, and he drowned himself in the pool."

Sundae sucked in a tiny gasp. "He's *dead?*"

"Mm-hmm. And his music died with him. His manager had taken all the records they'd pressed to the Riptide that night, and all of them were lost in the fire. The only thing left of him is that photo and a song on the old jukebox over there. But that thing hasn't worked in ages."

Sundae twisted on her stool to stare at the jukebox in the corner, which sat lifeless and caked with dust, its neon arch unlit. She turned back and looked at Holly Jolly's smiling face in the picture on the wall, his eyes gleaming with bright excitement instead of vacant silver. "*He* survived the fire, though," Sundae said. "He could have made new records. Why did he kill himself?"

Tony shrugged, straightening back up and swiping the glass he'd been wiping off the bar top. "That's not really something I can tell ya, Little Mermaid," he said. "I guess sometimes, if something bad enough happens to somebody, they're never really gonna be okay again."

Tony's words made Sundae's body go cold, like she'd just jumped into the deep end. *Is that the truth?* she wondered. *Will Mom and me just . . . never be okay?*

"Anyway," Tony said, shrugging again. "People say that ever since he drowned out there, he's haunted this motel."

"Tony," Sundae's mom snapped, coming up behind Sundae with an empty drink tray. "*What* are you telling her?"

"It's just a ghost story." Tony laughed nervously.

"Why would you tell an eleven-year-old a story about a man drowning in the pool at the motel *where she lives?*"

"Come on, it's no worse than what the kids see on their iPhones nowadays—"

"My daughter doesn't *have* an iPhone, jackass."

"Look, Liv, I'm sorry if I scared her—"

"I'm not scared," Sundae said, blinking the glaze of tears out of her eyes. She elbowed the bar to spin on her stool and face her mom. "It's okay, Mom. It doesn't scare me."

That wasn't totally true. It did scare her.

But she needed to see the man in the pool again anyway.

TWO

NOW

Sundae Valentine is glad she lived long enough to be crowned prom queen, even if it's the last thing she'll ever get to do.

"Holy shit," she says, squeezed breathless by the arms around her waist. "We are literally going to die today."

"Jesus, take the wheel!" Amber shrieks, throwing her hands up like the speeding Corolla they're crammed into is a roller-coaster ride instead of a death trap.

"Jesus can take the wheel out of my cold dead hands," Jackie says, long nails clacking against the top of the steering wheel as she casually dips into the next lane to pass a car that's driving only twenty miles over the speed limit.

"Jacqueline, I do not want to die south of a triple-digit parkway exit," Neelima says. Her arms, clamped tight around Sundae's waist, squeeze hard enough to crush a kidney as the car swerves back into the left lane.

Crushing six cheerleaders into a two-door Corolla for a nearly three-hour drive sounded fine in theory, when nobody was taking into account the fact that they'd be short a seat belt and that Jacqueline Salgueiro sees speed limits as a dare. But now, with only her best friend's arms anchoring her in place as they hurtle recklessly down the parkway, the joke Sundae made when they loaded into the car about sacrificing herself for the team is seeming kind of portentous.

Sundae leans forward and rests her elbows on the back of Jackie's seat. "If you crash this car, they're going to take our bodies to the morgue at"—she pauses to squint at the upcoming exit sign—"*Little Egg Harbor*. Like, that's *so* embarrassing."

"Oh my god, guys, we are literally driving to the end of civilization!" Francesca whines, her gum snapping in her mouth as she pushes it around her molars.

"Relax, Fresca, it's just the end of New Jersey." Jackie sighs, exhaling a vape cloud that fills the coupe with matcha-scented smoke.

"So? The only thing south of here is, like, *the south*," Francesca says. "I don't understand why we're not doing Seaside. You guys know my dad seriously, like, *owns* half of Seaside. We could have gotten into Karma, no problem. Everyone *knows who I am* there."

"As appealing as *Sleazeside* sounds, you know why we're going to Wildwood, Frez," Tasha says. She stretches across the back seat to snag Jackie's phone off the center console and thumb through her Spotify to choose a song. "Unless you want to do prom weekend *without the football team*, we don't really have a choice."

Sundae folds her arms over Neelima's, fingers curling and gripping at Neeli's forearms. It's not because of Jackie's driving. It's because every time she remembers where they're going, she has to grit her teeth against the scream caught in her throat.

She remembers how she first heard about it: She had been leaning toward the mirror affixed to the door of her locker, swiping glimmering pink gloss on her lips while Neeli performed a dramatic reading of the texts her ex had sent her the night before. Suddenly, the hall was filled with shouts and hoots, four football players thundering past as they bellowed—

"WILDWOOD, baby!"

"Wild-WOOOOOD!"

"Wildwood! Wildwood! Wildwood!"

Still bent toward her mirror, Sundae watched them go by in the reflection. They were pushing, shoving, stirring the crowd in the hall into a frenzy of excitement, but Sundae felt tension winding up her spine. Cold doused her like a dive into glass-blue water. Goose bumps crept up her arms, raising the golden hair dusting her skin. Neeli's phone chimed in her hand. At the same time, Sundae's phone buzzed inside her purse.

"Neeli?" Sundae whispered while she watched the shock on her best friend's features as she opened the message on her phone.

"It's Harper," Neeli said. "He rented rooms for the whole team at some motel in Wildwood."

"*What* motel in Wildwood?" Sundae asked.

Neeli looked up from her phone, meeting Sundae's eyes. "Not *that* motel."

Amber broke through the crowd, breathless with her tawny shag tousled like she'd been brawling her way over to them. Her long arm looped behind Sundae's back as she said, "Fuck, are you okay?"

Sundae nodded, but her hands were shaking so badly that she nearly snapped the wand of her lip gloss trying to put the cap back on. Amber pulled Sundae against her chest as Neeli vowed revenge on the Union Tigers' star quarterback.

"He's not gonna get away with this. I'm going to kick Harper McCall's balls so far up his ass he'll only be able to jizz out of his belly button for the rest of his life. I'm going to break his kneecaps. I'm going to set his fucking BMW on *fire*."

And Neeli wasn't the only one who was *pissed*. Following the announcement that Harper McCall had chosen Wildwood as the destination for Union High's post-prom weekend, all the cheerleaders were ready to jettison their prom dates and go somewhere else—Point Pleasant or Seaside or even Cape May—*anywhere* but *Wildwood*.

They would do that for her, of course. Even though partying on the Shore after prom is an indelible Jersey tradition and all of them had dreamed of that sun-soaked last hurrah all senior year. Even though the cheerleaders choosing a different destination from the football team could fracture the entire school population, throwing the party circuit into chaos.

But it wouldn't be fair. No one else should have to suffer for what Sundae had done.

So at first, she just said she wouldn't go. That they should all have fun in Wildwood and she'd stay home and catch up on *The Bachelor* and eat her weight in weed gummies. But it became clear pretty quickly that if *she* wasn't going, *they* weren't going.

So here she is now. Going to Wildwood.

Her mom isn't happy about it, but Sundae knew she wouldn't be. Sundae waited to tell her until they were snuggled up under a fleecy blanket, watching a cheesy Hallmark Christmas romance despite the fact that it was nearly June. When Mom had almost polished off her second glass of wine, Sundae finally turned to her and said, "I'm going to Wildwood for prom weekend."

Unfortunately, she'd said it right as Mom was taking another sip, and she ended up spitting her Franzia cabernet all over the new white area rug.

Like Neeli, Mom seemed ready for war at first. Sundae had to talk her out of calling Harper McCall's dad and telling him off for allowing his son to book the rooms in Wildwood. She even offered to pay for everything if the cheerleaders picked a different shore town. But Sundae knew her mom couldn't actually afford that, and after a few tense talks, Sundae finally convinced her that everything would be fine.

And everything *should* be fine. The Coral Cove Motel isn't even standing anymore—she'd looked it up for the first time in years and seen that the pink motel and its lit-up palm trees had been totally torn down, paved over to make way for a Dave & Buster's, of all things.

Whatever door *he* crawled out of is now closed for good. Besides, even if he *could* come back, Sundae knows the rules. They're what saved her life seven years ago.

He can't do anything to her. She's safe.

But as they fly down the parkway, Sundae holds tight to Neeli's arms around her waist. While Tasha picks a Beyoncé song that gets all the girls dancing in their seats, Sundae tries not to blink, lest she see a razor-tooth smile emerging from the dark behind her eyelids.

"Sun," Neelima murmurs, resting her chin on the curve of Sundae's shoulder to speak close to her ear. "You okay?"

"I'm fine," Sundae lies. "I just see my life flash before my eyes every time Jack switches lanes." She leans forward, grasping Jackie's headrest to steady herself as the car swerves erratically. "*Jacqueline*, can we make a pit stop? I have to empty my bladder so I don't piss myself when I die."

"Oh my *god*, you're all so *dramatic*," Jackie says, rolling her eyes as she cuts across three lanes to catch the rest area.

When the Corolla careens to a halt and lands crooked in a parking space near the entrance, Sundae jerks the door handle and slides out of Neeli's lap. It feels a little better to have her jelly sandals on solid ground, but the reality of what she's gotten herself into seems to chase her all the way into the rest stop.

The building smells like congealed pizza and bleach. Sundae's glittery blue sandals smack on the sticky tile. When she hits the bathroom door with both elbows, it swings open to a row of empty stalls and a barren line of sinks.

Stealing the moment of solitude, Sundae shoves her hands under the automatic faucet and cups a palmful of water. She slurps the water from her hands as if she's only nauseous on account of a hangover and not pure gut-twisting dread.

After she's swallowed a few mouthfuls of questionable rest-stop-faucet water, she grips the counter with both hands and leans toward her reflection. Long blond hair falls over her shoulders, tickling the bare skin exposed by her crop top. Eye to eye with herself, she whispers, "This is prom weekend, bitch. Get your shit together."

It'll probably be easier once she's had a few tequila shots.

Sundae dries her hands on her denim cutoffs and heads into one of the stalls. She takes her phone from her back pocket and glances at the notifications—comments on her prom pictures, tag notifications from everyone else posting theirs, likes, and story reactions—and then she places her phone on the toilet-paper dispenser for safekeeping.

The restroom door swings open as Sundae sits down to pee. She figures it's probably one of the girls. But after a second or two, something starts to feel . . . *off*.

Sundae narrows her eyes at the crack in the door of her stall. Whoever just entered the bathroom is now prowling slowly down the row of empty stalls. Sundae reaches for the toilet paper and tears off a handful just as the prowler reaches her. A tall dark figure passes the crack in the door and then stops in front of her stall.

Sundae feels her pulse spike when they don't move on down the line.

Now she *knows* something is off.

Sundae tugs up her shorts and fastens them. The thunderous suck from the toilet's automatic flush makes her jump. She reaches for her phone, still eyeing the crack in the door—but whoever is there is waiting just out of sight.

And then he says her name, and she knows who has found her here.

"Sundae?"

"Jesus *fuck*," she breathes, falling against the stall door. She unlocks the latch and throws it open, stepping through to face the prowler himself. "What are you *doing* in here?"

Luke Panagos, the Union Tigers' best linebacker, glances around nervously, as if angry women are going to burst from the stalls to tear him to shreds. He says to Sundae, "Sorry, I—I saw you run in here and you looked *freaked the fuck out* and I just— Are you okay?"

Sundae sighs, breezing past Luke to wash her hands at the sink. "I'm fine. I just really had to pee." She flicks her eyes up to watch him in the mirror's reflection and asks, "Are you following me or something?"

"Isn't Jackie driving?" Luke says.

Sundae rips off some paper towel and says, "Yeah."

"So you think we'd be able to keep up with her?" It's a valid point. Sundae nods, and Luke continues, "Nah, we stopped for breakfast. I needed some hash browns to soak up last night's Fireball before I punish my guts again. Our confluence is purely kismet."

Sundae watches a grin pluck at the corners of Luke's broad mouth. He thinks it's cute to get all AP English on her, reminding her that he's Not Like the Other Guys on his team. His boys are all meatheads and alpha-male wannabes, but Luke Panagos is the *sensitive jock*—he volunteers at an animal shelter, he had a poem featured in the school literary magazine, he has dreams of becoming an environmental lawyer and single-handedly destroying the companies that pollute the planet with his incredible oration skills.

But despite all of his idiosyncratic book smarts, he can't seem to figure out why his fantasy about being the world's White Male Savior makes Sundae gag instead of swoon.

The truth is, if Sundae made a ranked list of the things she likes about Luke Panagos, his mind wouldn't even make the top five. It'd be a little more like this:

5) All that thick black body hair that's giving Brawny Man porn parody.
4) The sweatpants he's wearing that cling in all the right places.
3) His warm honey eyes, framed by lush, ink-black lashes that flutter dreamily every time she touches him.
2) That tall, broad linebacker frame she could climb like a tree.
1) The way his thumb rubbed slow, languid circles on her clit while he fucked her.

Because all his sweet-boy posturing isn't an attempt to get in her pants. He's already done that—two months ago, in the laundry room at a house party. What Luke wants is to make Sundae his *girlfriend*, and *that* . . . well, that's a dream even more outlandish than the one where he saves the world by suing Nestlé into bankruptcy.

He would, however, make a great diversion right about now.

Sundae turns to face him, hands resting on the counter behind her. The pose elongates her body, all the smooth tan leg exposed by her short cutoffs, the sparkling rhinestone that dangles from her navel piercing catching the light, her thin pink T-shirt stretching across her braless breasts. And of course he's looking. His lashes flutter. Her glossy lips part in a smile.

"I don't know about kis*met*, but I think you should kiss *me*," she says.

It doesn't take more than that. He steps forward. Her arms wind around his shoulders, her long nails dragging up his neck and into his hair. His mouth is on hers, tasting like whatever fruity energy drink he must have chugged on the ride.

His hands grip her waist and he lifts her up onto the counter. She hooks her legs behind his hips, crushing the crotch of his sweatpants against the seam of her shorts. She moans into his mouth, rolling her hips. Her nails scrape his scalp as she grabs fistfuls of soft black hair.

He dips his head into the crook of her neck and kisses a hot trail across her pulse while his hand pushes up her ribs. His thumb swipes her nipple through the thin cotton of her shirt, just below the flocked felt letters ironed across her chest: YOU WISH.

The door blasts open.

Amber's snorting laugh echoes off the empty stalls. Jackie hoots, Francesca groans. Luke jerks away from Sundae, leaving her flushed on the counter, legs hanging limp as she grips the ledge between her thighs to keep from tipping forward.

"This is so depraved," Tasha says appreciatively.

"Woooow," Neeli jibes, coming in behind Tasha. "I can't believe you'd try to get a head start on the Slut Cup like this."

"Slut Cup?" Luke says.

"None of your business, turd," Jackie assures him, hip bumping the counter as she leans into the mirror to adjust one of the butterfly clips adorning her hair.

"Yeah, get the fuck out of here," Amber says, pointing at the door.

"Harper is out there looking mad lonely in the McDonald's food court," Tasha adds.

"I think he was crying into his Egg McMuffin," says Neeli.

Sundae giggles at the mental image and hops off the counter. She turns her back on Luke, checking her reflection—her lips swollen from kisses and her hair tumbled to one side, her cheeks aglow with rosy flush.

"Uh—okay, see you later, Sundae," Luke mumbles as he retreats to the door.

"Uh-huh," Sundae returns.

"Get *out*," Amber repeats, and Luke promptly obeys. Sundae giggles once he's gone, Neeli joining in as she sidles up beside her.

"I wasn't trying to cheat," Sundae assures Neeli. Sundae has utmost respect for the rules of the Slut Cup, the secret competition where the cheerleader with the highest body count on prom weekend is awarded the Slut Crown. "It was just a warmup."

"Sure, sure. A little dick pregame, so to speak." Neeli nods.

Sundae smiles at Neeli's reflection beside her own in the mirror. "Besides," Sundae purrs, "it's you bitches who are gonna need a head start."

THREE

NOW

By the time Lurch pulls into the parking lot of the Blue Velvet Inn, Lia is pretty sure the van's engine is about to burst into flames.

Honestly, it's a wonder the old Chevy G20 made it all the way down to Wildwood at all. Lia and her bandmates named their van Lurch after the Addams Family's faithful servant, not just because it was thematically appropriate considering the band's name—Morticia—but also because of its slow, lumbering qualities. It was already thirty years old (with two hundred thousand miles on it) when they acquired it for two thousand dollars from some sketchy dude Dallas found on Facebook Marketplace. And *since* acquiring it, the van has ferried the band and their gear to countless basement shows. Not that they've ever gone much farther than New Brunswick, which is only about twenty miles away from their hometown.

Well, except for the time they drove out to Philly, but Lia doesn't want to think about *that*.

It's hard not to, though, since the whole reason they drove the van nearly to combustion all the way to Wildwood is that Lia is kind of desperately trying to make up for what happened in Philly.

Booking Morticia a gig at the Blue Velvet is an act of atonement. It won't *really* make up for what happened the last time her band was supposed to play a show, because doing a set at Lia's aunt's motel in Wildwood doesn't quite compare to *opening for Spaced,* but Lia can't take back what she did in Philly.

All she can do is hope that it doesn't happen again.

"This kinda looks like the motel from *Devil's Rejects,*" Dallas declares, wrenching the back of the driver's seat as he shoves his head between Lia and Edison.

"Actually, it really doesn't," Edison says. "I don't know why you even think that."

"It's *blue,* dude," Dallas says.

"The motel in *Devil's Rejects* is, like, teal," Edison says. "This one's more of a cornflower."

"You're more of a cornflower," Dallas grumbles, dropping back onto the milk crate that has been his seat the entire ride, his gangly legs sprawled in front of him.

Lia twists the steering wheel as she guides the puttering van into a parking space, ignoring them both. Dallas and Edison are savants of weird media, constantly collecting knowledge of horror films and comic books for their YouTube channel, Ballbuster Video. Since the three of them have been best friends longer than they've been bandmates, Lia is used to zoning out during these kinds of debates.

"Rob Zombie makes no fuckin' sense to me, dude. How can a guy from Massachusetts pull off *Texas Chainsaw* hicksploitation so well, but totally shit the bed when he tries to do New England horror?" Dallas rants from his milk crate.

"*Lords of Salem* doesn't *totally* shit the bed. It did give us that scene where the lady from *They Live* spits on a baby," Edison says.

"Shit." Lia twists the key, killing the ignition with a long-suffering sigh. "I don't know what's more annoying, the way this van's fan belt has sounded like a dying pterodactyl for the past fifty miles, or you two numbskulls."

"That's the fan belt? I thought you were just playing a really long AC/DC song," Edison says, cracking open the passenger door to let the ocean breeze into the stuffy van.

"Good news is, if Lia deserts us again, Lurch can replace her and we can become an AC/DC cover band," Dallas says.

Lia's heart squirms in her chest. Even though they've talked about what happened in Philly (kind of), and even though Dallas and Edison claim they understand (kind of), Lia knows they haven't *actually* forgiven her for it.

Maybe after this weekend, they'll truly believe she'd never do it again, and they'll finally forgive her.

Just as long as she *doesn't* do it again . . .

As if he senses Lia's discomfort, Edison breaks the silence to ask, "So this is your aunt's place, huh? And it's . . . a motel *and* a museum?"

"And a diner. And a venue," Lia says, a little froggy from the tightness in her throat. She unbuckles her seat belt, the fabric dragging across the bare strip of stomach beneath the jagged edge of her cutoff Circle Jerks T-shirt as it recoils. She swings her door open, the wind blowing across the Wildwood boardwalk whipping her short black hair against her jaw. "Come on, asswipes. Let's check in, and I'll give you the tour."

It won't be the first time her best friends have met Lia's aunt Violet, but it *is* their first time seeing the Blue Velvet. The motel is all mid-century kitsch, painted milky blue and adorned with gilded stars and moon-shaped sconces, a celestial theme that carries over into the attached diner, where all the tables are lit by starburst pendant lamps and the booths are covered in shimmering blue vinyl. At the end of the parking lot, a pole rises up, and the yellow crescent moon atop it seems to dangle on the skyline above the boardwalk. The cat perched on the moon and the smooth cursive lettering that reads BLUE VELVET INN glow indigo in the dark, but right now, in the glaring sunlight, the neon coils are dead as empty seashells.

The back doors of the van fly open as Dallas tumbles out, his grubby white Chuck Taylors hitting the asphalt with a loud smack. Edison is slower to lumber out of the passenger seat, the sun catching on the buttons and spikes stuck to his denim vest.

"Should we grab the gear now?" Dallas asks, looking back into the van as he straightens his wrinkled silk shirt, a staple of his wardrobe ever since he came back from visiting his grandma in Seoul over winter break with a suitcase full of them. This one is black, and patterned with gold ropes and pink flowers.

"We'll come back for it," Lia says. She's getting that sweaty, nauseous, blurry-brained feeling she gets when she thinks about playing music lately, and she's afraid that if she picks up her guitar case right now, she might run across the boardwalk and fling it into the ocean.

Lia leads the way across the parking lot, keeping the boys at her back so they won't notice how queasy she looks.

It'll be fine, Lia reminds herself. They'll do one little set onstage in the diner attached to her aunt's motel, to a crowd that won't be much bigger than the ones they've played to dozens of times at basement shows before. It's no big deal. She can *do* this.

But as they step into the courtyard of the Blue Velvet Inn, Lia feels dread coil tighter around her chest.

Normally, Aunt Violet's motel attracts a specific sort of clientele. It is, after all, a carefully restored Wildwood relic, a testament to the doo-wop days of yore, with rooms named after music legends that have been part of the island's historic music scene. Plus, the motel is filled with artifacts, a shrine to Wildwood's place in rock and roll history. Stuff like the neon sign that used to sit above the entrance to the Rainbow Club, where Chubby Checker first performed "The Twist," which now hangs inside the motel's diner. Or the yellow vinyl booth seats from the lounge in the Hof Brau Hotel, where Bill Haley and the Comets played their first gigs, that now line the motel lobby. Or Diana Ross's feather boa, or Sammy Davis Jr.'s drum set from when he used to play in his father's band, or a poster of Bobby Rydell covered in lipstick kisses from his adoring fangirls.

Because of all this, the guests who choose to stay at the Blue Velvet tend to be old enough to remember the doo-wop days themselves, or at the very least they come to appreciate the aesthetic. But today, the motel courtyard, a blue horseshoe that surrounds the kidney-shaped pool, isn't populated by geriatrics and placid-faced Music History Aficionados.

No. The place is absolutely teeming with *teenagers.*

"Oh my god. It's prom weekend," Lia says, horror threaded through every word.

"Well, duh," Dallas says. His brown eyes narrow as he adds, "Wait. Did you seriously not realize it's *prom weekend*?"

"I mean, she's been a little preoccupied—" Edison starts to say, but he seems to think better of it when he notices the look on Lia's face.

"Right. Well. Surprise, it's prom weekend," Dallas says, waving his hands like a magician who just conjured an absolute nightmare out of a hat.

Lia *had* been too preoccupied to realize that their show at the Blue Velvet would fall on prom weekend. It isn't as if Lia or her bandmates even *went* to prom, and Lia doesn't pay much attention to all the coming-of-age bullshit that the general high-school population is preoccupied with. She's not even sure what the difference is between prom and homecoming. But maybe, if she hadn't been so strung out on her post-Philly mental breakdown, she would have realized that they were *going to the Jersey Shore on prom weekend.*

"Thanks, I hate it," Lia says as she recovers enough from the shock to keep walking across the courtyard, passing groups of kids just like the classmates who call Lia and her friends cruel names, the kinds of people who will look back on high school fondly because it's all downhill from here for them.

Lia finds Aunt Violet in the lobby, checking in a group of meat-head boys. Instead of sitting in her cushy rolling chair, Aunt Violet is standing behind the desk. But apparently not even her six-foot frame and full sleeves of tattoos can intimidate these guys into behaving themselves.

"Phone number?" Aunt Violet asks them.

"Sorry, you're not really my type," one of the boys says, and behind him, his crew of equally meat-brained buddies all laugh.

Aunt Violet is unfazed. Her dark eyes stare daggers into the boy, the rotating fan on the counter sweeping by to blow her long black hair back like coiling snakes. Calmly, she says, "You can give me the number you booked the room under, or you can go sleep under the boardwalk with the wharf roaches. Your choice."

"Just give her the number, Harper," one of the other guys says, rolling his eyes. He's taller than the others, and hairier, but what really sets him apart is that he kind of looks like a sad Labrador, while all the other boys around him are more like hostile Chihuahuas. He says in a petulant voice, "I want to have my room ready when Sunny gets here."

"Right. I forgot, we're doing—what were we calling it again? Operation Slut Shaming?" Harper says, turning to face his friend.

"Operation Taming of the Slut." The other boy sighs. "It's a Shakespeare reference. You wouldn't get it."

"Bro, you don't really think that Sundae Valentine is going to let you lock it down on prom weekend," says a guy whose lips are severely in need of Chapstick.

"What's that supposed to mean?" the Labrador boy asks, and the others laugh like he must be joking. Before any of them can answer, Aunt Violet interrupts by clicking loudly on the keyboard behind the check-in desk.

"All right. Wharf roaches it is," she says.

"Wait, all right, all right," Harper says, turning to her, holding up his hands as if in surrender. But there's a tone in his voice, like *she's* the problem. "They should be under McCall. Harper." He recites his phone number, and Aunt Violet reluctantly hands over a couple room keys, never breaking her cool demeanor.

"Thanks, Mommy," Harper McCall says as he takes the keycards from Aunt Violet. He laughs, and his friends do too, a perfect gaggle of sycophants. They head to the door, still pushing and shoving and shouting about some poor girl.

"Watch out, boys," Aunt Violet says as they go. "This is an old building, okay? It's made of hard laths and plaster. Don't punch any walls, you might hurt yourselves."

Lia and her bandmates step aside as the boys pass, none of them even seeming to notice the trio. That's fine—Morticia learned long ago that it's better to be invisible to that crowd, anyway. When they're gone, Lia turns again to Aunt Violet, who is coming around from behind the desk in her black slip and cowboy boots.

"Magnolia, remind me to take the energy drinks out of the vending machines. It's going to be a rough weekend," she says, even as she sweeps her tattooed arms around Lia to crush her into a hug.

"Hi, Aunt Vi," Lia grumbles against her aunt's shoulder.

Aunt Violet releases Lia, turning to give Dallas and Edison quick squeezes, too. The three of them have been friends for so long that Aunt Violet has watched the boys grow up alongside Lia, and she treats them like they're her own nephews.

"That was some impressive mean mugging, I do declare," Dallas says as he returns Aunt Violet's hug.

"Yeah. I think one of those dudes might have peed a little," Edison agrees.

"They suck. As if I needed a reminder of why I can't wait to be done with high school," Lia says.

"I hate to be the bearer of bad news, my love, but that little pack of Brock Turners won't get any better after high school. In fact, as their hairlines recede, they might even get worse," Aunt Violet says.

"Wow. Savage, Auntie Vi," Dallas says.

The lobby looks the same as the last time Lia saw it, except for one thing: The walls are still painted blue as a night sky, the lamp on the tall check-in counter still glitters with iridescent crystals dripping from gilded florets, and the yellow booths from the Hof Brau still frame the wide window. But in the corner, next to a big plastic palm tree, is a new addition.

A jukebox.

Lia isn't sure why it catches her attention, like a loose nail snagging the thread of a sweater. After all, the motel is full of stuff like it, and Aunt Violet is always acquiring new pieces for her collection. But the jukebox is looming in the corner of the lobby, where no sunlight seems to reach it, and Lia feels goose bumps crawl up the back of her neck as she notices how the dead lights seem to watch her like unblinking silver eyes.

She twists away from it abruptly, facing Aunt Violet.

"What's up with the jukebox?" she asks.

"Oh, that?" Aunt Violet says, casting it a glance. She turns her big dark eyes back to Lia and smirks. "The guys over at the Historical Society rescued that from the Coral Cove before it was demolished."

"Does it *work*?" Lia asks, doubtful.

"Nope. Apparently, it hasn't worked since the day Holly Jolly died," Aunt Violet says. She leans an elbow on the lobby counter and the yellow bulb in the gilded desk lamp slashes sharp light across the angles of her face. "The Coral Cove Motel is gone now, but in 1961, a doo-wop singer called Holly Jolly was staying there while trying to make it big in the Wildwood music scene. But when he finally got a gig, it was at the Riptide, the night of the fire, and he was the only survivor. Afterward, Holly Jolly went back to the motel, wrapped himself in chains, and drowned himself in the pool. Legend says that the pool at the Coral Cove was so haunted, the old owner had to put up a sign warning people not to open their eyes underwater, lest they catch sight of the specter of a drowned doo-wop singer."

The tale of a disastrous gig feels a little too personal right now. Lia swallows hard, then tries to play it off by croaking, "Wow. I bet the minivan families from Long Island love that story."

"Kids love ghost stories, Magnolia," Aunt Violet says. "Besides, that jukebox is a part of rock and roll history. I *had* to have it."

Here's the thing Lia doesn't get about her aunt's obsession with collecting this junk: Aunt Violet *is* rock and roll history.

Back in 1997, Violet Vial's song "Medea's Lullaby" was a chart-topping hit. It was an angry art-rock anthem with a catchy chorus and an iconic music video—so iconic several late-night comedy shows parodied it, reenacting the shocking-for-its-time ending where Aunt Violet kisses her ex-husband's new bride at the altar and then the two women run out of the chapel hand in hand.

But between the pearl-clutching from the religious moralists (who thought they were real clever when they started calling Violet Vial *"Violet Vile!"*) and the nonstop fetishization of her music video's controversial lesbian kiss, Aunt Violet recoiled from stardom. She stopped performing, ghosted her label, and vanished into obscurity.

All of it happened well before Lia was born, but she knows the whole story, and it feels like her entire life, Aunt Violet's failed music career has been Lia's personal boogeyman. The worst-case scenario that seems to creep into Lia's head every time she writes a song, steals her out of the moment at every band practice, makes her puke behind the van before every basement show.

And when her band finally landed their first big gig, maybe it's the reason all of Lia's worst fears came true.

"What's with the salt?" Edison asks.

That's when Lia notices it, too. A circle of salt drawn on the carpet around the jukebox. Aunt Violet heaves a sigh, rolling her eyes to the crack in the ceiling.

"It's for *protection,*" Aunt Violet says.

"Protection from *what*?" Edison says. "Burglars with hypertension?"

"Triffids," Dallas suggests, and Edison immediately turns to glare at him.

"That was salt *water,*" Edison says. "Seawater kills the Triffids in *The Day of the Triffids.*"

"Yeah, but clearly the *salt* is the important part, because they eat people, and people are sixty percent water," Dallas says.

"Actually, it's kind of a huge plot hole either way, because there's plenty of salt in the human body, too," Edison says.

"Au contraire, my friend. *The Day of the Triffids* is a British film, which means the titular martian man-eating plants are eating *British* people."

"True," Edison agrees. "Their bland and unseasoned cuisine would probably ensure theirs has the lowest sodium content of all human meats."

"Aunt Violet. What is it protection *from*?" Lia asks.

"I don't know. Theo insisted on it, it's some kind of witchy shit," Aunt Violet says.

Theodosia owns the diner attached to the inn, *and* she's Aunt Violet's girlfriend. Lia's not really sure what came first—the business partnership or the relationship. Either way, it seems to work for them. But when Aunt Vi described Theo as "a kitchen witch," Lia thought she just meant that Theo is a really good cook (which is evident enough if you've ever had a meal at the Blue Velvet diner.) She had no idea it might mean that Theo is *actually* into witchy shit.

"Does she think the jukebox is haunted?" Lia asks.

"She really does," Aunt Violet says, sighing again. "Look, me getting this jukebox nearly ended our relationship, so don't bring it up to her, all right? It's still a sensitive subject."

"Yeah, um, all right," Lia says, nodding. But with the jukebox lurking behind her, Lia feels like Theo might be right.

Or maybe it's just the specter of what happened in Philly, bearing down on Lia.

FOUR

NOW

The sun is setting over the boardwalk, and Sundae is trying her best.

On the surface, her best doesn't look so bad. She's got sapphire rhinestones sparkling on her lash line and her skin shimmers with glittery body oil. She's prowling the planks of Surfside Pier on a pair of skyscraper pumps like it's her catwalk, coconut rum on her tongue and the breeze in her hair.

She's even ahead on the Slut Cup, with two tallies on her scorecard so far: the first, a quickie with some boy from Vo-Tech who invited her to his motel room to hit his homemade gravity bong. The second was Monica Barnes, the fierce and heavily pierced power forward on the girls' basketball team, who fingered Sundae on the Sea Serpent earlier in the evening. But not even orgasming while the roller coaster plummeted down a 120-foot drop could make Sundae forget where she is right now.

Wildwood.

Still, Sundae's been pretending to be okay her entire life, so she giggles and throws her hair into the wind and walks arm in arm with Neelima down the boardwalk. Somebody made plans to meet a couple guys from the football team by Curley's Fries. Sundae and Neeli are the last to arrive—the other cheerleaders are already there, mingling with the boys. Tasha is making out with Imran. She'll tie with Sundae if she scores.

Sundae releases Neeli, who has her eye on Marcus Chambers as her first score. Nearby, Jackie is sitting on one of the tables, feeding Amber a steaming fry pinched between her bedazzled nails. The two of them are giggling, thighs rubbing, cheeks flushed. Sundae approaches them and asks, "Do you guys have any more?"

Amber walks her fingers across Jackie's hip and pulls a little baggie from the back pocket of Jackie's checkered shorts. There are two bright green pills stamped with alien faces inside, and Sundae takes the baggie, popping the zip to dump one of the pills into her palm. She swallows it with a slurp of rum-spiked soda from Jackie's cup.

Maybe once it kicks in, she'll finally be able to enjoy her prom weekend.

Sundae tucks the baggie containing the remaining pill into the clamshell purse dangling at her hip before she follows her friends down the pier. They ride the Tilt-A-Whirl, and Sundae helps Jackie chug the rest of her rum and Coke. She kisses one of the defensive linemen on the Matterhorn and lets him feel her up over her thin pink minidress. She rides the drop tower with Neeli, whose sheet of black hair stands straight up as they plummet toward the ground.

Neeli and Sundae are laughing and jelly-legged when they disembark from the ride, clutching each other's sweaty palms. As they exit the gate and rejoin their group, Jackie points farther up the pier.

"Let's do that one next!" she says.

Sundae follows Jackie's finger to a ride whose flat facade is lit by dark green floodlights. The plywood walls are painted with rows of distorted trees, their gnarled branches stretching up over the roof so that the spiky wooden leaves sit atop the ride like a holly crown. Steamy fog pours from the entrance, which is arched by letters dotted with red bulbs bright as poison berries that spell out THE HAUNTED FOREST.

Up on the platform, a chain of carriages waits under the sign's red glow, their shells painted like train cars.

Dread clutches at Sundae's chest, gluing her heels to the boardwalk as she stares up at the platform.

At first, she thinks it's just that the row of empty train cars looks too familiar, like an old recurring nightmare. Or maybe it's the fact that the twisted trees painted on the front are clearly *holly* trees, the plywood leaves jagged as knives atop the ride. But then, once she finally tears her eyes away from the crudely painted details, she realizes that *everything* about the ride is a little weird, and it's not just the waiting train cars that are empty—it's the whole platform, the whole ride. There's no one waiting in line to get on, no one coming in or out, no bored attendant to take tickets at the gate. The only sign of life at all comes from the figure standing behind the row of cars, face blotted out by shadow beneath an inky top hat, one hand gripping a lever to control the ride while the other waves to beckon them aboard.

"Ahhh!"

A sudden scream makes Sundae jump. She whips around, but it's just Francesca, whose prom date has snuck up behind her and grabbed her by the waist. The two of them cackle as they head to the platform, others following behind.

But Sundae can't pull her feet off the ground to move any closer to the facade of painted trees.

"Sunny?" Neeli questions, her voice soft.

"Um," she says, tearing her eyes away from the ride to look at Neeli. "I think I'll sit this one out."

Brent Fulbrook, a running back Sundae hooked up with a couple months ago, scoffs and says, "What, are you scared?"

"Shut the fuck up," Neeli snaps, twisting to glare at him. The venom in her dark eyes seems to slap some sense into him, because Brent immediately goes pale.

"Oh shit. Sorry, Sunny, I totally forgot—"

"Keep moving, Brent, or I'm gonna Sparta kick you off this fucking pier," Neeli hisses.

"Okay, okay, I'm *sorry*!" Brent insists.

Neeli turns back to Sundae, her hands gripping Sundae's upper arms, squeezing as she asks, "Are you okay, Sun? What's up? Is it just that the front of that haunted house reminds you of Brent's jacked-up teeth, or is something wrong?"

A laugh sputters from Sundae's lips, but she doesn't know how to answer the question. Because the truth is, Neeli doesn't know what this ride reminds her of—*no one* does.

That's the worst part of all of this. Everyone thinks they know what happened to her that summer seven years ago, but all they know is what the reporters clutching mics outside the taped-off entrance to Coral Cove *said* happened. What the police settled on, once they realized that no matter how much they questioned her, she was going to keep telling the same improbable story. What they put in the articles that pop up when you google her name, alongside the photo of her wrapped in a silvery shock blanket, drenched and baby-faced, surrounded by cops and paramedics.

They don't know the truth.

After everything happened, after Sundae and her mom left Wildwood, they settled into a small apartment in Roselle for a while. At first, her mom had seemed afraid that since their names had been on the news, Sundae's dad would come and find them—but eventually, the specter of *that* monster faded, overshadowed by something with sharp fangs and a crown of thorny leaves.

There was a lot of therapy, of course, and it helped a little, but she could never really be honest with the counselors who attempted to treat her. After all the police who made her tell the story again and again, trying to convince her it couldn't have happened the way she said it did, she learned to stop sharing the whole truth. No one would ever believe her, anyway.

Sundae was in her freshman year when Mom moved them to Union. The rented house was way nicer than their Roselle apartment, and Sundae made friends fast in her new school. So far removed from that summer in Wildwood, she thought no one would ever have to know about her past.

But then someone found out.

It shouldn't have been a shock, since the articles about it always come up if you google her name. Still, it's hard enough to be haunted by the memory of what happened. She didn't need the constant reminders in the form of pitying glances and hollow platitudes.

It kind of made Sundae want to leave Union altogether, and her mom seemed ready to move if she needed it. But ultimately, what kept her was Neeli.

Everyone else only knows what they can find out if they google Sundae's name. Neeli is the one person who has actually heard some of the story from Sundae herself. But not even Neelima knows about the man in the pool with the holly crown, or the things that happened once Sundae started talking to him.

And not even Neeli knows why that row of train cars turns Sundae's blood cold.

Of course, Neeli doesn't have to know *why* Sundae's freaked out by the ride they're all getting on to realize that she is. Her protective affection is comforting, and it reminds Sundae why she agreed to come to Wildwood in the first place—so that Neeli and the other girls wouldn't miss out on their perfect prom weekend.

Sundae shakes her head and says, "Sorry, I'm fine, it's fine, I'm just . . . I'm just gonna wait out here for you guys."

"I'll stay with you," Neeli says. She looks over her shoulder at Marcus, who is waiting nearby for Neeli to rejoin him. "I'm staying with Sunny."

"No," Sundae says, reaching up to pull Neeli's hands off her arms. She squeezes Neeli's fingers against her palms, and her best friend turns and meets her eyes again. "No, I'm fine. Please go. Have fun. Pretend you're totally creeped out so Marcus holds you extra tight."

"Are you sure?" Neeli asks, and Sundae nods, but before she can reassure Neeli again, someone else cuts in.

"*I'll* stay with her," announces none other than Harper McCall, the Union Tigers' star quarterback and the reason they're all here in the first place.

Sundae never liked Harper McCall to begin with. He's a bully, and bullies remind her of her father, and if there's one thing she hates more than remembering that summer seven years ago, it's remembering the man that Sundae and her mom came to Wildwood to get away from.

But the fact that Harper chose to book the entire football team rooms in Wildwood, despite knowing what he *thinks* he knows about what happened to her here, has definitely tanked Sundae's already low opinion of him. So when he makes his declaration, Sundae has to bite her tongue to keep from telling him that he's the *last* person she's interested in hanging out with this weekend, or at all, *ever.*

She's here because she *didn't* want to cause drama. Telling the king of Union High that she finds him repugnant is the exact opposite of *not causing drama*. So instead she smiles at Harper and says, in her candy-sweet voice, "Thank you, baby, but I'm fine. This is just not for me. I can't even watch *Hocus Pocus* without closing my eyes during the spooky stuff."

"Seriously? *Hocus Pocus* is a kids' movie," Harper scoffs. "I don't even close my eyes during *Saw*."

"Wow. So brave. Maybe you should go watch over everyone in there, then," Sundae says, tossing her hair over her shoulder as she smiles at Harper.

"Yeah, see, I'm kind of *too* brave for this stuff," Harper says. "I always end up punching somebody for popping out at me or something."

Sundae stares at Harper, a little wide-eyed, and then slides her gaze over to Neelima. They share a silent look, a promise that they will *definitely* laugh about this later. Then Neelima flashes a big smile and pats Harper on his meaty bicep.

"Great. Well, you keep that bravery to yourself, then." She kisses Sundae's cheek, her sleek black velvet hair brushing Sundae's shoulder, her lip gloss leaving a sparkly kiss on Sundae's face. And then she's off on Marcus's arm, headed to the platform, green floodlights clashing with red letters to bathe them in contrasting light as they climb the stairs.

Beside Sundae, Harper gives a big sigh. He looks down at Sundae, sweat glistening on his forehead, hair glued to his temples. Sundae imagines him showing the barber at Supercuts a picture of Ryan Reynolds, and she has to bite her lip to hold back her giggle.

"So. What do you want to do?" Harper asks her, as if he doesn't already have something on his mind.

"Do?" Sundae repeats, sounding as clueless as possible. "I thought we were just gonna wait out here for them."

Harper scoffs, arching his brows. Up on the platform, the train jerks into motion, and Francesca screams again.

"You wanna just stand here? Come on, that's boring. We'll meet up with them when they get out," Harper says.

Sundae knows what Harper's expecting. The same thing a lot of guys seem to expect as soon as they're alone with her. Sometimes they're correct. Sometimes, like in Harper's case, they're very mistaken.

She sighs, leaning back against the gate outside the platform and watching from the corner of her eye as the last train car—Neeli's—vanishes into the foggy cavern of the ride, leaving just the shadow with the top hat hunched over his lever beside the tracks. Sundae pops open her glittery clamshell purse and takes out her lip gloss and a mirror.

"If you wanted to do something exciting, Harper, you should have gone on the ride," Sundae says in her silky purr.

"Nah, that shit is corny. Why don't we go check out the beach?" Harper says.

Sundae twists open her lip gloss. When she lifts the heart-shaped compact to look at the mirror, she can see the green glow of the floodlights on the painted trees behind her. "The beach? The sun's not even out," Sundae says, in the most airheaded tone she can muster. Just daring him to say what's on his mind.

But he won't, of course.

Guys like Harper McCall think they can corner a girl into having sex with them. That with the right amount of time and pressure, every no becomes a yes. A big part of their strategy involves never actually giving her a chance to say no at all.

She can feel his eyes on her, sticky as day-old spilled beer. She dabs gloss on her lips, trying to ignore him.

"So? It's better in the dark," Harper says. "You're not scared of that, too, are you?"

Sundae keeps patting the fuzzy little sponge on the end of her lip-gloss wand against her lips. It sends pleasant tingles to the back of her skull, which means the MDMA must be kicking in. To Harper, she says, "I'm fixing my lip gloss. Don't distract me."

A sweaty knuckle presses against her thigh. Harper's hand drags up the outside of her leg, pulling up the hem of her skirt as he says, "Is *this* distracting?"

Sundae's reaction is instant, all the tension in her body snapping like a hair tie pulled too tight. She drops her lip gloss and twists, sending her elbow crashing into Harper's ribs. The fist of her battering arm is braced against the palm of her left hand, driving the full force of her rage into Harper's rib cage.

He clearly wasn't expecting Sundae's reaction, or her strength. But she's the team's flyer, every muscle in her body toned and controlled, and when she hooks her elbow into him, Harper reels back with a shout.

"Wow, what the fuck?" Harper gasps, taking a defensive step away from her while he hunches over, rubbing at his ribs.

"Whoops, sorry, guess I got a little *too brave*," she says, her voice so smooth and sweet that he doesn't even seem to realize she's mocking him.

Straightening up, Harper says, "You didn't need to totally freak out. I was just joking around."

"Baby boy, if your idea of a joke is unwanted touching, you really gotta work on your sense of humor," Sundae says.

"Oh, come on," Harper huffs, rolling his eyes. "Unwanted? You were practically giving your lipstick a blowjob, you knew what you were doing."

She tries to recall the moments before he touched her thigh, and she wonders if he's right—if, while enjoying the sensation of her gloss swiping across her lips, she might have made the action seem too sensual, sending a signal to Harper that she was inviting his touch.

"I was just putting my lip gloss on," Sundae says, but her voice is worn out as a pair of old slippers. "I'm sorry if you got the wrong impression, but I'm not going to hook up with you."

"Why not?" Harper snaps. "You were literally letting Nick feel you up on the ride earlier, and Luke told me he almost fucked you in the bathroom at the rest stop."

"So what?" Sundae says.

"So you're gonna fuck everyone on the team except for me? *I'm* the quarterback," Harper says.

"Nick and Luke are not *everyone on the team*," Sundae says.

"Sure, they're just the ones you've hooked up with *today*," Harper says. "The guys talk, though. Everyone knows about you."

Sundae stares at him, her mind split like an open clamshell, pink and runny and raw inside. There's this awful half of her that thinks that maybe he's right to be angry—maybe it's her fault for leaning on the gate with the hem of her too-short dress riding up in front of him, for going out with thick false lashes and her body rubbed with glittery oil, for fucking whoever she wants and expecting it not to have consequences like *this*: the gross presumptions of guys like Harper McCall, who think that being a slut voids her right to say no to anyone.

Her voice small, nearly smothered by the sounds of the boardwalk around them, she says, "I just don't want to hook up with you, Harper."

Harper scoffs. "Look, you're not even that hot, so I don't know where you get off being so stuck up."

"I'm not being stuck up, I—"

"You wear way too much makeup," Harper interrupts her to say. "And you dress like a stripper. Guys don't actually like that shit, you know."

"All right. Why are you trying to fuck me, then?"

"You're the biggest slut at Union High. I didn't think I'd have to *try*." Harper laughs.

Sundae plants her heels on the salt-stained boardwalk, shifting away from the gate she'd been shrinking against and standing up tall enough to look him in the eye. Her voice is velvet but her words are venom as she says, "You know what? The girls talk, too, and I know not a *single* cheerleader has *ever* fucked you. You wanna know why? Because you suck. You're the worst. Nobody wants to be touched by a dude who uses five-in-one body wash and thinks Joe Rogan is a style icon."

He steps in close to her, sweat glistening on his brow, and even though the way he's looking at her reminds her of the way her father's eyes would swim in fury after too many beers, Sundae isn't afraid.

Harper McCall is not the worst monster she's faced, of that she's sure.

"You think you can get away with anything just because everyone feels so bad for you. Well, not me. I don't give a shit if you got kidnapped as a kid or whatever. Get the fuck over it. It's not like he killed you."

An airy giggle bubbles from her lips and he freezes in shock. It's not the reaction he expected, and it's definitely not the one he wanted. There's nothing guys like Harper McCall fear more than a woman laughing at them.

Sundae tosses her hair over her shoulder and takes a step away from Harper, saying, "Harper, how about you get back to me on that when you're thirty and still haven't gotten over the fact that I wouldn't fuck you tonight."

She turns, the breeze off the black expanse of beach beyond the pier gusting against all her bared skin as she walks away from him.

And though she wishes his words meant nothing, the lights on the boardwalk blur in the tears that flood her eyes.

FIVE

JULY 2019

The balcony was empty, just like the last time she snuck out of the room. So was the courtyard, the pool water gently sloshing against turquoise tiles. But when Sundae padded down the pink metal stairs, she noticed that the lights were still on in the Coral Cabana, so it must not have been as late as last time.

She passed through the pool gate, the sign's red letters seeming to wink at her in the moonlight. DO NOT OPEN YOUR EYES UNDERWATER.

First, she walked in a slow circle around the edge of the pool, staring down into the bright blue water. In the shallow end, she spotted a lost pair of sunglasses at the bottom of the pool. There was a cluster of dead bugs and candy wrappers bobbing outside the skimmer vent, waiting to be swallowed up. Sundae noticed that one beetle floating on its back was still alive, its legs skittering against the sky. She paused, scrunching her nose as she reached a hand in and scooped it out, pouring it onto the pavers with a palmful of water. She couldn't just let it drown, even if it was kind of scary and gross.

What she concluded, in her examination of the pool's perimeter, was that she couldn't see the man with the shark teeth from outside the pool. So it seemed like, if she wanted to find him, she was going to have to break the last rule again and open her eyes underwater.

Circling back to the deep end, she stood at the edge. She glanced over her shoulder at the Coral Cabana, which looked empty even though the lights were on, the echo of fuzzy oldies whispering through the open windows. It was probably only Tony inside, closing up the bar.

She should be able to do this without getting caught.

Taking a big gulping breath, she jumped into the cold blue pool.

She sank like a stone to the bottom of the deep end. She felt afraid, but not in a bad way. Afraid like the feeling in her gut on a roller coaster cranking up to a drop. The tense windup of anticipation, the knowledge that when she sees the top, she'll have nowhere to go but down—even if it's scary, even if it seems too high.

The water glugged and bubbled against her ears. The shadows seemed to bend over her as she settled against the slick blue tile at the bottom of the pool. She looked into the black abyss of the darkest corner of the deep end, where she saw him last time, smiling with his mouthful of shark teeth.

For a while, she just floated, peering into the dark. Every glimmer of light cutting through from the surface made her jump. The chlorine burned her eyes. She bobbed there so long, the breath she'd taken started to thin, her lungs closing like a fist in her chest.

And then, in the echoey depths of the pool, she heard his growl.

Two silver coins danced out of the dark. He swam face-first, like a shark, his body undulating behind him. It carried him to her in a few quick thrashes, like the flicks of a fish tail.

She wanted to scream. To kick off the bottom, break through the surface, and throw herself out of the pool. But it was too late now. The roller coaster had reached the top. There was nowhere to go but down.

He bobbed in front of her, his silver eyes gleaming in the murky deep. The points of the holly crowning his head looked just as sharp as his teeth. The suit he was wearing looked similar to the one in the photo, only instead of dapper tartan, its pattern was like gnarled tree bark.

His lips curled into a smile, showing his black serrated teeth, and Sundae thought of what Tony said earlier. *Sometimes, if something bad enough happens to somebody, they're never really gonna be okay again.*

So she smiled back at him, even though he looked like a monster.

But there was only a squeeze of breath left in her lungs. She waved at him, not sure if she was waving goodbye, and then she kicked off the bottom of the pool.

Part of her was afraid, even though she felt guilty being afraid of him. As she zipped toward the surface, she *was* afraid that she'd feel his hands snatch at her ankles, afraid he'd pull her back down toward his saw-toothed mouth.

But he didn't grab her, and after a few frenzied kicks, Sundae broke through the surface and gasped a desperate mouthful of air.

She floated there, a little blond buoy in the deep end, paddling with her feet as she caught her breath and looked around. She twisted in the water, scared she'd find his shadow rising toward her, but she didn't see him at all until she made another spin.

And then there he was, mostly submerged, only his eyes and the top of his holly-crowned head poking over the waterline.

Sundae reeled back a little, because the way his eyes were glowing over the surface of the water reminded her of the way alligator eyes shine along the bayou in the nature documentaries her mom loved to watch. But then she saw the sadness wrinkling his brow, and she swept her arms through the water, carrying herself a little closer to him.

"Hi," she whispered across the ripples between them. "I'm Sundae."

It was nice to tell someone her real name, even if that *someone* was a ghost in a motel pool. He didn't say anything, so Sundae just went on. "I know your name. You're Holly Jolly."

With his lips still submerged, he growled softly in confirmation. Then he lifted his head a little more, chin breaking through the surface. His voice was like salt water, briny and coarse, flowing from between his rows of sharp teeth.

"How did you learn to hold your breath so long?" he asked her.

"I'm a Pisces," she said, shrugging. She could have told him she learned from swim practice, but the truth was, she could always hold her breath longer than the other kids on her team. She figured it was because of her Zodiac sign, the tethered fish, that she felt so comfortable in the water.

"Do you wish to swim faster? To have fins? To be able to breathe underwater?"

Sundae considered his question, arms sweeping leisurely as she floated like an ice cube in a glass. "No," she finally said, shaking her head. "Swimming would be no fun if it was so easy."

His eyes watched her, round coins beneath his furrowed brow, the berries in his holly crown red as the letters on the pool rules sign. She asked him, "Are you stuck here?"

He nodded, and Sundae sighed, restlessly gliding her arms to carry herself from side to side. "Me too. Me and my mom came here to get away from my dad. But there's just tourists here and I can't make friends with anybody, and I miss my swim team, and I miss all my stuff."

"You wish you could go back home," he said, not a question. But

Sundae bit the inside of her cheek and shook her head, blond hair swaying through the water.

"No. I don't want to go back there," she said.

"What *do* you wish for, then?" he asked.

Sundae giggled, bobbing a little closer to him to whisper conspiratorially, "I wish my hair turned pink from the sun." She knew it was silly, but she thought it would be cool if instead of getting more and more blond every day as she baked in the courtyard, her hair went from cotton candy to vibrant fuchsia.

But she stopped giggling when she saw the smile creeping up the corners of Holly Jolly's lips.

"I can make your wish come true," he said, his voice like waves sifting through sand.

Sundae felt a ripple of excitement. Her eyes widened as she asked, "How?"

He reached out across the water, long fingers unfurling to reveal something resting on his palm. Sundae looked down into his hand, where he held three swirled saltwater taffies wrapped in wax paper. Her gaze flicked back up, meeting his gleaming eyes in the dark.

"What are those?" she asked.

"Wishes," he answered.

Greedy desire stirred in her gut, making the pull of those candies nearly irresistible. Of course, her mom and teachers had always told her not to take candies from strangers, but no one ever said anything about taking *wishes* from strangers. She felt herself reaching out before she had even decided whether she should or not, and then her fingers were closing around the candies, pressing them into her palm.

Holly Jolly's smile opened wider, splitting upward toward the holly on his head.

Sundae opened her hand and stared down at the candies. It felt like looking at presents under the Christmas tree, each one waiting to be unwrapped, full of excitement and promise. She lifted her eyes, opening her mouth to thank him—

But he was gone.

She looked back and forth across the water, then down into the starless sky that expanded beneath her, but there was no sign of him there. No shining silver eyes, no dark mass in a bark-brown suit, no crown of thorny holly.

Sundae kicked toward the edge of the pool.

She dragged herself onto the pavers, concrete scraping at her legs as she climbed out of the pool one-handed, her other fist still gripping the candies he'd given her. She sat there on the cold ground, listening to the shuck-glug of the pool filter, the gentle laps of water hitting the walls.

She opened her hand again and looked down at her three bright taffies.

Wishes.

She picked one up and pinched the ends of the wax paper, pulling, the candy spinning as the paper unraveled. She held up the taffy between her wet fingers, and the pink-and-red swirl seemed to spiral in her vision, twisting like a windmill on the boardwalk.

She pressed it to her lips so she wouldn't have to look into the whirling center.

"I wish the sun turned my hair pink," she whispered. Then she popped the candy into her mouth.

It tasted like salt and bubblegum. Gnawing on the gluey shards sticking between her molars, she closed her eyes and imagined her long blond hair turning pink as the taffy she just ate. She smiled and licked the salty-sweet residue from her fingertips.

She got up off the ground and took one last look across the empty water. Then she walked out through the creaky gate, tossing the candy wrapper in the trash can on the way.

That's when she heard his growl again.

Only this time, it wasn't coming from the pool. It rumbled out through the open doors of the Coral Cabana, and instead of being muffled by the humming glug of the water, it was accompanied by tinkling instrumentation and a sneaking beat that sounded like waves drumming the shore.

Sundae twisted on her heel, crossing the courtyard to the open doors.

The Cabana's greasy floor was sticky under her bare feet. The tables were empty and the bar deserted, the only sign of life the clank and swish of dishes being washed in the back, through the swinging double doors behind the bar. Sundae looked up at the photo on the wall, at Holly Jolly, smiling without shark teeth, sprig of holly glinting on his lapel.

Then her eyes dropped to the jukebox, the one that Tony said never worked.

It was all lit up in red and bottle-glass green, neon lights glowing through the dust and cobwebs. A record was spinning behind the glass, playing a song through the crackling speakers. Sundae stepped closer as a voice like blue silk drifted over the melodic guitar.

"One, for a path I crossed.
Two, for my love I lost.
Three, and you will come for me,
Like the tide pulls the sand back to the sea. . . ."

"Hey, Little Mermaid, what are you doing down here?"

Sundae spun around, facing Tony the Bartender, soapy suds still coating his arms as he wiped his hands on a dishrag, a frown on his weathered face. His eyes flicked to the jukebox behind her, and she watched as shock arched his gray brows.

"What the hell?" he grumbled, stepping closer. He reached over her head, rapping his fist against the top of the jukebox. "Shit. That's weird. *Shit.* Don't tell your mom you heard me cursing."

Sundae giggled and said, "I won't, as long as you don't tell her you saw me down here."

"Ah. A little quid pro quo, I see." Tony grinned. He shook his head and gave the jukebox another punch. "Did you do something to this thing? This prehistoric hunk of shit hasn't worked since—well, practically since this damn island was all holly woods."

"I didn't do anything to it," Sundae said. It wasn't *technically* a lie, but it felt like one anyway.

"Weird," Tony said again, stepping back. "All right, you just wait here. I'm gonna go close up the back door, then I'll walk you up to your room, okay? I'm not gonna tell your mom I saw you, but you can't just be wandering around here all night."

Sundae nodded, and she turned back to the jukebox as Tony pushed through the swinging doors behind the bar. She'd missed some of the song, but the rest went—

"So let this song be a warning,
For the next one you come haunting.
The wanting hearts of dreamers here,
Will find only nightmares when you appear.

"One, for a path I crossed.
Two, for my love I lost.
Three, and you will come for me,
Like the tide pulls the sand back to the sea."

When the song died, so did the power to the jukebox—it burned out like a bad bulb, the record dropping as the lights went out. It left Sundae staring at her own reflection on the dark glass, her hair bright blond under the bar lights.

She looked down at the two taffies she still held and wondered what her next wish should be.

Then she heard a crash from the kitchen.

Her slippery feet spun on the grimy floor and she faced the swinging doors. She waited for another noise—maybe the sound of Tony cursing again as he picked up something that had fallen. But the sound had been *loud*, and whatever had fallen must have been *heavy*.

And now there was just . . . silence.

Sundae walked around the bar and approached the doors to the kitchen.

"Tony?" she called, but there was no answer.

She reached out a hand, pressing her palm to one of the doors. She pushed, slowly easing it open.

"Tony, are you okay?" she asked, but again, there came no answer.

Finally, she stepped forward, through the swinging door into the kitchen.

She felt something wet and warm beneath her feet. She looked down and saw red, spreading like a flood across the sticky tiles.

Her eyes followed the tide, and she found Tony.

The crash must have been him hitting the ground, because there he was, lying by the open back door. The summer breeze blowing in rustled his wisps of gray hair, but other than that, he was perfectly still.

Except for the blood that was rushing away from his body, pouring out from his neck, his throat split open wide as a shark's mouth.

Sundae screamed, and the whole motel heard her.

SIX

NOW

"Heyyy, you wanna party, bro?" Dallas says, brows waggling as he thrusts a neon-green slip of paper at a boy passing by in a gold-and-blue letter jacket. The boy jerks away as his buddies cackle and keep walking. Dallas sighs, hand dropping, flyer undelivered. "What am I doing wrong?"

"I mean, you could work on your approach," Lia says. She's sitting on the top rail of the boardwalk fence, her back to the moonlit beach, and she's had a lot more success wordlessly passing her flyers to the teens milling past than either Dallas or Edison.

If it was up to Lia, they might not be here passing out flyers at all. It's not like she really wants that many people to come to their show. There's a part of her that keeps thinking that the fewer witnesses they have, the better—especially if she ends up doing the same thing she did in Philly. But she knows she shouldn't keep thinking about that. She shouldn't be secretly telling herself it's going to happen again. She shouldn't want to run off and hide under the boardwalk until all of this is over and her best friends have finally given up on the band once and for all and let her dream die in peace.

But of course, Lia won't admit to any of that out loud. So here she is, drumming up interest in their show tomorrow at the Blue Velvet, even though it might just mean that there are even more witnesses to her potential humiliation.

Since the flyers were the boys' idea, they had pretty much full creative control over the design—which is how they ended up with a stack of neon-green flyers that read:

MORTICIA STARS IN PROM 2: PROM HARDER

AT THE BLUE VELVET INN

5/30 AT 8 P.M.

Complete with a hand-drawn depiction of Bruce Willis wearing a tiara.

Of course, they *are* playing to the lowest common denominator, so the joke seems lost on most of the kids who take a flyer. If they look at Edison's drawing of Bruce Willis with a questioning expression, one of the band members explains, "It's like prom, without the chaperones."

That seems to do the trick, even though it might be false advertising.

Dallas huffs and leans his long body back against the fence. "What's wrong with my approach? I'm giving them *Pump Up the Volume* Christian Slater energy."

"Sorry, but what you're giving is actually, like, *Encino Man* Pauly Shore," Edison says.

"Shit, not even *Bio-Dome* Pauly Shore?" Dallas groans.

"Dude. You keep saying shit like, 'How about a leaflet for my bro-sef?'"

Lia snorts and says, "What about when he gave that girl a flyer and said, 'Here's your license to ill,' and she gave it back and ran away?"

"Wait, don't forget the part where he screamed at her, 'Don't let me catch you illing without a license, then!'" Edison says.

Dallas blows out a big sigh and tips his face up to the warm purple sky, the ocean-spray haze hanging in the air stained by the neon lights of the boardwalk. "Look, what you have me doing here, it's like asking Ingmar Bergman to direct a Marvel movie, okay? I don't know how to appeal to this audience."

"You know how to hand out flyers, dickweed," Lia snaps. To demonstrate, she holds some out to a passing group of girls, who take the flyers she offers and continue down the boardwalk. "*See?* It's that simple."

"Boring. Formulaic. Uninspired," Dallas says, but when the next group shuffles past, he says nothing and hands them some flyers. He sighs after they walk away and says, "When in Wildwood, I guess."

"Wildwood isn't boring," Lia protests, plucking a joint from behind her ear. As she lights it with the etched silver Zippo her aunt gave her, she talks around the end pinched between her lips. "Did you guys know that it's the only boardwalk in America where your chances of being eaten by a lion are not statistically zero?"

"Bullshit." Dallas laughs. "This is South Jersey, not the freaking savanna."

"No, it's true," Lia says. She takes the joint from her lips and blows out smoke, passing it to Dallas. "Back in the 1930s, there was this act called the Wall of Death on the boardwalk. It was like, a big wooden bowl, and stunt riders would race motorcycles really fast up the walls. Well, there was this entrepreneur whose wife was a stunt rider, and he bought her a lion for her act. Like, a whole-ass lion. She named him Tuffy, and she'd do this thing where she'd put the lion in the sidecar of her motorcycle and ride the Wall of Death with him."

"You're absolutely shitting me," Edison says around an exhale of smoke from the joint.

"Old-timey people be chugging too much cocaine soda," Dallas says.

"Right?" Lia laughs, taking the joint back from Edison for another drag. Then she passes it and continues, "And besides the obvious abuse it probably took to get a lion to sit in the sidecar of a speeding motorcycle, this couple also kept the lion in a little cage whenever he wasn't doing his act.

"So, one day, Tuffy must have had enough. In the middle of the Wall of Death act, he suddenly lunged up and started mauling the stunt rider lady. She crashed the motorcycle, but Tuffy didn't stop. He tore her to shreds, then hopped out of the little sidecar and started attacking all the other stunt riders in the ring. Then he started in on the audience. Eventually the cops came and shot Tuffy, but by the time they put him down, he'd killed eleven people."

"Damn," Edison says on a sigh. "Poor Tuffy. He just wanted to be a lion."

In an impersonation of a vintage Transatlantic accent, Dallas says, "'He was a king and a god in the world he knew, but now he comes to civilization merely a captive! A show to gratify your curiosity!'"

"'We'll give him more than chains!'" Edison shouts. "'He's always been king of his world, but we'll teach him fear!'"

"Do you guys ever stop being weird?" Lia groans.

"Oh, *we're* weird?" Dallas says, black brows arching. "At least the lead singer of *our favorite band* didn't have to apologize for *our* behavior on stage."

It hits Lia like a punch to the gut, so hard she even doubles over slightly on the top rail, her dark eyes dropping to the salt-stained wood of the boardwalk. There's a stretch of silence between them that feels like it goes on for centuries, though it's probably only a couple seconds, while the waves roar across the beach behind Lia's back and the yellow tram car rolls by.

Then, finally, Edison says, "Dude, that was kinda fucked up."

"It's okay," Lia blurts out, even though it's not. But this is what she's been doing ever since that night in Philly, every time they even broach the subject of what she did when they got onstage at the Spaced show—she quickly cuts off the conversation, avoiding all the questions she's sure they've been wanting to ask her.

Because the truth is, Lia doesn't know what the hell is wrong with her.

For as long as she can remember, all she's really wanted is to make music. Like it's stitched into her veins, like her heart is a drum beating, like her breath only exists to carry her voice when she sings—it feels sometimes like music is the one reason she exists at all. And as a kid, that never scared her. From her earliest memories of making up songs while she banged her palms on the dining room table, to the day she asked Dallas and Edison to start a band with her, it's always come so innately that she never thought much about it at all.

But then there were all the times when she *couldn't* be making music. It wasn't so hard when she was small and the school days were short, and even in the classroom she could get away with some singsonging here and there. But as she grew older, the times she was expected to *work* and *focus* got longer, and everyone—her teachers, her parents, even her peers—seemed to expect her to be able to tuck her whole reason for existing away like a childhood toy.

School was bad enough, but at least she had music class, and at least she had moments where she could plug her headphones into her ears and tune out the clanging lockers and footsteps on linoleum and the shouting kids around her, retreating into the cocoon of her mind long enough to recover from some of the time spent feeling locked outside herself. But then, in the summer after her junior year, her mom made her get a job.

It's not that her mom's a total bitch or anything. She's always supported Lia's interest in music, always praised and encouraged her, always did her best to get her the gear and instruments she asked for. It's just that the older Lia got, the more her mom started to treat it all like a *hobby*, like something Lia should grow out of and set aside. As if she was trying to give Lia some kind of lesson in how to do that, she gave her an ultimatum: get a job, or lose her guitar for the entire summer.

So Lia accepted a job at the first place that would hire her, and she spent the whole summer before senior year working at a *Walgreens*, and if her mom wanted to prepare her for the misery of the "real world," there couldn't have been a better way to do it. Hours and hours spent without reprieve from the bile-colored lights that burned in the ceiling, the stuffy smell of her work vest, the screech of sticky shopping cart wheels, the constant barrage of disgruntled old customers who wanted her to be as miserable as they were. She'd only get one half-hour break each shift, just thirty too-short minutes to put in her headphones and leave the planet, and even then, some coworker sharing the break room would always interrupt the sanctity of her headphone time.

And what she learned, over that awful summer, is that she cannot handle a lifetime of *this*.

Sure, Walgreens was an especially shitty job, but no matter what she does, if it's not music, it feels a little bit like drowning. So if she graduates next month, and she has to go to college, or get a job, and accept that she's going to spend the rest of her life trapped in this feeling of perpetual suffocation . . . she's honestly not sure how long she'll survive.

Lia knows the only way she's going to make it out of this alive is if she finds a way to make music her job. She knows (and everyone's made sure to remind her) that a music career is a pipe dream—but when it's life or fucking death, anything is possible.

That's why it was such a huge deal when Morticia got invited to open for Spaced in Philadelphia.

They'd played so many basements, so many hole-in-the-wall stages at whatever VFW or restaurant some punk managed to book for a show, but most of those crowds were just the same local kids seeing the same couple bands again and again. Spaced is a *big deal.* Opening for them would put Morticia in front of a huge audience. It would also mean that Lia could brag that she'd *opened for her favorite band,* which would be a truly extraordinary achievement before she even graduated high school.

It was exactly what she wanted. It was exactly what she *needed.* Which is why she has no clue what possessed her to fuck it all up.

It'd never happened before. Sure, she gets nervous before shows, she's been known to puke behind the van before playing their sets, but what happened when she walked out onto the stage in Philadelphia is so much worse than all of that.

The show might have been a big deal for them, but it was still just a punk show on a rented stage, and there was no fanfare to announce their set. They were supposed to start whenever they were done setting up. But Lia *never finished setting up.*

In every technical way, she did. The guitars were tuned, she mumbled some checks into the mic, Dallas beat his drums a little, and they had their set list written up and ready. But every time they seemed about to start, Lia would say, "Hold on, one sec." Then she'd fiddle with her guitar, even though it was *definitely* in tune, or twist on her mic stand to adjust the height, or kick the set list around to make sure they could all see it.

Her hands were shaking. The crowd was restless. Dallas and Edison kept looking at her like she must have completely lost her mind, asking if she was ready, only for her to shake her head and tinker again with this or that. After she'd stalled for *way* too long, Dallas just started without her, launching into the drumbeat for the first song on their agreed-upon set list like he was pushing her right into the deep end.

And instead of swimming, Lia sank like a stone.

She stood there clutching her guitar, feeling like her boots were melting into the ground. Her fingers never moved on the strings. Her voice never found its way to her throat. And after a couple seconds, she left.

She just ripped the plug out of her guitar and jumped down off the stage. She pushed her way through the crowd, leaving Dallas and Edison by themselves, with no lead guitar and no singer.

After about a minute of stumbling drums and clunky bass playing, the two of them were booed off the stage. Their band wasn't invited back for Spaced's next show in Montclair, and Lia heard—though she didn't stick around to see it—that the band even jokingly apologized for their embarrassing performance at the top of the show.

Ever since that night, Lia hasn't been able to understand why she did what she did, let alone explain it to her best friends. It was supposed to be a dream come true. If playing music is like breathing to her, why hadn't she been able to do it?

Edison and Dallas have asked about it, of course, but Lia has only been able to give them half answers, and every time it comes up she must look so terrified that they end up dropping it anyway. She'd kind of hoped that getting them a gig at the Blue Velvet's diner would smooth things over, but she knows that it doesn't compare to the opportunity she ruined for them. And it still remains to be seen if she'll even be *able* to perform again.

Right now, it's feeling kind of unlikely, when even a mention of what happened at the Spaced show makes her want to jump over the rail and run into the ocean.

"No, Lee, I'm sorry, that *was* fucked up," Dallas says, face scrunching as he rubs the back of his neck. "I shouldn't've said it like that. It's fine. Who cares about Philly when we got this lowbrow jock-bait post-prom rager instead?"

Dallas isn't really making his apology convincing, and Edison shoots him another look, hugging his stack of flyers against his pin-studded denim vest like he's ready to curl up into a ball of misery. Edison's ash-brown eyes swing back to Lia, and he insists, "Actually, I think it's cooler that we're getting to play for like, a totally different crowd. I mean, a punk show's a punk show, but if we can get *these* shitbrains to pay attention to us, that really means something."

"Right," Dallas says, nodding. "Right. This is totally better."

"It's not," Lia can admit, but she appreciates their attempts to reassure her. "But whatever. We're still gonna play the best show these shitbrains have ever seen."

"Yeah, let's turn these meatheads into metalheads, baby," Dallas says. Suddenly, he throws his arms up, tossing the flyers into the air. They scatter like confetti, fluttering down on the crowd that's milling down the boardwalk. "Fuck all this. I heard the dude at the piercing place by the Dollar Hut sells fireworks out of the back of his shop. Let's do some pyrotechnics."

"Hell yeah!" Edison agrees, forcefully yeeting his own flyers into the crowd. The bulk of them crash directly against the back of some jock's head, and Edison's eyes bug out at the angry roar the broad-shouldered boy lets out as he twists around to hunt for the culprit. The three of them squeal, Lia hiding her remaining flyers behind her back as she leaps off the railing and starts running down the boardwalk with Edison and Dallas.

But even as she tosses the rest of her flyers into the wind, shedding the burden of the upcoming show, Lia can feel the weight of what happened in Philly hanging like an anchor between them.

And eventually, it might just sink them all.

SEVEN

NOW

Sundae feels like the only bitch in the whole world who has ever cried on molly.

It's prom weekend. She should be soaking in a happy high, sipping prosecco and dancing with someone beautiful to music so loud it vibrates her bones. Instead she's walking down a dark beach with her heels in her hand and sticky tears in her eyes.

And she's all alone in Wildwood.

Just like she was seven years ago, when she first saw him in the cold blue water.

Well, there *are* people around. On her left, the boardwalk is a rumble of noise and light, and to her right the waves crash under the low silver moon, shining on shapes of people playing at the breakers. If she screamed right now, *someone* would hear her.

But she's still alone, because she knows something none of them know.

Sundae picks at the rhinestones dotting her eyes, plucking them off one by one, the glue melted by her tears. She's careful not to drop any on the sand—she imagines the high tide washing them out to sea and a poor little fish choking on a blue plastic rhinestone, so she dumps them into the clamshell purse slung at her hip.

She's just peeling off the last tear-slick stone when she hears a shout nearby. "Hey! Watch out!"

And then something explodes right in front of her.

Sundae stumbles back as a blast of sand hits her bare legs. The initial boom and flash of light is followed by a keening whistle, and then, high above her head, another crack. An explosion of pink streaks across the sky. Sundae stares up at it, watching the light sizzle and die, like Pop Rocks on her tongue.

And despite the wet glimmer in her eyes, Sundae smiles.

Pounding footsteps approach her, shapes running across the dark beach. Panicked voices calling out. But she's still snagged in the spiderweb of glimmering smoke overhead, unable to look away until the last spark has burned out.

When she drops her gaze, there's a girl in front of her. Sundae thinks this girl must be the weaver of the light-web, because her eyelashes spike like spider legs and she has the energy of an unexploded ordnance. There is a gravity to her. The potential for shock and awe.

"Holy shit, are you okay?" the girl is asking as she comes to a skidding stop.

"Shit, she's crying." A boyish voice snaps out of the dark as two more barreling shapes arrive.

"Yeah, because Lia almost blew her up," a second boy says.

"*You* were supposed to be the lookout, limpdick," the web-weaver growls, spinning to glare at one of the boys before turning back to Sundae. "Oh my god, I'm *so* sorry—"

But Sundae stops listening, because she realizes something that sends a chill of panic through her body. She gasps, pressing her hand to her chest as she announces, "I dropped a rhinestone."

"You—what?" the girl says.

Sundae tosses her heels aside as she starts to sift her fingers through the sand. She feels them above her, all frozen, watching as she digs. Finally, the girl thuds to the ground beside Sundae and asks, "What are you looking for?"

"I dropped a rhinestone," Sundae repeats. "And now a fish is gonna swallow it and *die* because of me."

The girl is still for another second, a pause of disbelief, before she springs into action. Another bright flare—this time, it's the flashlight on her cell phone. She holds the bluish beam out and starts raking the fingers of her free hand through the sand.

"This weekend is getting really weird," says one of the boys—the one with long brown hair that makes him look like a pile of autumn leaves.

"Really? Passing out flyers to kids who want to stick our heads in the toilet wasn't weird enough for you?" says the other boy, the one with the slick blue-black hair and shiny silk shirt.

"I mean, don't get me wrong, that was weird," says the leaf pile. "But somehow not as weird as Lia nearly sending some girl's ass into orbit with a black-market firework dubiously labeled 'Pyro Viagra,' and us subsequently engaging in a needle-in-a-haystack-style search party for a rhinestone."

"I actually don't see you *engaging* in this search at all," the web-weaver—*Lia*—says, head snapping up to glare at her friends. "Why don't you get down here and start searching before your negligence causes a freaking fishpocalypse?"

A laugh squeezes out of Sundae, surprising her and everyone around her. It's watery and weak, still soggy from all her crying, but it's a laugh nonetheless. She rubs at the puddles under her eyes, and when her hands drop away she looks around at the trio surrounding her.

"I'm Sundae," she tells them, and Lia pauses in her search to glance at Sundae with a slight furrow to her brow, but the moment passes too quickly for Sundae to get a read on what might have perturbed her.

"Hey, Sundae," says the leaf-pile kid as he gets down, phone flashlight in hand. "I'm Edison, and I'm sorry for letting Lia almost blow you up."

"Dallas," says the boy in the silk shirt, hands in his pockets as he toes idly at the ground like he's part of their efforts.

"Dude," Lia snaps at Dallas, who is kicking sand where she's trying to sift. "Can you *actually* help?"

Dallas sighs and thuds down beside them, though he seems like he's not really that invested. Sundae doesn't take it personally. She's kind of distracted, too—she's scraping her pink claws through the sand like she's looking, but she's actually watching Lia's hands.

Sundae likes how Lia's agile fingers rub across the glimmering grains and how the dimples in her knuckles crease as her hands move. She likes the way the silver rings winding Lia's fingers look scratched and rough from wear. The way her thumb slides across the sand, leaving an indentation that sends chills down Sundae's spine as she imagines those hands on her skin.

"Oh, hey!" Edison shouts, picking something out of the sand. He holds it up to his phone light, electric blue and glinting between his fingers. "I think I found it!"

Sundae is jerked back to reality as her eyes tear away from Lia's hands, turning to the rhinestone pinched between Edison's fingers. She blows out a sigh and holds up her palm to accept it, nodding as she says, "Fishpocalypse averted." She tucks the rhinestone into her purse, then looks up at the sky and asks, "You guys have any more of those fireworks?"

"Hell yeah we do," Edison says, jumping to his feet, fumbling with his phone to turn the flashlight off.

"Just hang on to your rhinestones, okay?" Lia says, reaching one of her absurdly attractive hands out like she's about to brace Sundae from the force of the blast.

Sundae hopes the moonlight doesn't show the pink glow blooming across her cheeks too clearly as she snatches Lia's wrist, yanking playfully on her arm. "As long as you're not setting them off, I think I'll be safe."

"You'd rather trust *them* with explosives?" Lia laughs, pointing at Edison and Dallas, who are hiking up the beach to the stockpile of fireworks, Dallas drumming the air while Edison shout-sings in tandem.

"Mm-hmm." Sundae nods, giving Lia's wrist a squeeze before she releases it. "I always trust a man who's willing to say *dubiously* in front of the hos."

Lia snorts and settles in, sitting with her arms hooked around her knees while Sundae kicks her legs out and drops back on her elbows to look up at the sky. The sand sticks to the glittery oil on her bare legs, but her skin shimmers like the stars, so she doesn't mind.

"You weren't crying because I almost blew you up, were you?" Lia asks.

In the distance, there's a hissing fizz, followed by the blast of another firework. Sundae watches blue light explode across the sky as she shakes her head in answer to Lia's question.

"That was actually the least terrible thing that's happened to me tonight," Sundae says.

"Do you . . . Do you want to talk about it?" Lia asks.

Sundae shakes her head again. A burst of violet illuminates the sky. The molly she took makes every flare expand outward, prismatic and gleaming in Sundae's dilated pupils.

"Sometimes, when a man is annoying me, I try to guess what celebrity he showed his barber a picture of when he was getting his silly little haircut," Sundae says, her tone sweet and airy as a puff of whipped cream. Lia lets out a throaty chuckle that makes Sundae shiver.

Lia says, "How about . . . him trying to eat a banana in public, only he refuses to just bite into it, so he has to rip off each piece with his hands."

"Ick!" Sundae giggles as another firework pops across the sky. She says, "Him sniffing all the deodorant sprays at CVS, trying to pick a favorite."

"Oh my god. Him going camping and forgetting to bring the poles for his tent," Lia says.

A cluster of orange starbursts sizzle overhead. Sundae wiggles her toes in the sand and says, "Him trying to tell a joke, but he starts with the punchline by accident."

Lia whines with pained laughter and rubs at her arms like she's trying to stave off the chills.

"Him telling you about the tattoo he wants, and it's a Celtic cross that says *la famiglia*." Lia pauses for dramatic effect before adding, "Because he's Irish and Italian."

Sundae howls, throwing herself back against the ground just as another firework sprays light over the beach. She sprawls out, laughing from deep in her belly, sand tangling in her long blond hair as she watches the cinders fall from the sky.

Lia flops down beside her, her shoulder just an inch from Sundae's, their arms not quite touching. Sundae shivers when she feels the heat of Lia's body brushing against her skin, and she instinctively scoots a little closer, so their hips bump together. The rough denim of Lia's black cutoff shorts scrubs against the thin fabric of Sundae's mini-dress. She sighs, turning her cheek to the sand to look at Lia. The flare of another firework splashes Lia's face in pink light, catching the glitter in the inky purple eyeliner rubbed at her lash line, illuminating the sharp planes of her face and the high point of her nose.

Lia squirms a little against the sand. Sundae can feel the tension in her arm as she presses against it, the lithe muscle in Lia's bicep flexing. Her voice comes out awkward and throaty when she says, "These fireworks are pretty cool."

It's such a nonsense, nothing statement, and Sundae can't hold back the giggle that pours from her lips. "Am I making you nervous?" she asks, close by Lia's ear.

"Uhhh . . ." Lia gulps, then turns her face toward Sundae's. Her wide eyes seem to answer for her, molten brown and sparkling with the reflections of embers as they stare into Sundae's. "I'm just, like . . . always nervous."

Another firework explodes across the sky. Sundae scooches a little closer to Lia, their bare legs brushing. *"Always?"* Sundae says, a frown pulling at the corners of her mouth. "That must get in the way a lot."

"It really does," Lia murmurs. Sundae catches Lia's eyes flicking down to Sundae's lips. Their faces are close enough that Sundae could just tip her chin up and press their mouths together, and Sundae licks her gloss-sticky lips at the thought, but she won't do that. Not when Lia seems so tense.

Instead, Sundae fidgets a little, dragging her purse across the sand to dig her fingers inside. She draws out the little plastic baggie she tucked away earlier, one vibrant green pill still stashed inside. She holds it up over Lia's face and asks, "I'm not a doctor or anything, but have you tried drugs?"

Lia turns her head, eyeing the baggie pinched between Sundae's glittery nails. "What is it?"

"Molly," Sundae tells her. "If you think the fireworks are cool *now*, you should see them on this."

Lia lifts a hand, taking the baggie from Sundae. She brings it close to her face to squint at the pill inside. "Did you take one of these?"

Sundae nods, settling in against Lia's side again, leaving her purse open on the sand.

"Did you test them? Like, for fentanyl?" Lia asks.

"Amber did. She always does. She's a Cancer," Sundae says. "You don't have to take it if you don't want to. I'm not trying to pressure you or anything."

Lia looks to the baggie again, her other hand coming up to tentatively pop the zip. "I know. You're not pressuring me." She brings the baggie up to her lips and squeezes it open, letting the pill drop out into her mouth. She swallows, turning her cheek to face Sundae as she does. "How . . . long does it take to work?"

"It's usually like, a half hour," Sundae says, watching another firework explode in the reflection of Lia's dark eyes. Her fingers crawl across the sand, finding Lia's hand, linking their pinkies. "Let me know when you feel it."

Sundae looks up to the sky again, the fizz of the fireworks like champagne on her tongue.

For a while, she forgets how Harper McCall made her feel. She forgets the tears she cried. She doesn't think about what happened that summer seven years ago. She doesn't even think about being in Wildwood at all.

She just laughs, and lies on the sand with her pinkie hooked to Lia's, and watches the fireworks.

And sometimes she watches Lia, too.

She watches the way Lia pushes the heel of her boot idly across the sand, digging a little trench for her foot to rest. The way she pushes her hand through her glossy dark hair to drag it away from her face when she laughs especially hard. The way the collar of her cropped T-shirt hangs loose on her neck, the way the fabric looks worn so soft. Sundae wonders how the shirt would feel on her own skin if she stole it off the floor and put it on.

Her head swims in lusty bliss while the fireworks dazzle above.

Eventually, the boys tell Lia they're hungry, and they all decide to head up to the boardwalk. Sundae slings her heels back on when her feet hit the sunburned wood, and when they pass the dark window of a closed souvenir shop, she stops to check her reflection, fluffing the curled ends of her long blond hair and swiping the mascara stains from under her eyes—though unfortunately, there's really no salvaging her look at this point.

If she had known she'd run into such a total dream girl on the beach, maybe she wouldn't have cried all her cute makeup off.

"Sundae? Do you want pizza?" Lia asks, pulling Sundae's attention away from her reflection. She turns, and Lia is pointing to the red glow of a PIZZA sign ahead on the boardwalk.

"Sure. What's your order?" Sundae asks.

"Oh. Olives and red pepper, all the way," Lia says.

"Got it." Sundae spins on her glittery heels, walking backward. "You guys grab a table. I'll get the pizza."

"Wait—you want some money?" Edison frowns, digging in his pocket like he's searching for a wallet, but Sundae shakes her head.

"I'll come with you," Lia says, but Sundae waves her off.

"You guys did the fireworks, I got the food," Sundae insists. She turns away before any of them can argue further, stalking across the boardwalk.

Sundae steps up to the counter and smiles sweetly as she orders two pies. The sweaty cashier never mentions a price, and she never asks. She just takes them when they're handed to her and walks away from the stand, weaving through the crowded boardwalk to find Lia and her friends at a grease-stained picnic table nearby.

If Sundae's going to be here suffering the consequences of that summer seven years ago, she might as well reap the benefits, too. She usually tries not to abuse the power her second wish gave her, but with the sting of tears still puffing her eyelids, she thinks she deserves this little indulgence.

Sundae swings onto the bench beside Lia and sets the boxes down on the table. "Thanks for the show," she says, as Dallas tears one open and the boys snag slices.

"Oh, speaking of shows—" Edison starts to say, but Lia cuts him off.

"Where are you from?" she asks Sundae, meeting her eyes. It's brighter on the boardwalk than it was on the beach, and this close, Sundae can see the threads of gold stitched through Lia's warm brown irises.

Reaching for a slice of pizza, Sundae says, "Union. What about you guys? Are you here for prom weekend, too?"

"We're from Garwood," Edison says, before he stuffs an entire crust into his mouth.

"And we're *not* here for prom weekend. We didn't even go to prom," Dallas adds.

Sundae nearly spits out her food. She slaps her hand over her mouth as she swivels to look around at the three of them. Once she's safely swallowed the bite, she takes her hand away and says, "You didn't go to *prom*?"

"Fuck no." Lia laughs, shaking her head.

"Look, I know we seem charming and all, but the truth is, we're absolute social pariahs where we come from," Dallas says in a tone that makes it sound like he's bragging.

"Wow. Garwood must have no taste," Sundae says, shaking her head. A little smirk graces her lips as she eyes Lia. "If we went to school together, I would have asked you to prom."

Lia's cheeks flush deep as red plums, but after a moment in which she seems too frazzled to speak, she says, "Like, *seriously,* or as a joke?"

"Sundae!"

Sundae twists when she hears her name called out, her knee bumping Lia's as she looks over her shoulder. Neeli is rushing through the crowd, Jackie and Amber trailing behind. Neeli looks frazzled, her emerald nail polish chipped like she's been picking at it—which she only does when she's totally panicking.

Yet another needle of guilt pierces Sundae's chest, her heart a pincushion full of shame.

When they reach her, Sundae opens her mouth to apologize, but Neeli's arms lash around her neck before she gets a chance. Neeli squeezes so tight, Sundae can't suck in enough air to get a word out.

Amber is saying into her phone, "We found her, we found her, she's okay."

"Not if Neeli snaps her neck with that death grip," Jackie mutters.

"She's okay," Amber repeats to whoever is on the phone, side eyeing Jackie. "Tell Fresca we'll be there soon."

"I'm so sorry," Neeli is saying, muffled against Sundae's hair but close enough to her ear that she can hear it anyway. "I shouldn't have gone on the ride, I shouldn't have left you alone."

Sundae's fingers wrap around Neeli's wrists, and she pulls gently, coaxing Neeli to loosen her grip. "You didn't leave me *alone*," Sundae says once she can breathe again.

"I did. I left you alone with *Harper*," Neeli says. "That's worse than just *regular* alone."

"Did that fucking creep try something?" Amber asks, dropping the phone away from her face as she hangs up. There's a protective rage in her throaty voice that makes Sundae feel warm and fuzzy inside.

"I swear to god, that boy's a freaking sex pest," Jackie says.

Sundae looks over at Lia on the bench beside her. Lia's eyes are molten tar and her jaw is tightly clenched. Like she's filled in the blanks between what Sundae's friends are saying and the state Sundae was in when they met, and she's forming an idea of what might have happened to her. Lia's simmering fury and Neeli's tight embrace make Sundae wonder how she ever let Harper make her believe it was her fault he touched her without her consent. It doesn't matter how she was putting her lip gloss on, how short her skirt is, or how many other guys on the team she's hooked up with—Harper McCall is still the problem.

Sundae's hands squeeze at Neeli's arms. "I'm okay," she says. She twists in Neeli's grip and looks at Amber and Jackie, her lips curving into a rueful smile. "It's fine. I already told him off."

"Telling him off isn't enough. He needs to get lost at sea," Amber grumbles.

"We're not going back to Harper's motel block," Jackie says. "Fuck him and all his minions."

"Frez and Tasha are meeting us near the pier. We can sleep on the beach," Amber says.

"Yeah, they can have fun jerking each other off in their pussy-less Jacuzzi for the rest of the weekend," Jackie says. "Fuckin' losers."

Sundae giggles, and she pulls gently on Neeli's arms so they unravel from around her neck. She twists to face Lia and says, "How about that one? Him sitting in the hot tub with his boys, who all know he's the reason the cheerleaders ditched them on prom weekend."

"Ick, that *is* a good one." Lia smirks. "If they won't hold each other accountable, they'll just have to sit and marinate in each other's ball sweat."

Neeli snickers, Jackie cackles, and Amber gives an approving nod, so Sundae tells them, "This is Lia, by the way. And Edison and Dallas. They just saved the world."

"Well, that's a bit hyperbolic," Edison says.

"You never know. That rhinestone could have gotten sucked into the mouth of an orca, who then spits it into the engine of one of James Cameron's submarines, causing it to jam and explode, and then society utterly collapses due to the lack of new Avatar movies," Dallas says.

Neeli laughs and says, "Well, at least then he'd finally have to answer to god for acting like that door wasn't big enough for Rose and Jack to both get on."

Edison pipes up, saying, "I think it was never about the size of the door, I think it was a buoyancy issue—"

"Nope," Neeli says, holding a hand up to silence him. "Don't defend that ending to me."

"This is why I turn *Titanic* off at one hour and forty minutes in. That way, it's just a movie about an old lady telling one of her ho stories to a bunch of scientists," Sundae says.

"*Anyway*, we gotta go. Tash and Frez are waiting for us," Amber says, cutting through the chatter.

Sundae twists back to Lia and leans in, her long hair spilling off her shoulder to brush Lia's arm. "Are you coming with us?"

"Huh?" Lia grunts, looking surprised. She glances at Edison and Dallas, but they look like they're waiting for *her* to answer. So she brings her dark eyes back to Sundae. "Uh, we should head back, actually."

"Oh. That's too bad. I was really enjoying the fireworks," Sundae says in a velvet purr. She smiles, drawing back, sweeping her long legs over the bench as she stands up. "I'll see you around."

Then she turns away, Neeli's arm hooking around her waist, Amber and Jackie fencing her in from the other side as they wander off down the boardwalk.

Sundae walks away, totally unaware that the motel that they're not going back to also happens to be the motel Lia is staying at with her bandmates. Totally unaware that there's a jukebox in the dark corner of the lobby there, a jukebox that used to sit at the Coral Cabana seven years ago.

Totally unaware that when Lia goes back there tonight, he'll be able to smell Sundae on her, stinking of the wishes she stole from him seven years ago.

And this time, he won't let her get away without paying for them.

EIGHT

NOW

On the way back to the Blue Velvet, Lia starts to feel the effects of the pill she took from Sundae.

First, she notices how the boardwalk lights all look a little fuzzy, like they've grown fur made out of tinsel that sparkles in Lia's vision. And how the sound of the ocean waves smashing into the beach beyond the dark boardwalk seems to scratch an itch at the back of her skull. And how her clenched fist of a heart seems to be loosening, like soft fingers unfurling inside her chest.

By the time Lia and her bandmates make it to the room they're sharing at her aunt's motel, Lia is definitely high.

That doesn't stop her from taking the can of Modelo Edison offers her, but mostly she sits there on the edge of her bed, twisting the cold can in her hot hands and listening to the fizz of the beer bubbling inside. The boys have claimed the bed closer to the air conditioner, and they throw themselves on it with their beers in hand. They put on a movie and start talking about tomorrow's set list, but Lia is hardly listening.

She's too busy thinking about Sundae.

As if he can read her mind, Dallas abruptly cuts through Lia's fantasies to say, "I truly cannot believe you, by the way. You blew like, a hundred chances to ask that girl out."

Lia jumps, spilling a little of her beer onto her legs. The cold stings her skin, making goose bumps claw up her shins. She looks over at Dallas, wide-eyed like she's been caught in the act.

"Were you not into her or something? You should have at least let me tell her about the show tomorrow," Edison says.

"She doesn't want to come to our stupid show," Lia grumbles, purposefully *not* answering Edison's question.

"I bet she would," Edison says. "She's totally into you."

"She is not," Lia snaps, and even as it comes out of her mouth, she knows she's doing the same shit she always does. Objectively, Lia knows Sundae was flirting with her—but the problem is, that absolutely terrifies her.

Because of course she finds Sundae attractive. That's something she feels totally equipped to handle—it's as simple as never, ever, *ever* revealing that she thinks Sundae is weird and funny and extremely hot. After this weekend, they'll probably never see each other again anyway, so it should be easy to go a couple days without revealing that she has a bit of a crush.

But if Sundae actually likes her back, that's a big fucking iceberg in the hull of Lia's watertight plan to keep this crush on her a total secret. That's like, not enough lifeboats on the capsizing ship, that's a catastrophe, that's total chaos. There's no plan for that. Only sink or swim.

So she glares at Edison and Dallas and says, "Why don't one of *you* gormless freakwads try to hit on a girl?"

"Because none of the girls hit on us first," Dallas says.

"It's like they don't consider shock jocks a legitimate form of jock," Edison says.

"Maybe they will after I give you a traumatic brain injury," Lia growls.

"Whatever, dude. This is just like Philly, isn't it?" Dallas says.

Lia huffs when Dallas's words hit her, landing like a punch, her fist curling tighter around her beer as she stares at him. Bringing up Philly hurts no matter what, but bringing it up like *this*—that's a bull's-eye shot directly to the sorest, most shameful part of herself.

And the truth is, *it is*. Whatever stopped Lia from playing onstage at the Spaced show is the same thing that stopped her from reciprocating any of Sundae's advances, even though she *wanted to*. As they lay on the beach, she pictured doing it a thousand different ways. She could have used their linked pinkies to draw Sundae's hand closer, weaving their fingers together. She could have shifted her head across the sand and pressed her temple to Sundae's. She could have put an arm around her under the blooming fireworks; she could have even kissed her if she'd been brave enough. She could've told Sundae that if she'd asked her to prom, she would have gone, and she wouldn't even have hated it as long as Sundae was there beside her.

Or at the very fucking least, she could have *asked for her number* before they parted ways.

But she didn't. She didn't do *any* of that. She just lay there like a dead fish (one that had choked on a stray rhinestone, perhaps) and changed the subject any time Sundae tried to turn the conversation flirtatious.

Exactly like how she just stood there onstage, pretending to tune her guitar until she finally gave up and ran away.

And now, with the MDMA working to uncork the clog of tension in her chest, all the regret starts to pour out and flood her body. Feeling overwhelmed, she growls at Dallas, "Are you ever going to shut the fuck up about Philly?"

"You know, you're lucky we didn't kick you out of the band," Dallas snaps.

"Guys, come on—" Edison starts to say, but Dallas cuts him off.

"No, Eddie, don't try to play peacekeeper right now. She utterly *fucked* us, and you know it," Dallas says. He twists back to Lia, jabbing a finger in Edison's direction. "We talked about it, you know? We talked about kicking you out of the band. Because after that, how are we supposed to trust you?"

"How are you going to kick me out of the band when you don't *have* a band without me?" Lia says, her voice as strained as her fist around her Modelo, her fingers denting the sides of the can. "You guys couldn't even play that set on your own."

"Are you not hearing me? I'm trying to give you some kind of wake-up call, Lia," Dallas says, unraveling his legs to scoot forward on the bed opposite hers. He drops his feet off the edge, leaning forward to hold her eyes, his face half-lit in the blue TV light. "It's not just about what happened in Philly, okay? It's everything that came after, too. You never even *explained* what happened there, and I don't even think you know, but every time we talk about playing tomorrow, you get this look in your eyes like a cornered animal. Honestly, I think you're going to run away tomorrow, too. I really do. And if you were capable of anything else, then you would have asked that girl out tonight. But you're not. So I know we're not playing a fucking set tomorrow, to a crowd of brain-dead jocks or not."

Tears are burning her eyes, blurring her fuzzy vision further. Her head is a screaming mess of pain and shame and regret, because she knows Dallas is right. How is she supposed to stop herself from running away from everything she wants when she doesn't even understand why she does it in the first place?

Maybe it's something that can't be fixed. Maybe it's just as much a part of her as her blood, her breath, her music.

Lia jumps to her feet, her breath ragged and tear-choked. Edison is trying to say something to her, but she can't hear him. Her breath seems so loud, it's the only thing she can hear in the hollow dome of her head. She crosses the room, boots on the grubby carpet, and throws open the door.

The night outside is cool on her clammy skin. The motel courtyard is crowded with drunk kids, but they might as well be making no noise, because Lia only hears her sobbing breaths and her slamming heart. Movement out of the corner of her eye makes her turn, and she sees the door to the room she just left opening, Edison standing in the threshold, just a silhouette of hair with the TV light at his back.

"Leave me alone," Lia hisses at him before she twists away from the door and throws her back against the wall. She sinks down, crouching on the pavement with her spine pressed to the blue stucco, and if Edison is still there watching her, she doesn't know or care. She lifts the beer can that's still clutched in her hand, pressing it to her lips, tipping her head back as she chugs.

The froth sticks in her tight throat, but she coughs past it and keeps drinking.

Cold beer settles sourly in her stomach as she empties the can. Slowly, the sounds around her start to even out, the rasp of her breathing growing quieter. The thump of music from a speaker rattles the teeth in her jaw. There's the splash of bodies in the pool, the hum of voices and laughter.

Lia rubs at the tears soaking her face. She thinks, *again*, of Sundae, crying on the beach when Lia found her. What if she had just been brave enough to say the things she wanted to say to her? To do the things she wanted to do while they lay on the sand beside each other? Maybe then she wouldn't be here, realizing that her friends are right: She's a lost cause.

Suddenly, the sound of Sundae's name catches Lia's attention.

"Sundae sucked your dick?"

Lia's eyes whip across the courtyard. The boys she saw earlier are now by the pool, and they're *still* talking about Sundae.

It's an unusual name, and Lia remembered hearing it as soon as Sundae introduced herself. She'd been certain then that Sundae was the girl those boys had been talking about when Aunt Violet was trying to check them in. But if there *had* been any doubt, the name that came up when Sundae's friends found her would have dispelled it.

Harper.

They'd said his name like a curse, and Lia didn't miss the look that passed between Sundae and her friends as they called him a *creep* and a *sex pest*. She *knew* they were talking about *him*. And here he is now, stretched out on a lounge chair by the pool, still wearing the sweaty basketball shorts he arrived in earlier, still surrounded by a crew of pea-brained douchewads.

"Bro, she barely even waited for the ride to start. I had to stop her from doing it right there on the boardwalk," Harper says, smug laughter in his thick throat.

Judging by the tears on Sundae's face when they first met, whatever happened between her and Harper is nothing like what he's telling his friends now. Lia presses her spine against the rough wall behind her as she listens to them, letting it ground her as her anger starts to rise.

"What's up, Panagos? You still think she's wifey material?" one of the boys says.

"Shut the fuck up," the guy Lia thought had Labrador energy growls. He's in the pool, gripping the edge as he glowers up at his snickering friends. His eyes cut to Harper, and he says, "Dude, I know you're lying."

"I'm not lying. Your girl sucked it down," Harper says.

Another boy chortles as he says, "I told you, she's probably going to hook up with every dude in Wildwood this weekend."

"And every girl," says a boy who sounds like he's enjoying the thought a little too much. "She's bi, right?"

"She's pansexual," the Labrador says, pout deepening as he corrects his friend.

"The hell does that mean?" one boy questions.

"It means she'll fuck anyone," Harper says.

"Except for Luke, apparently," another guy declares.

The Labrador boy grunts and sinks back into the water. As he swims an angry lap, the other boys laugh, cruelty dripping from their mouths like sewer water from leaky pipes.

Lia's fury feels explosive, burning hot inside her as she watches. She wants to say something—she wants to storm over and tell them all off, wants to smash her empty beer can against Harper's smug face, wants to drive her boot into their balls so hard that all the bravado is crushed out of them.

Make a fucking move, she screams inside her own mind. *Do something, just to prove you actually* can.

But instead, she keeps crouching there in the shadows, back stuck to the wall like a fly glued to paper.

Her head feels like a fish tank. The beer she chugged loosens her clenched jaw a little, but it also seems to make her mind even hazier.

Slowly, the courtyard empties. The music dies, leaving just the hum of the boardwalk and the splash of pool water. Drunk kids haul each other to their rooms, leaving behind their trash, empty bottles and White Claw cans tossed across the pavement. The moon dips low on the horizon.

And then, in the quiet of the abandoned courtyard, there comes another sound.

At first, it sounds like waves sweeping the sand, as if the courtyard has gone quiet enough that Lia can hear the ocean from all the way across the boardwalk. But then she realizes that it's not cresting waves she's hearing but a soft slinking beat, coming from somewhere beyond her left shoulder.

She twists against the wall, looking down the row of closed blue doors. Her vision is blurred, like she's seeing the world through a foggy lens. Maybe someone's playing music in their room. But then her eyes fall on the wide window trimmed with gold curtains at the other end of the courtyard, and cool dread winds its way through her chest.

It's not the window to one of the rooms. The blue neon letters over the glass door beside it read LOBBY, and because Aunt Violet went to bed hours ago, it *should* be locked up. There's a call button on the wall that buzzes Aunt Violet's room if someone needs her, but other than that, the lobby should be dark for the night.

Except it's not.

There's a green glow emanating through the window, staining the gold curtains chartreuse. From the direction of the light, Lia can tell it's coming from the dark corner by the plastic palm tree, where the jukebox that doesn't work sits lurking in the shadows.

Except clearly it *does* work. Because when Lia rises to her feet and slowly creeps closer to the lobby, she can see it through the window, all lit up in green and red. And the music she hears is coming from the speakers, muffled by the plaster walls of the lobby, but growing louder as she gets closer.

When she reaches it, she shoves on the door, but the lobby is locked. Through the glass, she can see the jukebox in the corner, a vibrant green arch of light with little ruby buttons. There's a record spinning on the platter inside the dusty cover, lit up like a yellow half-moon. The rhythm of the song sways like a boat in a lashing sea, and a smooth voice crackles through the old speakers of the jukebox.

"One, for a path I crossed.
Two, for my love I lost.
Three, and you will come for me,
Like the tide pulls the sand back to the sea."

Lia presses her hands to the lobby door, leaning in close to listen through the glass. The song is soft and dreamy, and the singer's croon sounds like heartbreak. It's so intoxicating, Lia almost doesn't notice the sound that's coming from *behind* her now.

But then it cuts through the music, a sound like crab legs skittering across concrete, only worse somehow—like crab legs made of knives.

Lia turns too fast and her brain seems to wobble in her skull. She stumbles back against the lobby door, her elbow catching the push bar to steady herself. There's no one left in the courtyard, just Lia and the jukebox alone in the buzzy silence.

Well. Lia, the jukebox, and the man in the pool.

It's somewhat of a stretch to even call him a man. Yes, he's wearing a suit brown as tree bark, and he has arms and legs and a face like a man—but as his hands claw up the edge of the pool, his fingers sharp as claws, Lia finds that *man* seems like a wholly inadequate descriptor.

The leafy crown on his head is green as the glow from the lobby. His eyes catch the moonlight, reflecting cold silver. He hangs there on the edge of the pool, water dripping from the thorny leaves of his crown, running in rivulets from his slicked-back hair.

She must be hallucinating. *Does molly make you hallucinate?* It must. That must be what's happening. The man in the pool ducks down so only his silver eyes peer up over the edge. When she stares at him, she even feels a sense that she's seeing something at the fringes of consciousness. Like when she learned about optical illusions in psych class, and there were these illustrations that could look like two things at once. Something about him reminds her of the moment when the illusion would "switch," when she would find herself able to see the second image hidden within.

Slowly, she takes a step away from the lobby door, inching toward the edge of the pool. The music coming from the jukebox behind her seems to grow louder, like someone has cranked the volume up. The blue voice sings,

"Here in the Wildwoods,
Where you once stood,
All clothed in green . . ."

The man in the pool pops back up, his face tipped to the light. A kind smile spreads across his face, so pleasant it nearly negates the sharpness of his teeth. Lia's heart gallops when she sees them, black and serrated behind his grinning lips.

"What the fuck," she whispers, freezing a couple feet away from the edge of the pool. "What are you?"

"I'm just like you," he answers, and his voice sounds like the one coming from the jukebox, but slightly distorted, the way sound echoes inside a seashell when you press it to your ear.

"Um. I don't know about that," Lia says.

"It's true," he says. He pulls himself up higher, propping his elbows on the edge of the pool. "I wanted what you want. I wanted to make music. I wanted the whole world to hear me. I wanted to write a song so perfect, it would be sung long after I was gone."

Lia frowns, twisting to glance back at the green glow coming from the lobby. The jukebox is still playing, his voice resonating from the fizzy speakers. She turns back to the man in the pool, who has now climbed up to sit on the edge, one leg dangling in the water while the other bends, his elbow resting on his knee. His palm is open, showing three candies wrapped in wax paper.

"Are you, like, the ghost of Holly Jolly?" she asks, remembering the story Aunt Violet told her about the singer whose last song is stuck on the jukebox.

"Ghosts are dead things. You hear my music, don't you?" He pauses, and Lia nods. "Then I will never die."

"Okay. Um. I'm probably hallucinating," Lia says, matter-of-factly.

"Then there's no harm in making a wish," he says.

"A wish?" Lia repeats, wobbling a little when she tries to cross her arms over her stomach and thinking better of it, instead squaring her stance so she doesn't fall over.

The man at the edge of the pool holds up his hand, presenting his palmful of wrapped taffies to her as if on a silver platter. "Here. Take them."

"What . . . are they?" Lia asks.

"Wishes," he says, and bares his serrated black teeth in a smile.

"Wishes for *what*?"

He tilts his head, the courtyard lights shifting across his crown of holly. His smile widens as he says, "You are a hungry thing, aren't you? You can wish for whatever it is you want the most."

Whatever it is she wants the most.

There *is* so much she wants. So much she's always too afraid to take.

Just like she's afraid to take these candy wishes, offered up by a ghost.

Maybe she'll never do anything. Maybe she'll never be brave enough to stand up to guys like Harper and his crew. Maybe she'll never make it as a musician. Maybe she'll never even play music again. Maybe she'll never tell Sundae how badly she wanted to kiss her tonight.

Maybe this is just a dream, conjured up by the pill she took, trying to tell her that no matter how much she wishes things were different, she can't change this about herself.

But what if she *does* take the taffy?

What if she *can* change?

Her fingers stretch for his open palm. The candies seem almost magnetic, as irresistible as if she were starving and they were the first food she'd seen in ages.

"What do you wish for?" he asks her.

The taffies are in her hand now. When she looks down at them, the swirled colors seem to twist hypnotically beneath the waxed paper.

She picks one up and pulls the ends of the paper, unfurling the twist, exposing the sticky taffy inside. The music from the jukebox in the lobby gently sways, and the water in the pool splashes like the tide, and the taffy smells like the blond cascade of Sundae's hair when she leaned in close to Lia on the bench outside the pizza stand. Like sweet coconut with a bright lemon bite.

"I wish I'd just been brave enough to ask her out," Lia whispers.

She pulls the candy out of the wrapper with her teeth and bites down, her mouth flooding with sugar and salt and, underneath it all, a coppery spike of blood.

And after she's gnawed it down and swallowed it all, she balls the wrapper up in her fist and looks to the edge of the pool.

But the man is gone, and the music has stopped, and now Lia really is all alone.

NINE

NOW

A beast has been let loose on the boardwalk, and he is hungry.

Starved, even. He's spent seven years waiting with an empty stomach, in a skin that has grown ragged on him, like a snake trapped in its own shed. Seven years, waiting in the shadows, her unpaid debt a blade dug into his side.

When he opened his eyes at sunset he could smell her on the boardwalk. Even from all the way in the dark place where he roosts, tucked into the seam of the veil, he knew she was near. Reeking of stolen wishes, the afternoon sun sinking into her hair, staining the strands pink as strawberry taffy. Pink as a cat's tongue. Pink as drops of blood blooming in water.

Yet the rules hadn't changed. He needed a way around them. He needed a way to get to her.

Then came that sad little singer, with her dark eyes big as mussel shells and her wanting heart shining like the beam of a lighthouse, cutting through the dark. And best of all, there was the scent of stolen wishes clinging to her, sticky and thick as congealed blood dried to her skin, and he knew whose company she'd been keeping that night.

The singer made a wish.

She set him free.

The one who stole from him is not hard to find. She still carries the wanting heart that drew him out of the dark all those years ago. She is a hungry thing that covets and craves, and her desire is his chum, luring him through the shadows all the way to her like a shark hunts the scent of gore.

He crawls between the beams beneath the boardwalk and finds her on the hazy beach. Salt water drips from his teeth as he watches her.

She isn't alone. She's surrounded by friends, girls like bunches of grapes, ripe for the picking. He imagines how each would spurt blood like burgundy juice between the saws of his sharp teeth.

She lounges on the sand with them, their limbs entwined like tree roots, and she's laughing, careless. Like she's forgotten the debt she owes. Like she's forgotten *him*.

He will show her that *he* hasn't forgotten.

Slithering out from the black gap beneath the boardwalk, he crawls across the sand, his jaw hanging open and his rows of black teeth chomping the air. He creeps up on their island of fuzzy towels and suntanned legs, so close he can taste their hunger. There's a girl beside her with long black hair, a girl who aches for a vision of her future that seems to center entirely around fine dining with her friends. She wishes for enthralling chatter and gourmet cocktails and golden sunsets streaming through the windows of restaurants with prix fixe menus.

Another hungry thing.

All the girls are hungry.

But none as much as *her*.

He reaches for her, the pink-haired thief, ready to snatch her by the throat and *finally* taste her blood. But as his hand slithers across the sand, a sudden pain rakes through his body. His silver eyes roll up, reflecting the orange glow at the ocean line, the rising sun staining the sky egg-yolk yellow.

The dawn has come.

It burns like a hot iron, right down to his bones. He lets out a pained snarl, and one of the girls jerks around at the sound, but she only catches sight of his back as he ducks into the dark beneath the boardwalk, escaping before the sunlight catches him.

TEN

NOW

When Lia woke up in the late morning, sweating on the floral comforter of the bed across from Edison and Dallas, the holly-crowned man who came out of the pool felt like a distant dream.

The boys were already awake, watching a movie on Edison's phone, and they greeted Lia like nothing had happened the night before. Even Dallas, who normally holds a grudge (*clearly*) showed no signs of residual rancor. It made her wonder if all of it—the fight and the bizarre encounter she had in the courtyard afterward—was a dream, just the anxious turning of her mind as she slept off the pill Sundae had given her.

It seems real when she closes her eyes, when she runs her tongue over her teeth and remembers the taste of sugared coconut and salt water. But when her eyes are open and the sun pours in, it slips away like sand between her fingers.

So sitting in the bright, glass-paned diner attached to her aunt's motel, it's easy to forget about all of it.

The diner is on theme with the rest of the motel, the baby-blue walls cluttered with vintage posters and ephemera from Wildwood's doo-wop days, the tables topped with pearly white laminate like the inside of an oyster shell, the smell of cracked vinyl and french fries in the air.

Aunt Violet's girlfriend, Theo, is in the kitchen now. Lia can see her over the saloon doors, behind the counter, dressed in a halter top and bell-bottom blue jeans, her hair the color of spice cake piled high in a messy updo. Lia almost went back there to ask Theo about the salt she poured around the jukebox, the salt Aunt Violet said was for protection—but now that Lia's on her second cup of coffee and the taste of taffy and blood has been washed out of her mouth, that seems ridiculous.

"You're such a weenie," Lia says, and Edison scoffs, his breath scattering the steam rising off his coffee cup.

"I'll never swim in the fucking ocean, dude, I'm sorry," Edison says.

"You swam in the Paulinskill when we went camping," Lia points out.

"So? That's a *river*. There are no sharks in rivers," Edison says.

"Actually, that's not necessarily true," Lia says. "Have you heard of the Matawan Man-Eater?"

"The *what*? What the hell is the *Matawan Man-Eater*?" Edison says, brown eyes wide and fearful.

"I don't know, but that's a sick band name," Dallas says, putting down his menu, suddenly interested in the conversation.

Lia's smirk widens across her lips. She lowers her voice, leans closer, and says, "In 1916, the Jersey Shore was plagued by a series of shark attacks. The initial attacks occurred right off beaches like this one, but then, a few weeks after the bloodbath began, a sea captain living in Matawan said he'd spotted an eight-foot-long shark in the Matawan Creek. No one believed him, until a group of boys swimming in the creek were attacked by the shark. The shark took one of the boys, and the ones who escaped ran into town for help. A bunch of men went out to the creek to search for the missing boy, thinking there was no way it was really a shark that had gotten him . . . until one of the men was attacked by the shark in front of a crowd of witnesses—"

"Dude. What is going on?" Edison interrupts her to say, his voice cracking unsteadily. "We're in *fucking New Jersey*, not the Outback, what is up with all these animal attacks?"

"What's next? Are you gonna tell us there's a crocodile in Menlo Mall?" Dallas says.

"No, but there *was* an anaconda in Lake Hopatcong," Lia says.

"Well, slap my ass and call me a Bloomin' Onion, 'cause it's 'No rules, just right' out here," Dallas yells, loud enough to attract a couple confused looks from the surrounding tables.

"Cool. Now I have a bunch of new things to be paranoid about," Edison says. "Thanks, thanks for that."

"Oh, look," Dallas says, suddenly lowering his voice. Lia follows the direction of his gaze and sees that the door is swinging closed behind a group of girls who enter the diner laughing, arms linked, one unified mass of muscular limbs and windswept hair.

And at the center of them all is *Sundae*.

Lia's guts give a lurch like she's fallen down a flight of stairs. She sinks low in her seat, whipping her menu up to hide her face because it feels like the blood in her cheeks is singing Sundae's name.

"Hm?" Lia hears Edison grunt. He twists in his seat, looking over the back of the booth at the cluster of cheerleaders by the door. "Ooooh," he coos, and Lia sinks even farther down into her seat.

"Shut up, both of you," she growls into her menu. She peeks around the corner just long enough to see that a waitress is taking the girls to a table across the diner, which is honestly a relief. Maybe Sundae won't notice Lia's total panic over her mere presence.

"Quit being weird. You're not even gonna say hi to her?" Edison says.

"Yeah, what happened to all the game you had last night, Casanova?" Dallas laughs.

"Don't be a fucking dickhead," Lia says. Maybe Dallas *is* still holding a grudge, after all . . . but when Lia glances over her menu at him, he looks confused by her venom, like he wasn't mocking her at all.

Then there's a gust of warm coconut-scented skin beside her, and a sugar-sweet voice asks, "You're a water sign, aren't you?"

"Me?" Lia says, her voice coming out tight and breathless as she stares up at Sundae, who stands beside their table with a sly smirk tucked in the corners of her pink glossed lips.

"Of course *you*, silly."

"Oh." Lia gulps and nods her head. "Um, yeah, I'm a Scorpio."

Something about Sundae looks different, and for a second Lia thinks it's just the shock of seeing her in the light of day after they met last night in the dark. But it's not that, and it's not the fact that she's wearing nothing but a pink bikini etched with iridescent flames, or the way the sun has toasted her cheeks and the tops of her shoulders, or the way her eyes have lost the fresh-cry puffiness they had last night. It's her hair, which has taken on a soft pink hue, like the bags of pastel cotton candy that hang all over the boardwalk.

Dallas, who clearly noticed the same thing, butts in to say, "Hey, Barbarella, Queen of the Galaxy, did you dye your hair?"

Sundae giggles, glancing over at Dallas. "No. It's just magic, baby."

Honestly, Lia kind of believes it is. When Sundae throws her hair over her shoulder, strands of it seem to sparkle, like glimmering shocks of pink tinsel. Sundae smiles as she drops into the booth beside Lia, the rhinestone dangling from her pierced belly button flashing.

"Do you like it?" she asks as she reaches across Lia to snag a menu off the table. Sundae meets Lia's gaze, her eyes blue as the Icee machine churning behind the diner counter. Lia can feel her heart beating in her throat.

"Yeah, it's cool," Lia chokes out. "How was, uh, the rest of your night?"

"Severely lacking in fireworks," Sundae says with a sigh, her nails pattering against the plastic pages of the menu in her hands.

The waitress arrives to take their orders, and Lia is so interested in what Sundae likes for breakfast (a Nutella waffle and a strawberry milkshake) that she forgets what she wanted in the first place, so she just asks for eggs and toast.

When the waitress leaves, Lia clears her throat and says, "We have more."

"Hmm?" Sundae hums, twisting a lock of bubblegum hair around her finger as she turns to Lia. She's sitting close enough for Lia to see every grain of glitter stuck to her lash line, every freckle blooming on her sunburned cheeks, every lick of pearly pink in the pastel waves of her hair. Sundae bites her lip as she holds Lia's gaze in the swallowing blue of her eyes, and Lia's brain feels as melty as the milkshake the waitress brings to their table.

"Fireworks," Lia barely manages to say. "We have more fireworks."

Sundae smiles, swirling the straw in her gloopy pink shake. She takes a slurp, then says, "Baby, the fireworks are right here."

Lia could honestly slide off the booth and onto the floor. Her pulse is pounding in her neck, her cheeks are burning hot, the vinyl seat is sticking to the sweat on the back of her knees. She thinks she couldn't possibly be more overwhelmed, but then Sundae looks down into her milkshake and says, "So, my dress is blue, if you want to match tonight."

"Match? Tonight?" Lia repeats.

"Yeah, I'm your prom date. Remember?" Sundae says.

Lia glances across the table at Dallas and Edison, who appear pretty concerned about Lia's total stupefaction. The looks they're giving her seem to say, *What the hell is wrong with you right now?*

She thinks back to what Dallas said right before Sundae approached their table. How he asked what happened to the game she had last night, which was confusing, since Lia would say she had whatever the exact *opposite* of game is. Every time Sundae tried to flirt with her, she clammed up like a clenched fist. But whenever she froze, there was always something she *wished* she had the guts to say—and then, suddenly, she remembers.

The man with the holly crown and the rows of sharp black teeth. The three candies in his palm, and the wish she made.

It must have happened when Sundae said she'd have gone to prom with Lia if they went to school together. The thing Lia wanted to say but didn't was this: *Then be my prom date tomorrow night. My band is playing at the Blue Velvet. We'll dress up and take awkward photos together. I bet Eddie and Dallas would even make us a balloon arch.*

Instead she'd changed the subject. At least, that's how she remembers it. Lia digs her fist into her thigh, the silver rings circling her fingers pressing against her skin like she's trying to punch some sense into herself. Is she seriously about to believe that she made a wish on a ghost's candy last night, and it *actually* came true? There has to be a more logical explanation. Maybe the ecstasy messed with her memory. Maybe it peeled away her inhibitions enough that she *did* ask Sundae to be her date. Maybe the dream about the man that came out of the pool was some kind of hallucinatory vision quest.

That has to be it. Because there's no way she ate magic taffy last night that caused them all to leap into an alternate universe where she somehow had the balls to flirt with Sundae.

Still, for an instant, Lia finds herself glancing toward the saloon doors to the kitchen, where Theo is at the range frying up a heap of peppery potatoes, and she thinks again of the moat of salt around the jukebox, of the way its green glow illuminated the lobby, of the smell of rotten seaweed and sour berries and blood that wafted off the man at the pool's edge. . . .

But Lia rips her eyes away from Theo, turning them to Sundae, who is staring back at her like she has no idea there is a universe in which Lia didn't ask her to be her date to the show tonight. And whether it was a wish on a ghost or a pill that killed her anxiety, Lia decides it doesn't fucking matter. *Sundae is going to be her date tonight.*

"Right," Lia says through the panicky tightness still clinging around her throat. "I can . . . I can wear blue."

"Cool," Sundae says. "I told my friends. They're coming to see your band play, too."

Lia tries not to think about what will happen if she gets onstage and she *can't* play, because it was embarrassing enough to chicken out in front of her favorite band—is she really about to do it in front of the girl she's crushing on, too?

Taking a deep breath, Lia turns to Sundae and holds up a pinkie, saying, "All right, but you have to pinkie promise that you'll still hang out with me after, even if you think we suck."

Sundae smiles, a laugh bubbling from her lips as she hooks her pinkie around Lia's and squeezes tight. She pulls on their linked hands, yanking Lia a little closer as she whispers, "I promise I'll hang out with you, no matter what."

"You might change your mind after she starts constantly telling you about freak animal attacks," Edison says.

"I don't know. It's pretty hard to scare me," Sundae says, pulling her straw out of her milkshake to lick a swirl of whipped cream off it. She winks at Lia as she stabs her straw back into her glass.

And Lia wishes she could say the same, but the truth is, she's fucking terrified.

ELEVEN

JULY 2019

The boardwalk was sunny gold, and Sundae's hair was pink as strawberry ice cream.

It had been a week since she made her wish, and every day since, her hair had bloomed a deeper shade—from pale candy floss to vibrant bubblegum. Of course her mother noticed, but Sundae played dumb and said it must be the pool water, or maybe the cheap shampoo in the little plastic bottles Mom pocketed from the maid service carts.

Mom accepted this explanation. But maybe she wouldn't have, if she hadn't been so distracted by the murder.

Since Sundae was the one who found Tony, she had to talk to the police when they came and filled the pink courtyard of the Coral Cove Motel with their loud radios and stomping boots. There was an officer named Detective Morton who made Sundae sit in one of the lounge chairs by the pool while he asked her things like: Had she heard Tony talking to anyone that night? Was anyone else in the Cabana? Why was *she* in the Cabana? Did she talk to Tony at all? Did he seem nervous or afraid?

She answered these questions honestly, while her mom sat behind her on the pool chair, squeezing her shoulders through the cold, wet towel they'd given her to wrap around her soggy bathing suit. But when they asked her if she'd seen anyone strange around the motel that night, she didn't know how to answer. Looking at the deep end of the pool, she thought of Holly Jolly and how he'd come out of the darkness, eyes shining like silver coins.

But then she remembered the two candies she still had, the taffy swirls in wax paper, each a wish she could make for anything in the world—and she said nothing.

They probably wouldn't have believed her, anyway.

After Detective Morton was done asking Sundae questions, Mom had wound her arms around Sundae and clutched her tight as she leaned over and asked the officer, "Do you have any idea who might have done this?"

"No, ma'am," said Detective Morton.

"Well, I— To be honest with you, my daughter and I came here to get away from my husband, and I'm just worried—"

"Ms. Valentine, do you think he had something to do with this murder?" Detective Morton asked.

"No, no, probably not," Mom said.

"*Probably* not?" Detective Morton repeated with a scoff.

"I'm sorry. I just—I only brought it up because I want to make sure our names are left out of . . . any news reports or anything," Mom said.

"I don't control the news, Ms. Valentine. I wish I did, trust me," Detective Morton said. He chuckled, but his laugh was bitter as a cherry pit, and Mom hugged Sundae tighter as he got up and walked away, joining the other officers who were drinking Styrofoam cups of lobby coffee as they stood around outside the Cabana.

For a while after it happened, Mom wouldn't let Sundae out of her sight. But the lady on the news with the neat brown hair said that it was a robbery gone wrong, and no one ever mentioned Sundae being the one who found him, and eventually Mom seemed to relax again.

She still couldn't go back to work, though.

The Cabana was a crime scene, so until the cops took the yellow tape off the door, the bar couldn't open. Sundae knew they were running out of money, because Mom was feeding her cheese sandwiches on stale bread, and soup packets boiled in the coffee maker. But Sundae didn't mind so much, because even though she hated the chicken soup packets with the mushy strings of noodles, she and her mom would eat them together while watching silly TV dating shows, and they would laugh like there was no one to come and yell at them for laughing, so those dinners felt like the best meals Sundae had ever eaten.

Mom would spend the days with Sundae, too. Most of the time, they went somewhere away from the motel—the first day, Mom even brought Sundae to the aquarium, where she saw fish and eels and got to pet a smiling stingray, and had to ignore the way that every toothy shark made her think of glinting holly and silver eyes emerging from the dark.

Now, a week after Tony's murder, Sundae and her mother were walking the boardwalk at noon, cooked from a morning spent on the silky sand of Five Mile Beach. Both of them were sunburned, their hair stiff with salt water, and Mom bought them a cup of Curley's fries to share, even though it cost more money than Lipton's soup packets.

So when Sundae saw the hermit crabs and felt that familiar pang of greedy wanting, she knew she couldn't ask her mom to buy her one.

She had seen them before, out in front of the cluttered souvenir shops along the boardwalk. Alien creatures with bugged-out eyes, climbing the screen walls of their enclosures with pointy legs and tiny claws. Sundae liked the way they scuttled sideways on their speckled limbs, the way they disappeared inside their shells whenever the shopkeepers opened the cages to pluck one out. Sundae knew Mom didn't have the money, but every time she saw their eyes staring at her as she passed them, her heart wanted to pop like a bursting bubble. And this time, as Sundae approached the screened-in hutch full of crabs with painted shells, she wondered if maybe she didn't have to ask her mom to buy her one after all.

Maybe, if she made the right wish, Mom would never have to pay for what Sundae wanted ever again.

Mom was distracted by a phone call from Aunt Colleen, so she wasn't watching Sundae closely as she wandered over to the hermit crabs. Sundae leaned in, scanning the clambering little crabs until her eyes settled on one in particular. It had paprika-red legs and a shell painted iridescent lilac, gilded with stripes of shiny gold, and Sundae knew she had to have it.

She reached into the pocket of her shorts and drew out the candies Holly Jolly had handed her, staring down at them as they rested on her palm. One was blue and white, the other licorice black with a starburst of red. She chose the blue one, and when she pulled on the ends of the wax paper, the white swirl at the center churned like a cresting wave.

She peeled the candy off the paper and looked at the hermit crab with the lilac pearl shell.

"I wish . . . I could have whatever I want, and never have to pay for anything."

She popped the taffy into her mouth and bit down. Salty blueberry gushed across her tongue. She chomped down every sticky bite, and when she'd swallowed it all, she walked right up to the man behind the shop counter and said, "I want a hermit crab, please."

And he came around to get it for her.

She pointed out the crab with the lilac shell, and she chose a tank with a glittery pink cover to put it in. She picked out a craggy sponge and a ceramic castle to place inside the tank, and asked for a container of crab food, which the shop keeper handed over, too.

He never asked her to pay for any of it.

And Sundae knew her second wish had come true.

Toting her new hermit crab down the boardwalk in its pink carrying case, Sundae admired how the sun shimmered on its iridescent shell. Her mom asked her how she'd gotten it and she'd had to lie, just like she lied about her pink hair—this time, she told her mom that she'd guessed how many hermit crabs there were in the cage, and the shopkeeper had given it to her as a prize.

And her mom accepted this explanation, once again, probably because she was too distracted by the murder.

After their dinner of mushy soup packets, while her mom was in the shower, Sundae snuck out of their room at the Coral Cove and went barefoot down the balcony to the vending machines. She got her mom a sleeve of Lorna Doones from the machine (she only had to press the right buttons, and out it came, no quarters needed). On her way back to the room, she stopped to lean over the balcony railing and wave at the empty blue pool in the courtyard, wondering if her friend was somewhere at the bottom, hiding in the dark of the deep end.

When her mom came out of the shower, Sundae presented her with the yellow packet of cookies, and though her mom gave her a skeptical look when she claimed that she'd been saving some change to buy it for her, it *was* her most favorite snack in the world, so she didn't ask too many questions.

She just fell into the bed beside Sundae and kissed her twice on the cheek, then once more for good luck, before she ripped open the box of cookies. They shared the crumbly dry shortbread squares while they watched another episode of *Project Runway*, and when Sundae dozed off, it was to the buzz of the TV and the feeling of her mom cradling her close, smelling like motel soap and sunburned skin.

But when she woke up, it was to the smell of rotten seaweed and the sound of her mom screaming.

Her eyes flew open, and there he was. *Holly Jolly*. Only now his shark-toothed smile split his face, and he was raising a black handsaw up high, the sharp tip pointed at her.

No, not at her.

At her mom.

Cold water splashed from his sleeve as his hand swung down. Sundae's mom threw an arm over her, shielding her as the saw sank toward her chest.

But it never landed.

His hand was frozen, the saw blade hanging just an inch from her mother's heart. His silver eyes were wide, reflecting the flickering light of the TV as he stared at his own stalled limb.

He raised the saw back up and tried again.

Again, his arm froze like an invisible hand had grabbed his wrist.

"Who are you? What do you want?" her mom yelled.

He didn't answer.

He only growled, low and rumbling and full of rage.

His arm swept down, but this time he wasn't aiming for Mom—this time, he was coming for Sundae. Her scream ripped out as he scooped her up around the middle. She kicked and thrashed in his hold, her hands grappling for her mother, who was grabbing for her and shrieking.

Mom followed them through the motel door, pounding her fists against his back, though all her punches could do was splish-splash against his waterlogged suit. She scraped and clawed at him, but he was unmoving as a tree trunk and strong as a tidal wave as he carried Sundae out to the balcony.

"Let her go! Leave us alone! Stop—*Sundae!*"

She heard her mom yell her name as he launched over the balcony, soaring off the second story.

They landed in the cool blue of the pool, water rushing into Sundae's mouth as she screamed.

TWELVE

NOW

Sundae is laughing as she steps into the pink glow before sunset, her heels thudding against the balcony outside the second-floor motel room she and the other cheerleaders had crowded into to get ready. When she told her friends about her prom date with Lia, they were instantly in on the theme. Everyone pulled their prom dresses out of the trunk of Jackie's car, where they'd stuffed them before they drove down to Wildwood the morning after all their prom-night debauchery.

Sundae is wearing the outfit that nearly got her dress-coded at the door, a baby-blue Poster Girl minidress that's so tight it might as well be painted on her skin. Her legs, long and tan and bare, shimmer with pinprick sparkles from her glittery body oil.

And of course, she's wearing her crown.

Everyone said she'd be prom queen, but Sundae didn't believe it until they called her name. It seemed so funny to her, to walk up onstage in a dress that clearly showed the outline of her nipples and take the tiara, much to the annoyance of half the school faculty and many of her peers. And it's funny to her now, to strut out in her feather-strapped Pleasers and skimpy little dress, with the crystal-covered crown topping her soft pink hair, to meet Lia in the motel courtyard.

As she heads down the stairs to the courtyard of the Blue Velvet, she's holding hands with Neeli, whose hair falls like a black velvet curtain down her bare back. Neeli's wearing a sleek emerald gown held up by a gold chain around her neck, Jackie's in the fiery orange-red jumpsuit she wore to prom, and Amber is showing off her muscular limbs in a neat black minidress as she puffs skunky clouds from Jackie's bejeweled vape.

The courtyard is crowded, the party already in full swing, even though the sun has yet to set. Some faces are familiar, but Sundae's classmates aren't the only herd of seniors in Wildwood for the post-prom revelry, so there's plenty of fresh meat, too. None of them interest her at the moment, though.

It's Lia she wants.

At the entrance to the diner, there's the balloon arch Lia promised. Sundae giggles as she passes under it. Inside, all the tables are lit by starburst pendant lamps, the tall windows along the walls opening to a view of the boardwalk and the sky streaked in pink and gold.

There are two women behind the bar, one with her reddish hair in a Pam Anderson updo, the other tall with long black curls and lots of tattoos and big dark eyes that bear a striking resemblance to Lia's. The two of them are watching the rowdy crowd filling the diner with furtive smirks on their lips, leaning close to share private murmurs that make each other laugh, each with a drink in hand—a glass of red wine for the taller woman, while the cinnamon-haired Pam Anderson holds a dirty martini.

They're not only watching the crowd, though.

Sundae follows their eyes to the stage. It's not, like, a *big* stage—it's just a step up from the floor, a half circle in the corner with some warm gold lights and a smattering of art deco stars painted on the dark blue wall behind it.

And standing at the center of it is Lia, her head bowed over a violet electric guitar, her thumb plucking at the strings as the notes buzz over the sound system.

Sundae's heart goes pop-fizz at the sight of her. She's wearing an ocean-blue gown overlaid with beaded black mesh, the thigh-high slit revealing her beat-up combat boots. Her hair falls back from her face as she lifts her lips to the microphone in front of her, muttering into it, "Check, check—" but she cuts off when she notices Sundae in the crowd. The mic catches Lia's little intake of breath, and Sundae shivers at the sound.

"She's, like, a little rock star. I love that for her," Jackie says.

"Damn, Jack, you're almost as good as my mom at making a compliment sound condescending," Neeli says. "I think she's giving nineties leather jacket Winona Ryder."

"Grand theft Winona Ryder," Amber says, her voice mucky with weed smoke.

Sundae is barely listening to them. She's too busy watching Lia, who looks a little wide-eyed, like she might be low-key panicking. Her shoulders are tense against the thin straps of her dress, and her hands grasp her guitar like it's the only life raft in a stormy sea. But her eyes—those wide, frightened eyes—are on Sundae, and Sundae feels her feet carry her across the checkerboard floor, all the way up to the stage.

The lights shine on Lia's metallic blue eyeliner and long black lashes, spiky as spider legs. Sundae tips her face up, a smile on her glossy pink lips.

"Hey," Lia says, accidentally speaking into the microphone so the whole diner hears her. Plum-red blush blooms on her high cheekbones, and she steps away from the mic before adding, "Um, thanks for coming."

"Not for the last time tonight, I hope," Sundae says on a candy-sweet purr, and Lia's blush deepens.

"Nice crown, Barbarella. Are you the prom queen?" Dallas says, snapping a drumstick against the edge of his hi-hat as if to punctuate the question.

"Mm-hmm. To be fair, I did kiss most of the electorate, so they might have been a little biased," Sundae says.

"Dude. Lia's got a date with the prom queen," Edison says, looking over at Dallas. "This feels very 'directed by Judd Apatow,' doesn't it?"

"Yeah, this is definitely some Apatow-esque nerd wish fulfillment," Dallas agrees.

Lia huffs, rolling her eyes to the stage lights above. They catch in the gold that threads through her irises, and Sundae's heart does that little explosive pop again. "All right, how about you two shut the fuck up and start playing now?"

"Now?" Edison says, looking incredulous.

"*Now*, now?" Dallas echoes, sitting up straight, drumsticks poised in the air.

"*Yes*, now," Lia snaps, squeezing her eyes shut. "*Go*."

And they do.

Dallas cracks his drumsticks together twice before slamming them down, launching into a raucous beat. Edison strums his bass, long hair covering his face as he bobs along. And with her eyes still closed, Lia's hand moves over the strings of her violet guitar, strumming a rhythm that blows little goose bumps up the back of Sundae's neck.

Then Lia's molten brown eyes snap open, and she leans into the mic and starts to sing.

Sundae's friends find her in front of the crowd, squeezing in beside her to dance to the music. It's fun and fast and melodic, but even as Sundae jumps on her sparkly pumps and swings her pink hair around, she barely takes her eyes off Lia—and most of the time, she finds that Lia's eyes are on her, too.

Lia's voice matches the music, snarling with attitude, and her presence seems to fill up the whole diner. All her inhibitions drop away, shaken off like an empty mortar, leaving her to soar onstage, bright and explosive and impossible to look away from.

Sundae is holding hands with Neeli, the two of them jumping to the rowdy beat, when a tall shadow darkens the corner of her eye.

Sundae yelps in surprise as a hand falls on her shoulder.

"Sundae," he yells, louder than he needs to.

And Sundae twists to face Luke Panagos.

"Baby boy," Sundae says, releasing Neeli's hands to slap a palm over her heart. "You have *got* to stop jump-scaring me like this!"

"Sorry, sorry," Luke chuckles. His hand squeezes at Sundae's shoulder, his thumb prodding at her collarbone. It's kind of annoying, but then again, so is his presence in general. Sundae would way rather be enjoying Lia's music.

"I just— Do you *like* this emo music?" Luke asks Sundae, sounding perturbed.

"This isn't emo, this is *punk*, you ignoramus!" Neeli shouts over the sound.

"Okay, cool!" Luke says, in the tone of someone who hates being corrected. To Sundae, he says, "I just didn't know you were into this stuff."

Sundae tilts her head and swirls a lock of cotton-candy hair around her finger as she asks him, "What stuff?"

"You know. This kind of music," Luke says.

Sundae giggles and says, "What kind of music did you think I was into?"

"Don't you listen to like, Taylor Swift?" Luke says, and Sundae just laughs. He seems confused by the ambiguity of her response, but he soldiers on. "Do you mind— Can we talk for a second?"

"Aren't you already talking?" Sundae says.

"I mean—could you just, like, step outside with me?" Luke says. When he senses Sundae's reluctance, he adds, "*Please?* It's really important."

Sundae sighs and glances at Neeli, who rolls her eyes. But Sundae still nods, and she trudges through the crowd, leading Luke through the side door.

They step out onto the boardwalk, and when the door closes behind them, the sound of Lia's band is muffled by the steel siding of the diner. Still, Luke seems compelled to draw her farther away from the restaurant, and Sundae's irritation rises as she trails after him down the darkening boardwalk.

The sun is just peeking over the shoreline in the distance, bright as a tangerine, and the sky is vibrant violet. It would look so pretty through the windows of the diner, framing the stage where Lia is playing right now. But instead, Sundae's out here looking at it behind *Luke.*

"Luke?" Sundae says, planting her feet on the boardwalk, waiting until he stops walking away. He turns around, a petulant expression on his face. "Why are we walking? I thought we were supposed to be talking."

"Um. Right," Luke says, nodding. He steps a little closer to her, a frown creasing his lips. "Yeah, um, so, I was thinking . . ."

As if he's just said something dismaying that she's pretending to sympathize with, Sundae coos, "Oh no, baby."

Luke snorts. He rubs his hand through his thick black hair, takes a breath, and finishes the sentence he started. "I was thinking . . . you should stay in my room tonight. With me."

Ugh. Did he seriously drag her out here for *this*? Sundae slumps against the boardwalk railing beside her, leaning into it as she tosses her hair into the breeze and takes a deep, calming breath of salty air.

"I'm not your girlfriend, Luke," she reminds him. Her voice is silky, but her tone is firm.

"No, no, I know," he says, but his head nods even while he says no. "I get that, totally. It's just like, I know it must be hard for you . . . being here. I want to make you feel safe. You could be right next to me, in my arms, all night—"

"This is prom weekend, baby boy," Sundae cuts him off to say, a giggle on her lips. "Were you planning on *sleeping*? Because I'm sure as hell not."

"Well, we don't have to actually *sleep*," Luke says, his lips cracking into a grin. "But I heard you girls stayed on the beach last night, and I was really worried about you out there like that."

"You don't have to worry about me, silly," Sundae says. "I snoozed on a float in case the tide came in."

"I wasn't worried about the tide, Sunny. You know as well as I do, there's creeps out there."

Annoyance spikes Sundae's pulse. She sighs, her eyes rolling as she says, "There's creeps everywhere, Luke. Some of them might even be your friends."

Luke's face tenses, his brow furrowing. He steps in closer to Sundae, his head bowing toward her as he says, "Be honest with me, did Harper do something to you last night? Because . . . he's been saying stuff about you, and I think he's full of shit."

The question shocks Sundae, her wrist freezing mid–hair flick as she stares at him. Sundae glances around, like Harper might be lurking somewhere on the dusky boardwalk. But the only thing she notices is that when she looks back at Luke, there's a green light on the horizon behind him.

Sundae's almost *positive* it wasn't there before. She's been looking at Luke and his stupid lovesick face for most of this terrible conversation, and she's pretty sure she would have noticed it. Because when she squints her eyes and focuses on the source, there's no mistaking it—the glow is coming from a ride on the pier, where the facade of painted holly trees is illuminated in verdant green, the cutout leaves like a thorny crown against the darkening sky.

Was it just not lit up yet?

Or was it not there at all before the sun set?

Sundae wraps her arms around her chest, a tremor shaking her body. She looks to Luke, who is still waiting for an answer, and she manages to ask him, "What . . . What is Harper saying?"

"You don't want to know what he's saying," Luke says, fast as a slap. "But I know how he is, and I want to make sure you're okay."

"Oh, how gallant," Sundae says, once again all sugar to hide the sour. "Question, what do you mean when you say you 'know how he is'?" Sundae's fingers make air quotes around his words, her glittery claws flashing.

"That's not really relevant," Luke says.

"It is, though. Because I think what you're saying is that you're aware your dear, *dear* friend is a sex pest, and you want to know if he forced himself on me or not, because you know that's what he does to girls."

"If that's what he did, you need to tell me. Because I'm not okay with that," Luke says.

"But you *were* okay with it, when he was doing it to other girls. That makes me feel so special, baby," Sundae says, so sweetly that she thinks it should be obvious she's mocking him.

"Are you being facetious?" he asks, and Sundae giggles like he told a joke. Luke rubs at his temple, grumbling, "Please, just tell me what really happened."

"Why do you need to know so bad?" Sundae says.

"Because if he did something to you, I'm going to fuck him up," Luke snaps.

"What good would that do? It won't take back what he did to me."

"So he *did* do something." Luke squares his shoulders, his eyes darkening behind his thick lashes. But beneath the righteous anger, Sundae senses something else—a thread of relief unwinding from his brow as he settles on a target for his rage.

She tilts her head, a soft smile parting her lips.

"You weren't worried he'd forced himself on me at all," Sundae says. "You were worried he hadn't."

"Huh? No— Hey, no way." Luke reaches out for Sundae's arm, but she twists away from his grasp before he can touch her. "Sunny, come on. He's been going around saying shit about you. I'm going to call him out. I just wanted to make sure—"

"Look, Luke, baby, here's the thing," Sundae interrupts him to say, her bubbly voice never slipping. "You and I are never gonna be boyfriend-girlfriend, so if that's the only reason you care what happened between Harper and me, you can get over it and go back to silently endorsing his predatory behavior, okay?"

Sundae glances again at the pier behind Luke, all the rides chugging and whirring, their shiny metallic cars full of people, lines crowded around them beneath the blinking jewel lights . . . except for one ride, which sits in the shadows all lit in green, empty train cars crouched beneath the glowing red HAUNTED FOREST sign. Chills crawl up her back like skittering crab legs, and she returns her eyes to Luke and reaches up to give him a quick pat on the shoulder.

"If you don't mind, I'm gonna get back to the punk show. It was so fun talking to you, though. Bye-bye."

She turns away, heels clipping down the boardwalk as she returns to the Blue Velvet.

Sundae ignores the urge she feels to look over her shoulder as she walks, to make sure the Haunted Forest ride is still there, or to search the crowd for a set of shining silver eyes. It's all in her head, she reminds herself—the Coral Cove is gone, and he's not coming back for her.

And she's not going to let *him*, or Luke, or Harper fucking McCall ruin her prom weekend.

Sundae shoves the diner door open and steps back inside. The windows are fogged up now, obscuring the view of the boardwalk, turning the diner into its own little snow globe. And at the center of it all is Lia, standing on the stage with the lights making long shadows of her spidery lashes.

Sundae pushes back to the front of the crowd, and she feels all the cold dread in her chest turn to hot melty infatuation when she's locked in Lia's tar-pit eyes. In the sticky heat of the packed diner, she laughs and dances and shares a whiskey-spiked strawberry milkshake with her friends, totally oblivious to the hungry thing that's following her scent across the dark boardwalk.

And this time, he's not hunting alone.

THIRTEEN

NOW

Luke Panagos is pissed off, but it's not like he can just give up now.

Sure, the talk with Sundae didn't go the way he wanted it to. In fact, nothing this weekend has really gone the way he wanted it to. It was his idea, after all, to come to Wildwood for prom weekend. It wasn't about upsetting Sundae, it was about *helping* her. His AP Psych professor mentioned that hypersexuality could be a symptom of PTSD, and it all clicked—the reason Sundae Valentine is such a slut is because of whatever happened to her in Wildwood when she was a kid.

So maybe, if Sundae could make new memories here with him and all their friends, she'd finally get over it and realize she should be with *him*.

He floated the idea when he was beer-buzzed with Harper and the boys, and even though they teased him about being a simp for Sundae, they still vowed to help him. Harper especially, who booked the rooms for the team and acted like Wildwood had been *his* idea, so that Sundae wouldn't be mad at Luke when she found out about it. But maybe involving his friends in this was a mistake, because now, if he admits that Sundae *still* refuses to be his girlfriend, they're going to roast the ever-loving shit out of him for the rest of his natural-born life.

The fact is, he *needs* to get Sundae this weekend, no matter what.

Still, he doesn't go back to the Blue Velvet after Sundae walks away from him. He doesn't want to deal with his boys giving him shit about Sundae—especially Harper, who is probably lying about what happened between him and Sundae last night. And he *really* doesn't want to be anywhere in earshot of that screaming girl onstage inside the diner, because it annoys him that Sundae might enjoy that kind of music.

It makes him feel like he doesn't really know what she likes at all.

But of course he does. And one thing he's sure she likes is *candy*, because he saw her eating a lollipop once and he jerked off to the thought of it for, like, a week straight. So when he notices a candy shop glowing green on the boardwalk, a totally brilliant idea pops into his head.

Maybe he doesn't notice anything weird about the place because he's too busy picturing exactly how Sundae will react to this freshly plotted romantic gesture. (Obviously, she'll be besotted, and finally quit acting like such a fucking brat.) Or maybe he's just the kind of guy who never experiences trepidation, because the world has never been a dangerous place for him.

So Luke doesn't notice that the green light emanating from the shop windows seems to drift out like curling smoke, wafting strangely across the boardwalk. He pays no mind to the way the bell on the door rings a sour note when he walks inside, or the fact that there's no one in the shop but him and the burly man with a striped apron behind the counter. He doesn't even notice the way the sickly sugar-sweet scent on the air smells almost like rotting meat, or the cleaver that the man behind the counter is holding in his hand.

What he *does* notice is the maggots.

It's hard not to. The cellophane bag he takes for the candy is crisp and clear, so when he pours a scoop of peach rings in, it's impossible to miss all the squirming white worms that come along with it. He shouts in surprise and drops the bag, spilling peach rings and maggots on the red tile floor.

The man behind the counter lets loose a high-pitched giggle.

"What the *fuck*, man," Luke starts to say, but when he twists to face the man behind the counter, his complaint dies on his lips. Because the man behind the counter—the man with a belly like a wine barrel straining against his apron and arms as wide as shovel blades—is holding a cleaver up to his face, one rolling wild eye peering at Luke through the hole in the slick metal.

The man giggles again, in a breathy falsetto like he's imitating the sound of a child's laughter.

It's only then that Luke starts to notice all the *other* weird things about this place. Like how the chocolates lined up in the display case are covered in cobwebs. Or the stains on the floor in the shapes of sprawled-out bodies, like corpses rotted into the tiles. Or the way some of the candy bins are full of sugar-crusted bones, or teeth, or eyeballs . . .

But he's realized it all too late, because by the time he starts screaming, the man in the striped apron is already on the other side of the counter.

Luke spins and tries to run for the door, but one of his sneakers skids on a maggot-covered peach ring, and he nearly loses his balance. He recovers, but he can hear the thunderous clomps of the big man running up behind him, can hear his warbling giggle getting closer and closer—

And when the cleaver splits into his skull, Luke's last thought is that all of this happened because of Sundae Valentine.

FOURTEEN

NOW

This might not be opening for Spaced, but to Lia, it's the best night of her life.

Maybe it's because she was afraid she'd never be able to do it again, so picking up her guitar and screaming into the crowd feels somehow miraculous, like stretching out a limb she thought she'd lost. Maybe it's the fact that this is such a different audience for Morticia—the prom weekend partiers are definitely *not* the gleefully thrashing punk kids they normally play for—that makes the enthusiasm catching through the crowd extra heady. Maybe it's the way Aunt Violet is there, watching from behind the bar, her proud smile and watery eyes visible even from a distance.

Or maybe it's just Sundae.

She can't get over how good Sundae looks in her tight baby-blue prom dress, dancing excitedly to Lia's music. The way her pink hair flashes like tinsel in the light as she jumps and shimmies and spins with her friends, the way she smiles and sings along to every song once she learns the chorus. It makes Lia's heart gallop in her chest, and it brings something out in her that she's never had onstage before—a kind of triumphant elation that carries in her voice, pushing out all her doubt.

Lia's mood did hit a speed bump when the ridiculous Labrador guy came in, put his hand on Sundae's shoulder, and somehow convinced her to step outside with him. A jolt of irritation made Lia shriek louder into the mic. Not out of jealousy, but anger—because Lia could tell by the look on Sundae's face that he was bothering her. Luckily, she wasn't gone for long, and when Sundae returned, she just kept on dancing like nothing had happened.

When Lia thrums her last chord and the music fades out to shouts and applause, she takes a moment to bask in it. She looks out at the crowded diner, and then she glances over her shoulder at her best friends, Dallas sweaty and wild behind his drum set, Edison looking a little shocked by all the attention as he stands frozen with his bass.

Lia nods at them, grateful to see the exhilaration on their faces, grateful she didn't end up disappointing them again. Grateful Dallas was wrong about what he said during the argument that might or might not have happened last night. Grateful she isn't still stuck in the universe where she didn't have the guts to play a show or ask a girl on a date, no matter if it was a wish or a pill that got her here.

Theo switches on the house music again, piping some '90s club hit through the speakers for the kids to keep dancing to. Nobody seems to mind that the song is old; the beat is good. Lia slings off her guitar and sets it down. She grabs something she hid behind the amp before the show and hops down off the stage to stand in front of Sundae, who is waiting there with her cheeks flushed and tendrils of pink hair sticking to her sweaty temples.

Terror and joy fill Lia in equal measure.

But she was brave enough to stand in front of a crowd and play her music, and even though she can't remember it, she *was* brave enough to ask Sundae to be her date tonight. So she faces Sundae, one hand pushing back her dark hair while the other holds the gift out to her.

"Here, um . . . I wanted to get you a corsage, but this is all I could find."

It's a kitschy boardwalk souvenir, a bracelet of pearly beads and little rosettes made out of pink cowrie shells. As she offers it up to Sundae, she can feel the blush heating her cheeks, and there's a part of her that fears that Sundae might just laugh in Lia's face for trying to give her something so silly. But Sundae's blue eyes go wide, her glossy lips parting on a delighted gasp of breath.

"Oh! My god! This is so much better, because it'll never die," Sundae says, holding out her hand so that Lia can slide the bracelet onto her wrist.

But Lia hesitates, a certain foreboding freezing her for a moment.

It's something about Sundae's words. They remind her of a voice like claws dragging against sand saying, *"You hear my music, don't you? Then I will never die."*

Lia shuts her eyes, the flare of stage lights burned into the back of her eyelids like fireworks in a starry sky. She shakes it off, then opens her eyes and slips the bracelet onto Sundae's wrist, tightening the hemp-rope knot that fastens it. Before her hands can drop away, Sundae grabs one of them, squeezing Lia's fingers against her palm.

"Thank you," Sundae says, raw and earnest. "I love it. Almost as much as I loved watching you sing."

Lia opens her mouth to stammer out thanks, but then Aunt Violet cuts her off with a loud, "Holy shit, Magnolia. That was some real fuck-you music."

"Yeah. That was a kick in the teeth," Theo says in her airy, dream-drenched voice. She's hooked in Aunt Violet's tattooed arm, and the two of them are looking at Lia like a couple of proud parents, which makes Lia want to crumble to a pile of ash where she stands (in the best way possible).

Instead, she chokes out, "It was fine. I kind of went too fast on 'Happy Enough to Stay Still.'"

"Yeah, thanks a lot for that, by the way," Dallas shouts as he gets up from behind his drum set, rubbing gingerly at his shoulder when he springs down off the stage. "Pretty sure I tore my rotator cuff trying to keep up with you!"

"You're just mad it wasn't *you* putting us on hyperspeed this time," Edison says as he steps down behind Dallas.

"And who is this?" Theodosia asks, her always-sleepy eyes on Sundae.

"Oh, right, sorry—this is Sundae," Lia says, her cheeks flushing even more as she realizes that she's been standing there holding Sundae's hand in front of her friends and family like it's no big deal, when it *is* most definitely *a big fucking deal*. "Um, Sundae, this is my aunt Violet and her partner, Theo."

"Sundae," Theo repeats, her cinnamon brows arching. "What a sweet name."

"Really, dad jokes already, Teddy?" Aunt Violet sighs.

"It just sounds familiar," Theo says, tilting her head, her sleepy eyes a little more awake. "Have you been to Wildwood before, sweet Sundae?"

Lia feels Sundae go tense. Her hand tightens, crushing Lia's fingers as she takes the tiniest step back, as if she's fighting the urge to flee. Still, she keeps her voice as candied as ever as she answers, "Of course it sounds familiar. I'm not the only sundae on this boardwalk, am I?"

"Wow. Well, this saloon ain't big enough for two dad-jokesters," Lia says. She turns to Sundae, meeting her eyes, squeezing her hand in return—though much more gently than Sundae is squeezing hers. "How about we get out of here?"

Sundae nods, and when her blue eyes meet Lia's, it's clear how desperate she is to do exactly that, so Lia doesn't make her wait a moment longer. She twists on her beat-up boots, guiding Sundae toward the door that leads out to the boardwalk.

"Have fun! Don't ruin my dress! It's older than you!" Aunt Violet shouts at Lia's back.

"You know I always respect my elders!" Lia calls back as she pushes open the door, letting a blast of ocean breeze into the steamy diner. She pauses in the doorway to turn, looking back at Aunt Violet, who raises a middle finger at her. Lia returns the gesture, then steps out onto the boardwalk with Sundae.

Sundae sighs with relief once they're out of the diner. Her long pink nails graze the back of Lia's hand, and Lia hopes the pounding of her heart isn't visible through her rib cage.

"Sorry, was that weird for you? Are you all right?"

"I'm okay," Sundae says, and now that they're alone, she *does* look okay, the tension melting off her spine.

Still, Lia asks her, "Do you want to talk about what happened with that guy in the middle of the show?"

"Actually, yes," Sundae says, anger sharpening the velvet tones of her voice. "I'm sorry, but did he *only* bring one pair of shorts to wear this entire weekend? If you've been wearing the same nasty basketball shorts for two days, you should already *know* you don't have what it takes to be with a girl like me."

Lia laughs, watching Sundae strut alongside her, looking totally unbothered by the situation despite her obvious annoyance with whatever the guy said to her. It's kind of awe-inspiring, this ability she has to seem like nothing could shake her footing. Even last night, when Lia first met her, Sundae somehow made crying on the beach look very glamorous and cool.

Lia can't help but ask, "How do you do that?"

"Do what?" Sundae says, touching a hand to her tiara like she's checking it's still in place.

"I don't know, you just . . . You seem like you're really not afraid of anything," Lia says.

Lia must have struck a nerve, because Sundae draws in a quick breath between her teeth, like it stings a little. The bustle of the boardwalk moves around them as they walk, a cacophony of lights and sounds, but all Lia sees is Sundae.

"What are you afraid of?" Sundae asks Lia.

"Honestly . . . sometimes it feels like I'm afraid of literally everything," Lia answers.

"Give me *one* thing you're afraid of, then," Sundae says.

"I mean . . . I'm scared of heights." Lia shrugs. It's true, but it's not the most limiting of her fears—still, it seems like the only one she can mention without making this conversation way too intense.

"So let's go on the Ferris wheel," Sundae says, pulling on Lia's hand, starting to draw her toward the giant wheel twirling at the end of the pier.

"*What?*" Lia balks.

"If you want to know how I stopped being afraid, it's by having everything I could possibly be afraid of happen to me already," Sundae says. "So if you want to stop being afraid of something, I guess you just survive it once, and know you could do it again if you had to."

Lia gives up any resistance she had against Sundae's pull, letting herself be tugged toward the Ferris wheel. Sundae's words settle over her, sinking in like peroxide on a cut, stinging the whole way down.

What Sundae's saying is the opposite of what Lia did after the Spaced show, when she felt like all her worst fears had come true, and her response was to tell herself she might never play again. But she's pushed herself past that, so why not this, too?

"Okay. Let's ride the Ferris wheel, then," Lia says, even though the thought makes her want to throw the fuck up.

Maybe if she stares at Sundae the whole time and never looks down, it won't be so bad.

They head to the end of the pier, where the massive wheel spins toward the sky, the rainbow lights blurry in the ocean mist like an oil-slick halo against the asphalt-black night. The bored boy at the gate doesn't ask them for tickets, which strikes Lia as odd, but then again, Lia feels like Sundae probably has that effect on people.

"Are you sure you want to do this?" Sundae asks Lia as they climb the steps to the platform.

Lia glances up and instantly regrets it, her stomach dropping when she sees how high the Ferris wheel towers over her. She drops her eyes back to Sundae and says, "I definitely don't *want* to do this, but let's do it."

Sundae giggles and tugs on her hand, and the next thing she knows, she's falling into the swinging cart beside Sundae and the gate is locking shut behind them.

The wheel jerks into motion, lifting them away from the ground.

Sundae's arm is coiled around Lia's, and she's pressed close against Lia's side as they rise. Lia tries not to crush Sundae's fingers with the squeeze of her rings, but Sundae's hand is her anchor and it's hard not to cling to it.

"This is way cooler than the *actual* prom, by the way," Sundae says. "Especially since no one stopped me to tell me my nipples were showing."

"Jesus Christ," Lia says through gritted teeth. She can't help glancing down, as if she hasn't already noticed how the aqua-blue fabric of Sundae's dress is so tight that it's obvious she isn't wearing anything but a thong underneath it. Sundae giggles when she catches Lia looking, her hips shifting, like she's making sure Lia has a good view.

Lia bites the inside of her cheek, which is already bitten raw from the past two days. Her pulse is spiking—and not just from the height their cart is climbing to.

"Anyway, joke's on them. These tits made me prom queen," Sundae says, free hand patting her tiara.

Lia shakes her head in awe, dragging her eyes up to Sundae's face. She wishes she could show a past version of herself this moment and gloat that one day she'd nail the best show she ever played and then ride the Giant Wheel with a scorching-hot pink-haired prom queen. Maybe then she'd have gotten bolder sooner.

But since she can't change the past (any more than she already has), Lia decides to be bolder right *now*.

Her one hand still squeezed tight in Sundae's, she lifts the other and skims her knuckles against Sundae's cheek. Her fingers uncurl, combing into Sundae's hair, the pearly pink strands catching in the flashing lights. Sundae leans in, too, her hand finding Lia's leg through the slit in her dress. The feeling of Sundae's sharp nails against the skin of her thigh sends shivers up Lia's spine.

Sundae's lips part, a pleased sigh escaping between them.

Lia catches it in her mouth and kisses Sundae, and neither of them notice the silver eyes watching from the boardwalk below while the Ferris wheel spins them up toward the sky.

FIFTEEN

NOW

Sundae's favorite thing about kissing Lia is that she can feel the exact moment when Lia stops holding herself back.

Just like when she was playing her music, there's a point in their kiss where Lia seems to break free of her apprehension and become downright explosive. When Sundae feels it happen, she shudders in Lia's arms, letting Lia's sudden intensity pulse through her as their kiss goes totally volcanic.

Lia has one hand in Sundae's hair and the other on her body, and Sundae's dress is so thin she can feel Lia's rings on the underside of her fingers as her palm drags up Sundae's ribs. Sundae melts back against the bench, pleased Lia's hands feel just as good as she'd imagined they would.

She's just about to slide her hand farther up the slit in Lia's skirt when she hears it.

It's so faint, it's a wonder she catches it at all. But that song has played so often in her nightmares, she could recognize it by a single note, by the barest whisper on the breeze.

Sundae rips away from Lia's lips. Lia's eyes snap open, deep brown shot through with gold, and she asks in a throaty whisper, "Sundae? What's wrong?"

"Shh," Sundae hisses, her breath ragged and quick. "Do you hear it?"

"Hear *what*?"

It's playing through the speakers on the ride. The ones down below, which were blasting a loop of *Souvenir de Cirque Renz* just a moment ago, are now buzzing with a familiar melody and a crooning voice that sings,

> *"One, for a path I crossed.*
> *Two, for my love I lost. . . ."*

The cart they're in has nearly reached the top of the ride. Their faces are washed in flashing light from the neon bulbs studding the steel bars all around them. Suspended high above the boardwalk, surrounded by nothing but inky blue sky, it feels a little like floating in the deep end, a smiling beast at her back. Sundae is shivering, cold fear running through her body as she leans away from Lia and looks down over the side of their cart.

"Sundae?" Lia murmurs, concern clear in her tone. "What's going on?"

Sundae finds him instantly by the red in his crown of holly, by the shine of his metallic eyes. He's standing on the platform at the bottom of the Ferris wheel, his face tipped up so she can see the smile that splits his mouth.

Sundae's scream cuts the night as his hands grasp the bars of the ride, and he starts to climb, scaling the wheel as fast as a spider climbs a wall while his smile grows wider.

"No, no, no—" Sundae repeats, panic taking over as she shrinks away from the edge of the cart, pressing her back against Lia. She feels Lia's hands grip her shoulders as she crushes her against the corner of the bench, but it's no use.

There's nowhere to run.

She's trapped, and he's coming for her.

"Sundae, please—" Lia starts to say, but if she's about to ask what's going on again, she stops short. Because the music from the speakers below is getting louder, booming up to ricochet off the canopy of their cart, and Sundae's hands cover her ears as she screams again.

"Three, and you will come for me,
Like the tide pulls the sand back to the sea. . . ."

And then his face rises over the side of their cart, the spinning lights dancing across rows of wet black teeth as he smiles at her.

No matter how many times she's relived the memories of him, no matter how many times he's appeared in the dark space of her dreams, she's still not prepared for the terror she feels seeing him again. All the thoughts in her mind become a frantic scream, like the one that rings from her mouth as she presses even harder against Lia on the bench.

He thrusts his arms into the cart and scuttles over the bars to perch on the opposite bench. He crouches like a beast ready to pounce, his penny loafers balanced on the edge of the seat as he leers over them, dripping seawater, smelling of low tide.

"Oh god, this can't be happening," Lia whimpers close to Sundae's ear.

"You've kept me waiting for such a long time, little fish," Holly Jolly says, his voice like waves scraping the shoreline. "Are you ready to settle your debt?"

"Leave me alone!" Sundae shrieks. Her sweaty hands slip on the slick metal of the bench, and she kicks at the floor so she doesn't slide any closer to him.

"Don't be so selfish," he says. "Do you think it's fair that everyone should have to pay but you?"

"What do you *want* from her?" Lia asks. One of her arms crosses Sundae's chest and her other hand grips the safety bar behind them, like she's ready to anchor them in place if he tries to drag Sundae away.

The wind rushing through the cart rustles the holly crowning his head as he reaches out, unfurling his long fingers toward Sundae. A single taffy waits on his palm, black as his teeth and swirled with blood red.

"I want what she owes me," he says with his cold eyes locked on Sundae. Lia's arm flinches on Sundae's chest, a quick gasp escaping her lips.

"No! I'll never do it!" Sundae yells, her cry tapering off into another scream as he lunges for her.

Sharp fingers clasp her legs and pull, nearly yanking her from Lia's grasp. Lia lets out a throaty shout as she releases the safety bar to wind her other arm around Sundae, and both of them are flung off the bench, the cart lurching violently as they crash to the floor. Sundae lands on top of Lia, who bears the brunt of the impact, her head hitting the steel with a loud thud.

Still, even with the breath knocked out of her, Lia doesn't release her hold.

Sundae's hands clamp to Lia's forearms, clinging desperately as a raw sob rattles from her throat. The cart swings to and fro, rocking like a boat in choppy waters. He swoops down from above, the taffy pinched between his fingers as he looms over them. He reeks of rot and brine, his face pushing close to hers, his unblinking eyes wide as silver dollars as he stares at her.

"This is the last chance I will give you to surrender," he says in a salty whisper as he dangles the taffy over her mouth. "Open up. Make your wish."

Sundae keeps her lips sealed shut, cringing away from him and shaking her head. She closes her eyes so she doesn't have to see his teeth bearing down so close to her face, but fetid seawater drips onto her prom dress, soaking through the thin fabric, reminding her that he's there.

She feels Lia shifting underneath her, stretching one leg out toward the opposite end of the cart.

"No!" Sundae screams back at him, her eyes opening again, his shadowy shape blurry through her tears. "I know you can't hurt me! Not unless I make that wish!"

Even through the glaze in her eyes, she can see the smile widening on his face. Fear feels like needles all over her body, making her writhe and whimper. Slowly, he reaches his hand into his brown suit jacket and draws out his saw blade.

Its serrated teeth glint in the moonlight.

He holds it up high and lets out a silty laugh. "The arrangement has changed," he says.

And then his blade plunges toward her chest.

Something thunks by their feet and Lia's other boot comes down to press against the floor.

The safety gate swings open into the wind.

"Sundae! Go!" Lia cries against her ear.

She doesn't have to say more than that for Sundae to understand what she's supposed to do. They rear up together, Sundae driving her heels into Holly Jolly's gut while Lia pushes against his shoulders. His saw scrapes Sundae's upper arm, biting into her skin and then sliding back out as they fling him through the open gate, into the sky over the boardwalk.

For a thrilling moment, he seems to vanish from sight, falling past the edge of the cart.

Then Sundae realizes she's moving, and she looks down to see his crab-leg fingers wrapped around her ankle, dragging her toward the open gate.

People are screaming below, but Sundae can't hear them over the rushing wind and the sound of her own keening yell as she flies out of the cart. But she jolts to a sudden stop, and so does he, pulling so hard on her leg that she screams out in pain. It takes her a second to understand why she stopped at all.

Then she realizes it's Lia's arms around her again, elbows looped beneath her armpits, hands clasped against her rib cage. Lia has her boots braced on either side of the open gate, anchoring them against his falling weight, and her eyes are wide, like she's shocked she managed to catch Sundae before she fell.

Sundae looks down. First at the boardwalk, so far below her dangling feet. Then at him, one hand clasped to her ankle, his holly-crowned head tipped toward her. Slowly, he reaches his other arm up, the wrapped black taffy pinched between his fingers.

"Take this, little fish," he says. "Soon you may find yourself with nothing left but a wish for death."

His words send a chill up Sundae's spine, and despite herself, she reaches out and takes the candy he offers her.

"Sundae, don't," Lia grunts.

But Sundae curls her fist around the taffy, pressing it to her palm, and his grip slips from her ankle.

He drops like rotten fruit from a tree. Sundae watches him as he falls, his face pointed up to her the whole time, a smile on his lips. He lands on the control panel at the bottom of the ride, driving it into the platform with a shower of sparks and the sound of twisting metal.

The crowd below becomes a roar of screams and pounding feet as people run and push in every direction, some of them to get a closer look, some to get away. Meanwhile, Lia is dragging Sundae into the cart, and when she hits a point where the small of her back touches the floor, Sundae is able to scoot her hips and legs the rest of the way in.

She twists in Lia's arms, curled up halfway in her lap on the diamond-plated metal. The wind rattles the open safety gate and blows through Sundae's pink hair as she meets Lia's eyes, her arms coiling around Lia's shoulders.

"You saved me," she murmurs, voice worn raw from all the screams.

"Sundae, what . . . the fuck . . . was that?" Lia says through panting breaths, her hands resting on Sundae's waist.

"*That* was the thing I survived," Sundae says.

"Is it *dead*?" Lia asks, craning to the side just enough to peek over the edge of their cart, down toward the boardwalk.

"I doubt it," Sundae says.

Sure enough, he's moving, pulling himself out of the crater of crumpled metal made by his impact. The control panel he crushed is still emitting sparks, sizzling against his wet brown suit as he gets to his feet.

His silver eyes find their dangling cart and a smile splits his face. Then he hops down from the mangled platform, stalking off into the crowd.

Sundae loses sight of him in the stampeding throng, but her eyes follow him just long enough for her to guess where he might be headed.

And if he's going to the Blue Velvet, where all her friends are partying and unaware, then his warning could be right.

Before this night is over, she might very well wish for death.

SIXTEEN

JULY 2019

He dropped like an anchor, dragging Sundae by the ankle into the deep end of the pool.

The only air in her lungs was the scream caught in her throat. Sundae stared up at the courtyard lights shining on the surface as she sank down and down and down.

She never hit the bottom.

Bright aqua fell into darkest blue. The bubbles around her winked like stars in the sky. She felt her oxygen running out, her vision closing into darkness.

And then suddenly, they broke through, rearing out of the water.

Sundae gasped for breath, her eyes flying open. But she wasn't in the courtyard at Coral Cove anymore—she was somewhere strange and unfamiliar, where bright lights and loud sounds assaulted her senses.

She was too disoriented to make sense of it, and he hauled her up, carrying her under his arm.

He set her down in a hard wooden seat and swung himself up beside her.

He'd taken her to some kind of ride, several connected carriages painted to look like train cars. Sundae rubbed the spots from her vision and looked around as the engine bucked forward, chugging down the tracks.

It was a ride that reminded her of the one she'd ridden once at the carnival with her mom, the one called the Tunnel of Love. Only instead of passing through glowing rows of hearts in the dark, the train crawled past scenes that reminded Sundae of being lost inside a bad dream, of nightmare places that look like real life but feel all wrong.

The first one they rumbled past depicted an underwater landscape, the walls lined with wrinkled blue foil to resemble an endless sea. Black lights made the fish suspended on wire glow in the dark, and mucky green seaweed reached up from the floor like grabbing hands.

And as Sundae stared into this papier-mâché ocean scene, a hulking, huge shark swam out of the deep.

It didn't look fake, like everything else around it. The glide of its massive body was too smooth for any hydraulic motion. Its silver skin glistened with every twist of its tail. When it opened its mouth, Sundae could smell rotten fish and blood.

It lunged toward the train car with jagged black teeth bared, and Sundae screamed, covering her face and turning away from the beast.

She expected to feel its teeth rip into her, but even when they didn't she stayed curled up with her knees pressed to her chest and her hands over her eyes. She kept her head bowed, fear shivering through her body as tears leaked down her damp cheeks.

There were strange sounds all around her. The churn of the ride's motor, the whisper of crashing waves, the chatter of seabirds in the sky. And louder than all of it, the song she'd heard on the jukebox in the Coral Cabana was piping from hidden speakers somewhere above, echoing through the ride.

"One, for a path I crossed.
Two, for my love I lost.
Three, and you will come for me,
Like the tide pulls the sand back to the sea. . . ."

There was a sound like creaky tree branches now—they must be chugging through a new scene—but Sundae didn't look. She squeezed her eyes tight and moved her hands to her ears, crushing her fingers against them to try to muffle the hum of his voice.

But she could still hear the song, no matter how hard she pressed.

"All along, I knew the cost.
But I always thought I could stop.
That I would dig just one grave.
That my love could be saved.
But now that I've paid the price,
I'll wish to forget what I've sacrificed."

Sundae felt the ride slowing. The air was filled with the smell of sulfur and sea muck. She jumped when something brushed her legs, and her eyes snapped open to see long wisps of blond salt grass stretching up into the train car from either side of the tracks as they rolled through a marsh surrounded by walls with a painted wooden skyline.

The train made it halfway through the scene before it suddenly started to buck like it was jammed on the tracks. Sundae screamed as the ride began to tilt to the side, leaning toward the thick tall grass.

She looked beside her, expecting to see Holly Jolly sitting there, but he was gone.

The rumble of the train's engine died, and in the quiet that followed, Sundae could hear the hiss of the wind through the grass and the splash of the ocean hitting the mud.

And then there came the sound of screams.

Sundae twisted around, looking at the train cars behind her, but they were empty. She whipped forward again, clawing up the tilted seat, away from the thick of the marsh.

As she sat on top of the tipped-over ride, she saw the words painted along the side of the row of train cars—THE WEST JERSEY RAILROAD COMPANY.

Clawed fingers sank into her shoulders and she was wrenched into her seat as the ride suddenly jolted back to life, turning upright on the tracks to keep crawling along. She looked up just long enough to see Holly Jolly on the seat beside her again, before she covered her eyes as the song returned, crooning down the track.

"Here in the Wildwoods,
Where you once stood
All clothed in green.
Now my love is gone,
And before the dawn,
You will be clothed in me."

The song mingled with the sounds of the scenes they were passing, but Sundae wouldn't look at them. She smelled hot sticky sugar, burning rubber, smoldering embers. She heard things that made her yelp and sob: a noise like teeth gnawing bone, the roar of a hungry beast, strangled voices crying out.

And from unseen speakers, his voice still crooning:

"So let this song be a warning
For the next one you come haunting.
The wanting hearts of dreamers here
Will find only nightmares when you appear.

"One, for a path I crossed.
Two, for my love I lost.
Three, and you will come for me,
Like the tide pulls the sand back to the sea."

The train finally slowed, and Sundae's hands fell away from her face as she took in the final scene.

This one was the Coral Cabana, the walls painted with a mural of the tiki-themed bar, perfect replicas of the amber glass lamps hanging from the ceiling, even the dusty jukebox in the corner glowing green like it did when it turned on the night she made her first wish. On the floor behind the bar sprawled a waxen model of Tony, red silk ribbons pouring from his neck.

The train crept on, pulling through the doorway of the Cabana, to a re-creation of the courtyard. In the center of the scene was a miniature version of the pool, and Sundae could see that around it there were wet handprints and splashes of water.

She tried to remember the moment when he'd first dragged her through the dark at the bottom of the pool and they'd emerged in this strange place, but she'd had to hold her breath for so long, and everything was fuzzy and unclear. Still, she thought, this might be the way they'd come—which meant it might be the way back out.

Sundae twisted in her seat, looking up at Holly Jolly, a smile still splitting his jagged mouth. She flinched away from him, cowering into the corner of the bench.

"What do you want from me?" she asked in a whisper.

"Your last wish," he said, and lifted his hand, a black taffy swirled with red held out on his palm. "Make it now."

Sundae looked down at the taffy, blurred through the tears in her eyes. She kept her hands on her shivering knees and shook her head. "No," she said. "I don't want to."

A chuckle hissed from his sharp teeth. "But you were so greedy before."

Sundae shook her head again, winding her arms around her legs, shrinking back against the wooden bench beneath her. "I'm sorry," she whispered, though she didn't know what she was apologizing for. "I don't have any more wishes."

"What a lie. You are full of wishes, little fish. It is what drew me to you. I only come out when I find something as hungry as me," he said. He pushed his open hand closer to her, the red swirl at the center of the taffy twisting beneath the paper wrapper. "Your last wish. Make it now."

"No!" Sundae snapped, tipping her chin up to glare at him. "I won't do it!"

"Make a wish!" he commanded, thrusting the candy at her again. "Now!"

"Fine! I wish you'd leave me alone!" Sundae shouted back at him, snatching the candy. But before she could unwrap it, he closed his long fingers over her hand and stopped her, clicking his tongue.

"You cannot use your wishes against me. You cannot bind me, you cannot stop me. Not if that is the intent of your wish, anyway. You were only able to keep me from collecting the cost of your second wish because you truly believed there was no price for your vain little demands when you wished to have whatever you want without paying. A lucky trick you found." Another cruel laugh breezed from his mouth, a laugh that made her feel small and silly and stupid for believing that his wishes had been offered in friendship alone. He continued, "A trick of ignorance, but a trick nonetheless."

Sundae stared at him, her hand crushed in his grip and his sharp teeth far too close to her face. This wasn't the first time she'd been cornered by a monster. Of course, the last monster didn't have jaws full of pointy teeth or skin that shimmered like fish scales. But still, Sundae's father had taught her a thing or two about his kind.

And she knew, from the rage in his eyes, that if Holly Jolly *could* hurt her right now, he *would*.

But instead he just sat there, holding that piece of candy, demanding she make a wish. Which gave Sundae the impression that until she did, he couldn't do anything to her at all.

The realization was like cool water on the frantic flames of her fear, but she tried not to let it show that her terror was fading. The other thing she'd learned about monsters is that they are calmest when they think they are in control. Sundae let her voice tremble as she said, "You didn't tell me the wishes *had* a cost."

"Nothing comes without a cost," Holly Jolly said impatiently.

"I thought they were a gift," Sundae said. "If—if you just tell me what the price is, I'll pay for them now, and you can let me go."

"You did pay for the first wish," he told her, his hand twisting in a circle to point toward the scene in front of them. "It is the debt for your second that is still outstanding."

Sundae looked where he pointed, across the pink courtyard, to the model of the Coral Cabana where the wax figure of Tony was lying on the floor with ribbons of blood spilling out of his throat.

The comfort she'd felt knowing that Holly Jolly wasn't able to hurt her sliced away instantly as she realized what he meant.

"Tony?" she whispered, whipping her head around to look at Holly Jolly again. "Did Tony die because of my wish?"

He answered her with a laugh that purred from his throat like a lion's growl. The guilt dropped hard on Sundae's chest, knocking out an anguished cry as she covered her face again. Palms pressed against her eyelids, she still saw Tony with his head tipped back and his throat torn open—only it wasn't the wax replica, it was the real thing. And it was all her fault.

"You can wish he were alive again," Holly Jolly said softly. "Go ahead. Use your last wish to bring him back."

Sundae dragged her hands down her face, her fingertips pressing against swollen cheeks as she looked at the candy in his hand again. Now the red swirl seemed to pulse like a heartbeat at the center. Sundae lifted her eyes, watching him through the blur of tears.

Maybe he was telling the truth. Maybe she could wish for Tony to come back to life, and it would be like she never caused him to die at all.

But Sundae had a feeling that if she made that wish, something very bad would happen. She wasn't sure what, or how it could be worse than Tony dying, but she was certain Holly Jolly wouldn't be trying so hard to get her to make the wish otherwise.

And though she knew enough about monsters to be sure it was dangerous, Sundae kept her eyes locked on his, and her chin lifted high as she declared, "No. I'll never make that wish, and you can't make me!"

Then she jumped out of the train car, because she had escaped a monster before, and she could get away from this one, too.

She heard his roar behind her, but she didn't turn around. The train tracks were rough against her bare feet as she scampered up onto the staged Coral Cove motel, the pink pavers bouncing like Styrofoam as she ran across them.

Hoping she was right about the pool, she took a big gulping breath and jumped in.

The water wrapped around her, cold and salty as the sea. It burned her eyes, but she kept them open as she swam down deeper, praying she wouldn't see the bottom of the replica swimming pool coming up to meet her. Which is how she spotted it, out in the murky blue water—a dark shape, moving toward her across the seemingly endless length of the pool.

Her limbs faltered, slowing her descent for a moment as she took it in. Skin silver as a knife, gleaming in the beams of light that cut through the water. An undulating tail, slicing back and forth. The sharp dorsal fin, stabbing up toward the surface.

It was in the water with her now. The shark that had lunged out of the first scene in the ride.

She had to bite down on the scream that wanted to escape her as she kicked, sweeping her arms to propel herself back into motion. Regaining the momentum she'd lost, Sundae swam faster than she ever had before. As the massive shark got closer, she could feel it—the way its tail displaced the water, sending bubbles cascading past her eyes.

And when its teeth tried to snap down on her leg, it made a noise like a thunderclap, booming against her ears.

She glanced back as it drove toward her again, its open mouth so massive it could swallow her whole. Fear wanted to seize her muscles and turn her held breath into a shriek, but she swam faster instead.

Whipping her head forward, she realized she could see light playing against the surface of the water. She wasn't swimming down anymore—she was going up.

Up, up, out of the deep end.

She broke through the surface in the pool at the Coral Cove Motel. The *real* one, not his painted re-creation.

The sky was streaked with purple and gold, and the courtyard was teeming with people—cops in their blue uniforms, stomping and jangling their belts, just like the night Tony died. They didn't even notice her as she paddled desperately through the water, because they were too busy marching around with their big boots.

Sundae opened her mouth to shout for help, but all she got was a swallow of water as something pulled her back under.

She expected the gnashing jaws of the shark, but when she twisted in the bubbling blue, it was Holly Jolly in the pool with her. Only, as little stripes of early dawn sunlight sliced through from the surface, they beamed across his face, and like the facets of a prism, she saw other things—the gnarled bark of a tree, the golden eye of a hungry beast, gaunt gray skin stretched across a hollow cheek, a round chin speckled with silver hair like granules of sugar, little peeks of other faces that glimmered in the light.

She didn't understand what it meant.

But she *did* understand that the sunlight was bothering him.

It was the way he thrashed his face to and fro, the light catching one side, then another, like he was trying to shake it off. He bared his teeth, and sometimes they were black and serrated like a shark's, and sometimes they were twisting tree roots, and sometimes they were rotten and yellow or bright pearly white or fanged like the mouth of a savage big cat.

"Wish!" he screamed into the water, and his voice was a dozen voices all at once, refracted like a hall of mirrors. "Do it *now*!"

If there had been any doubt at all, it was gone. He couldn't hurt her unless she made that final wish. And he desperately needed her to.

Sundae shook her head, and he shrieked, a sound like snapping branches, like shattering bone, like a throaty croon sliding out of tune.

He released her, his sharp fingers grazing her arms as he flailed in the blue water. He shot down toward the bottom of the pool, but when he reached the tile floor, he crashed into it, like the doorway to the replica Coral Cabana had been closed.

Holly Jolly beat his fists against the tile, his screams piercing Sundae's ears as the sunlight flooded in from above. Sundae kicked her legs, bobbing up to the surface, her pink head breaking through the water.

Finally, the cops in the courtyard noticed her, and her mom was shouting her name.

But Sundae ignored them all. She took a big gulp of air and then dropped back below the waterline, looking down at the bottom of the deep end, where Holly Jolly was writhing against the floor. Chlorine burning her eyes, she tried not to blink as the light seemed to cut through him like knives.

Sundae watched as he twisted and floundered and started to shrink. Someone jumped into the water near her, the waves making her bounce, but she didn't look away from the thing that seemed to be dying in the deep end.

He was folding in on himself like crumpling tissue paper.

Just a scrap of black shadow.

Two bright silver coins fell to the blue tile with a soft plink-plink.

Then someone grabbed Sundae and pulled her out.

Water plastered her pink hair to her face as she was dragged up to the surface. When she shook it back and looked around in the warm gold dawn, she saw that it was the same cop who had questioned her the night Tony died, carrying her out of the pool. *Detective Morton.*

Her mom was waiting for her, kneeling on the pavers, her arms outstretched.

As she took Sundae from the panting police officer, struggling to swim in his boots and heavy belt, Sundae collapsed into her mother's arms. Drenched and cold, blinking salt and chlorine from her eyes, she curled up in her mother's embrace and looked back down into the dark belly of the deep end.

But she didn't see the two silver coins at the bottom anymore.

"It's over. I've got you, baby. It's over," her mom was whispering against the top of her head.

And for the next seven years, Sundae believed she was right.

SEVENTEEN

NOW

Skilled as she is at catastrophizing, if Lia had tried to imagine all the things that could go wrong at the top of a Ferris wheel, she's pretty sure that getting attacked by a shark-toothed psycho killer wouldn't have made the list.

Sundae is shivering in her arms, her pupils blown wide with adrenaline and fear, blotting out the blue of her iris. There's blood leaking down her bicep from the gash carved by that holly-crowned beast's saw blade, and she's looking through the open safety gate at the boardwalk below like she might be able to spot him somewhere in the crowd.

"Sundae, please, tell me what's going on," Lia says.

"Something is different," Sundae murmurs, without turning away from the gate. "Something changed. He shouldn't be able to hurt me."

"*What?*" Lia says, horror spiking her voice. Because as hazy as last night is, Lia is pretty certain that whatever just attacked them is the same thing she saw by the pool. The same thing that handed her three wrapped taffies, just like the one he gave to Sundae.

A taffy she ate, wishing she had asked Sundae out on this date—only to wake up and find that her wish had come true.

"Sundae, what *was* that?" Lia asks, practically pleading now.

"His name is Holly Jolly," Sundae says. She pulls away from Lia a little, looking straight down to the platform below. "I think they can't get the Ferris wheel moving again."

"Holly Jolly? Like the doo-wop singer?" Lia says. "Didn't he drown himself, like, sixty years ago?"

"He broke the control panel," Sundae says, sitting back up, twisting to face Lia. "We're stuck up here."

To Lia, this seems like a far less pressing issue than the matter at hand, which is *why the hell is an undead doo-wop singer trying to kill Sundae?* (And why did Lia herself see him last night, and why did she take those goddamn wishes from him. . . .) But she leans forward anyway, cautiously peeking over the edge of the diamond-paned floor of their cart at the platform below.

There are cops there now, at the front of the crowd staring up at the Ferris wheel. The police are talking to the ride operator, who is pointing up at their cart, and when she cranes her head out farther, she can see the mangled mess of what is left of the control panel, totally caved in by Holly Jolly's impact.

"It's all right," Lia says, sitting back up, trying to convince herself as much as Sundae. "They probably have emergency controls. They'll get it moving again soon."

"I'm going to climb down," Sundae says, reaching for the straps of her heels and starting to unhook them.

"What the fuck?" Lia balks, her eyes going wide. "Sundae, you can't *climb down*, we're like a hundred feet in the air—"

"A hundred fifty-six," Sundae corrects, kicking her shoes off her feet. She stands, balancing barefoot against the sway of the cart. "The Giant Wheel is a hundred and fifty-six feet high."

"Okay, all the more reason why you can't *climb down from here,*" Lia snaps, standing too, so abruptly that the cart gives a jolt that makes Lia's heart drop into her gut. She steadies herself against the violent rocking and meets Sundae's eyes. "They'll get it moving soon, you don't have to—"

"I have to get down there *now,*" Sundae says, interrupting Lia. She steps up to the open gate, the wind whipping through her long pink hair as she looks back at Lia. "I have to do this. In the time it takes to get it moving, he could kill them all—Neeli and Amber and Jackie and your friends and *your aunt* and her rude girlfriend—"

"Sundae, *please,*" Lia interrupts, her body tense as she reaches out for Sundae, grabbing hold of her arm though she doesn't dare get any closer to the edge. Somehow, it seems much scarier when she's standing up, like she might accidentally tip forward at any moment and careen toward the ground.

156 feet. 156 feet, down to the ground.

Lia shudders, her grip tightening on Sundae's arm. "*Please,* don't do this."

"I'll be okay," Sundae promises, and she sounds so sure, just as confident as her stance in front of the unlatched gate, turning to Lia like she isn't afraid of the open sky at her back, the lashing waves below the pier, the sweaty faces watching from the ground. "I just have to get to the middle, then there's a ladder the rest of the way down. It'll be fine."

"Sundae, I can't—I can't do this," Lia says, her throat tight.

"You don't have to," Sundae says, lifting her hands to frame either side of Lia's jaw, her long nails pushing back into Lia's thick hair.

"You can stay here and wait for the ride to start working. But I need to go."

Sundae's hands drop away and she turns, reaching out to grasp one of the bars crossing the frame of the Ferris wheel, her other hand holding on to the side of their cart to brace herself.

"Sundae!" Lia cries, but there's no use.

Sundae steps off the edge, her bare feet finding another bar.

The crowd below chatters and roars as they watch. The other carts are swinging, the rest of the riders trying to get a look at what's going on. There's a knot of horrified dread in Lia's throat, choking her as she watches Sundae start to descend the crossed bars.

Lia really doesn't want to follow her.

But she thinks she might have to.

Because . . . what if this is her fault? Sundae said *something had changed.* And hadn't Lia's wish changed *everything*? It rewrote history, made it so that Lia said the thing she'd been too chickenshit to say to Sundae, the thing she remembers wanting to say but never saying.

She saw the man with the shark teeth and holly crown, sitting at the edge of the pool last night.

She made a wish.

And now he's here, trying to kill Sundae.

It's got to be her fault. And if she doesn't follow Sundae now, there's no telling how long she might be trapped up here, waiting for someone to figure out how to get the ride going again. Which means that if Sundae runs into that . . . *thing* again, she'll be on her own, without Lia's help. And while Lia certainly doesn't consider herself any sort of hero, she can't deny that Sundae needed the backup just now.

If he gets her when she's alone, Lia has a feeling it's going to end badly.

She still can't wrap her mind around it all, how this impossible being has arrived to kill Sundae, but it doesn't seem like there's time for analyzing the *how* right now.

There's only time to decide if she's doing this or not.

Lia inches closer to the edge of the cart, her hands lifting to grip the bars on either side of the open gate. First she looks straight down, which is a huge mistake. The height is a punch to the gut, making her instantly recoil from the doorway.

But then she looks out at Sundae, whose agile limbs move her from one bar to the next. Just watching her, you'd think she was on her way down a little ladder, not descending a stalled Ferris wheel a hundred-plus feet off the ground. She looks fearless, but maybe that isn't because she's not afraid. Maybe it's because she's more afraid of what could happen if she *doesn't* do it.

And Lia thinks she might be more afraid of that, too.

"Fuck," Lia mutters to herself, stepping back from the edge. She grabs Sundae's heels and loops the fabric of her long skirt through the straps, knotting it at her thigh so it's out of the way.

"Fuck," she grunts again, her breath quick and panicked. "I can't believe I'm fucking doing this."

Lia strides forward, and before she can change her mind, she reaches through the open doorway and grabs hold of one of the bars.

She draws in a deep breath and steps out onto another beam, her boots squeaking against the slick metal.

The wind blasts against her, tossing her short dark hair around her face. The frame of the Ferris wheel emits low thunks and groans near her ear as she clings to it. For a moment she's frozen there, hands stuck to the bar, knees locked in place. But she looks across the web of white bars to Sundae, climbing toward the center of the wheel, her prom queen crown glimmering beneath the bright jewel lights, and she knows she has to keep moving.

She doubts Sundae will wait long for her at the bottom of the platform. If Lia intends to stick with her in case Holly Jolly shows up again, she's going to have to try to catch up.

The crossed pattern of the beams is disorienting. Lia has to move slowly, careful not to misstep or let her sweaty grip slip off the bars. The heels tied to her skirt bounce against her thigh in the thrashing wind. The boardwalk and the ocean bleed together in her periphery, just an endless sprawl of moving lights. Focused on her progress, she doesn't pay attention to the shouts of riders in the carts she passes on the way down, or the rumble of voices from the crowd below.

All she can do is follow Sundae's path, a climb straight down into the center of the ride, one beam at a time. And even when her hands slide a little, even when her boots almost miss their mark when stepping down to the next bar, she keeps on going.

Just like Sundae said, when Lia reaches the center of the ride, there's a ladder that runs along one of the support beams. It's steep, and it's still a good seventy feet off the ground, but it's easier than navigating the crisscrossed lattice of beams, and the slight slope makes the descent feel less terrifying.

At the platform, Sundae is waiting for her.

Lia drops, her boots landing with a thud on the metal. Behind Sundae, the twisted wreckage of the control panel is still sending feeble little shocks into the air, which makes Sundae look kind of ethereal, like she's got angel wings made of fizzy sparks. She also looks *pissed*, her arms crossed over her chest and her bright blue eyes narrowed on Lia.

"I told you to wait up there. Why did you climb down after me?" Sundae demands.

Lia loosens the knot she tied in her skirt. She holds up Sundae's heels by the ankle straps and says, "I had to bring you your shoes."

Sundae's eyes widen and a disbelieving little laugh escapes her lips. Her arms unwind from her chest, and she shakes her head as she leans in, one hand hooking her shoes while the other rests on Lia's shoulder. She presses a kiss to Lia's cheek as she takes her heels, murmuring, "Thank you."

Sundae pulls away to sling her shoes back on. Lia's cheeks are turning red, so she tips her face up to hide it, which just causes her to look straight at the Ferris wheel towering over them.

It still makes her stomach drop, same as it did before they got on. If it weren't for the fact that her heart is still pounding and her palms are slick with sweat, it'd be hard for her to believe she really climbed all the way down from way up there. She *did*, though, and the truth is, she isn't any less afraid of heights now.

But Sundae was right. As much as the climb down terrified her, she knows she could do it again if she had to.

Just like Sundae is going to survive Holly Jolly again.

Lia drops her eyes back to Sundae, who is straightening up on her towering heels. Warily, Lia asks, "Sundae, why is a dead doo-wop singer coming after you?"

"Because . . . he thinks I stole a wish from him," Sundae says, brushing her pink hair behind her ear. Then she holds out her hand to Lia, nodding in the direction of the Blue Velvet Inn. "Come on. I'll explain on the way."

Lia presses her palm to Sundae's, their fingers weaving as they hop off the platform. But there's a cluster of cops waiting by the gate, and they close ranks to block the girls' escape.

"Ladies," one of the cops says. "We're gonna need to have a word with you."

"Here's a word: no," Sundae says as she tries to walk past them.

"Hey, now," another cop snaps, his arm swinging out to catch Sundae. She stops short to keep from running into it, then spins on her heel to glare at the two officers.

The one who stopped her drops his hand to his duty belt, palm resting on his gun.

"We have some questions, ladies. Setting aside the criminal act *you two* just engaged in, I've been informed there was an incident involving a man who climbed this wheel to attack you girls in your gondola. Can you tell us why he did that?"

Like so many times before in her life, Lia knows exactly what she *wants* to say in this moment. And as usual, she's about to bite her tongue—but then she looks over to Sundae, whose blue eyes are blazing, and she reminds herself that she's done being such a fucking coward all the time.

Lia swings her face to the cop and says, "So all these people just told you a man climbed the Ferris wheel to attack us, but your question is, what did *we* do to deserve it?"

"Hey, that's not what I was asking," the cop says, holding up both hands. "I'm just trying to understand what happened here."

"You will *never* be able to understand what happened here," Sundae says. She tries to charge forward again, but this time the cop grabs her by the arm and holds her in place.

"Are we gonna need to take you two down to the station?" he asks.

Sundae glares up at him, her hand squeezing Lia's tight. But as she looks into his eyes, and he looks into hers, they both seem to realize something.

"Wait a second . . . I know you," he says.

"I know you, too," she murmurs.

"That's it," the cop—Detective Morton, according to the silver nameplate pinned to his chest—says, pulling on Sundae's arm as he looks to the other officers. "I'm placing these girls under arrest."

"Are you serious?" Lia says, laughing in furious disbelief.

"Sure am," Detective Morton says, twisting Sundae's arm as he steers her out through the gate. Another cop grabs hold of Lia's shoulder, and Sundae's fingers are ripped out of Lia's hand as they're drawn away from each other.

Still, Lia can hear Detective Morton as he leans in toward Sundae and says, "We're not doing this again, all right? You caused enough trouble seven years ago."

Seven years ago? Is that how long this thing has been after Sundae?

Lia watches Sundae stumble as the cop pulls her through the gawking crowd, the glitter on her skin winking beneath the boardwalk lights, her full pink lips set in an angry pout. And though Lia already knew Sundae was full of surprises, there's something shocking about looking at her shimmery bubblegum exterior and trying to reconcile it with the things she's learning now.

It was bad enough to imagine Sundae terrorized by a monster. But if all this started seven years ago . . . then this thing has been after Sundae since she was a *child*.

And Lia desperately hopes that her stupid wish isn't the reason he might finally be able to kill Sundae.

EIGHTEEN

NOW

If Sundae had known she was going to wind up in the back of a police car on prom weekend, she would have assumed it would be for something more fun than *this*.

Like, she and the other cheerleaders could have paired ski masks with their bikinis and robbed a bank, or sunk a Republican congressman's yacht docked off the pier. But getting arrested for defending herself and running for her life from her childhood boogeyman?

That's truly such a fucking bummer.

The cops searched Sundae and Lia and zip-tied their hands behind their backs before shoving them into the back seat of Detective Morton's cruiser. Now he's trying to drive through the crowd on the boardwalk, but no one seems particularly motivated to get out of his way, and Sundae is trying to hold in the scream that wants to push out of her chest.

"You have to let us go," Sundae says, breathless with the panic she's feeling. "Please, you don't understand, he's out there—"

"Who's out there?" Morton asks, though he doesn't sound

particularly interested. He's too busy glaring at the people milling down the boardwalk, as if they're breaking some kind of law for walking in the way of his cruiser.

"Holly Jolly," Sundae snaps.

"You're still telling this story, are you?" Morton scoffs. He angrily blasts the siren for a moment, as if that might clear the crowd.

"I'm still *telling the truth*, yes," Sundae says. "There's a monster on this island, and he's probably out there killing people *right now*!"

"Unbelievable," Morton says, shaking his head. "That headshrink they made us bring in said you were making it up to deal with the trauma. But I don't think your trauma looks very dealt with."

At that, Sundae catches his eyes in the rearview mirror. They run over her glitter-caked face and her tight little dress like he's sizing up her appearance. Like he thinks *that* is some manifestation of her trauma. This is nothing new to Sundae—in fact, it seems to be a pretty common misconception. Still, when she's trapped in the back of a cop car with her hands zip-tied while a monster could be hunting down her friends, this assumption is particularly infuriating. She feels anger pulse through her, but she isn't the one who responds first.

Lia is.

She slides forward on the seat, leaning close to the plexiglass divider. Glaring at the back of Morton's head, she says, "Gross. Keep your eyes on the road before you hit someone, jerkass."

"Hey. You're not gonna sit back there and be disrespectful," Morton says, twisting around to shoot Lia a stern look, totally taking his eyes off the people crossing in front of him. "Everything you're saying right now *will* be part of my report."

"Oh, good. Make sure you put on your report that I said you're balding, and that if all my friends get murdered by Holly Jolly tonight, it's your fault," Sundae says, shifting against the cold leather seat beneath her. As if the zip ties crushing her wrists aren't uncomfortable enough, of course Morton is blasting the air-conditioning like he's trying to turn his cruiser into a cryogenic chamber.

Like he wants to show off more of his receding hairline, Morton fully turns in his seat. He reaches back, wrenching open the center panel of the plexiglass divider, so there's nothing between his angry face and them. "That's enough with the bullshit. Because of you and this Holly Jolly story, the first murder case I ever got put on is *still* unsolved. There's no such thing as killer ghosts—"

He's cut off by a loud crash from the front of the cruiser.

At first, Sundae thinks they've hit something—but actually, something has hit *them*. A projectile smashes through the windshield, punching a hole in the glass as it flies through.

And it keeps on going, straight through Detective Morton's skull.

His eyes roll back as the metal spike pushes out of his forehead and finally comes to a stop. His mouth drops open in a death-rattle groan. Blood dribbles down his gasping face, and when he turns slightly, Sundae realizes that the object piercing his head is attached to a rope that runs out through the broken windshield.

And as both the girls start screaming, something pulls on that rope.

Detective Morton's chest slams into his steering wheel and the horn blares loudly, but it's drowned out by the sound of screams coming from all around the boardwalk. Another yank on the rope, and he's being dragged up the dashboard by the harpoon through his head. Morton's body breaks through the rest of the glass in his windshield, leaving a streak of blood on the hood of his cruiser as he's pulled across it.

Finally, Sundae can see the attacker on the other end of that rope.

But . . . it's not Holly Jolly.

A man in a tattered button-up shirt and old-fashioned breeches stands there, twisting the rope around his arm as he hauls Morton toward him. He's got long wild hair and wind-burned cheeks, and Sundae thinks he might have silver eyes like Holly Jolly, but then she realizes that his eyes are covered by round silver coins, stuck like two buttons sewed to the face of a rag doll.

The coins make it hard to tell if he's looking through the broken windshield right at them, but Sundae is pretty sure he is.

"Holy shit, holy shit," Lia is repeating, quick and panicked.

"We gotta get out of here," Sundae says, twisting in her seat to grope behind her, bound hands searching for the door handle. She finds it, but a few quick tugs confirm that they're locked in the back of the cruiser.

Lia's already shaking her head like she knows the door won't work. Instead, she shifts on the seat, craning her neck and shoulders through the open panel of the divider. She struggles a bit without the help of her hands, but eventually she shimmies forward enough to dangle halfway through before her hips catch.

"Give me a push," she calls back to Sundae.

"Oh my god. This is *not* what I pictured when I thought about grabbing your ass for the first time," Sundae says as she presses her shoulder against Lia's butt. It would be better if she could use her hands, and not in a sexy way (well, not *completely* in a sexy way).

Sundae shoves, and Lia falls forward into the front seat, landing awkwardly on her side. She hisses as she collides with the center console and broken glass digs into her skin. Sundae winces, scooting forward to stick her face through the open panel.

"Are you okay?" she asks.

"Fine," Lia grunts.

She sits up, and Sundae looks past her, out the windshield, where the man with the coins for eyes is bent over, prodding at Detective Morton with some kind of rusty two-pronged hook like he's inspecting his catch. Sundae shudders in horror, throwing herself back against the seat and sliding over to the door.

"Let's get the fuck out of here," she whimpers.

Lia grabs the driver's-side door handle and tumbles out of the cruiser. She flings herself against the back door, bound hands grappling behind her spine. Finally, the door pops open, and Sundae swings her feet out and plants her heels against the boardwalk.

"Let's *go*," she says, and they run.

The boardwalk is a mass of stampeding bodies, shoving and screaming in their panic. Most of them probably don't even know what they're running from. The cops who had been following behind Morton's cruiser are yelling from the windows of their car, telling the crowd to *remain calm*.

As if.

With her hands behind her back, Sundae's balance is off, and the push of the crowd nearly knocks her over. She calls out to Lia and nods to a nearby T-shirt stand, a pocket of stillness at the edge of the crowd.

Sundae's almost mowed down by a man who barrels into her on the way, but once they cross the threshold into the souvenir shop, Sundae recovers her footing on the salt-stained carpet. The store is totally empty save for racks of shirts and junk.

"We gotta get these zip ties off," Lia mutters, and she starts prowling through the shop. Under the bright fluorescent lights, Sundae can see all the little bits of glass stuck to the back of Lia's shoulder. Clearly, the spaghetti strap of her dark blue dress didn't provide much protection when she landed headfirst in the front seat of Morton's cruiser.

Lia lets out a satisfied laugh when she locates a selection of knives and bongs in a glass case at the front of the shop. "I had a feeling this place would have some Gravy Seals shit. I could tell by the *These Colors Don't Run, They Reload* T-shirts."

Lia goes around to the back of the case, and Sundae anxiously watches the open doorways, where the teeming throng is still wrestling against each other as they go by. As chaotic as the scene on the boardwalk is, her eyes are only searching for a crown made of holly, or for two silver coins set in a hollow face.

Sundae jumps when Lia knocks over a bong and glances over to see her straightening up with one of the knives in her hand, giving Sundae an apologetic look.

"Come here. It's not super sharp, but be careful," she says, and holds the knife at her back with the blade facing out. Sundae turns, brings her wrists to the knife, and slides them up and down to saw through the plastic zip ties, careful not to catch the bracelet Lia gave her. Her knuckles brush Lia's hands, and Sundae marvels at the way it makes her heart flutter, even in this anxious moment.

The bindings on one of her wrists pops open, finally separating her hands, and she takes the knife from Lia. She slides the blade under the other zip tie and slices it off, letting it fall to the grubby carpet. As she wraps a hand around Lia's arm and carefully starts to cut through the ties, she murmurs, "I don't know who that guy was. With the fucking . . . *harpoon* or whatever. I've never seen him before."

Lia nods and breathes out a relieved sigh as her hands are freed. She twists to face Sundae, rubbing at the raw skin on her wrists as she says, "Great. So is there, like, more than one murderous dead man after you now?"

"I don't know. But we *have* to get back to the motel and warn everyone," Sundae says, glancing at the doors again. There are more cops now, shouting through megaphones as they herd the crowds off the boardwalk.

"They might be looking for us," Lia says. "The cops, I mean."

"Cool. What's worse, cops or killer ghosts?" Sundae says.

"Well, until somebody tells me the ghosts are killing people to uphold a social order rooted in race and class exploitation, I'm gonna say the cops are worse," Lia says, and Sundae blows out a breathy laugh as she bends to reach into the glass case full of knives. She picks up the biggest knife in the case and the leather sheath it's displayed on top of, which she uses to strap the knife to her thigh.

Sundae straightens up, holding out another sheathed knife to Lia. "Here, take this," she says.

Lia does as she's told, but her eyes don't leave Sundae as she props her boot up on the side of the counter and loops the strap of the sheath around her thigh. "I'll have you know, I had my sexual awakening to Boris Vallejo paintings, so this look is really doing something for me."

"Don't get used to it. I'm not usually a knife-wielding kind of girl," Sundae says as she traces her fingers over the gash Holly Jolly's saw left on her upper arm when he tried to stab her. The blood is clotting, but the wound is still raw and sore.

She just can't understand what has changed since the last time she saw him.

Seven years ago, when Holly Jolly dragged her through the pool to his weird dark train-car ride, Sundae knew he desperately wanted to hurt her. But he *couldn't*. And it seemed so clear, based on how adamant he was that she make her last wish, that he couldn't do anything to her unless she ate that final taffy.

So what's different *now*?

It doesn't make sense, but in this moment it doesn't matter. Seven years ago, it wasn't just *her* he couldn't hurt—he hadn't been able to stab the point of his saw blade down into her mom's chest, either. If he can kill *Sundae* now, that means he can probably kill everyone she loves, too.

"We have to get back to the motel," Sundae tells Lia, for what feels like the millionth time. "We have to warn everyone."

"All right, but first, could you warn *me*?" Lia says. "Because I still don't know what the fuck is going on."

"There's no time—" Sundae starts to say, but her mouth clamps shut when the boom box behind the counter suddenly switches on.

Static drones through the speakers, radio interference snapping loudly in the quiet of the store. Then a familiar melody sneaks up through the buzzing static, a voice lilting as it sings,

"One, for a path I crossed.
Two, for my love I lost.
Three, and you will come for me,
Like the tide pulls the sand back to the sea."

Fear jolts through Sundae. She reaches out to grab Lia's hand, fingers weaving with hers as she pulls. "Come on, come on, we have to run!" she says pleadingly.

But Lia plants her boots on the ground and shakes her head, yanking Sundae back. Sundae stumbles on her heels, and Lia puts her free hand on Sundae's waist to steady her.

"Wait," Lia says, her dark eyes wide as she stares into Sundae's. "Hold on. Listen to the song."

"I've heard the fucking song," Sundae snaps, but a look from Lia makes her quiet down. She bites her lip and does as Lia says—she *listens*.

"All along, I knew the cost.
But I always thought I could stop.
That I would dig just one grave.
That my love could be saved.
But now that I've paid the price,
I'll wish to forget what I've sacrificed."

Suddenly, the radio cuts out again, taking the sneaking drumbeat and smooth guitar with it. But the voice remains, singing from somewhere nearby, bright and clear without the radio static accompanying him.

"Here in the Wildwoods,
Where you once stood,
All clothed in green . . ."

Sundae turns around, and there he is.

Holly Jolly.

Only . . . he looks different. There's no crown of holly on his slicked-back hair, no silver eyes gleaming in the night. His suit is soft forest green instead of brown as gnarled bark—though it's smudged with ash like he's been around a blazing fire. His teeth are straight and pearly white. He looks exactly like the photo of Holly Jolly that used to hang behind the bar at the Coral Cabana, the one that Tony had pointed to when he told her the story of the doo-wop singer who drowned in the pool.

But Tony didn't mention the chains.

This version of Holly Jolly is wrapped in them, metal links wound around his shoulders like a silvery blanket and falling to trail behind him. They clatter down the now mostly empty boardwalk as he walks slowly toward the front of the shop they've sheltered inside.

He looks so sad, his brows crumpled as he sings his blue song.

"Now my love is gone,
And before the dawn,
You will be clothed in me."

"Okay," Lia says, her voice tight with fear. "I've heard enough. *Now* we run."

Sundae doesn't need any more motivation than that. The two of them burst out of the T-shirt shop, dodging the chain-wrapped Holly Jolly as they take off down the boardwalk.

NINETEEN

NOW

Lia can't stop thinking about those lyrics.

One, for a path I crossed. Two, for my love I lost. Three, and you will come for me, like the tide pulls the sand back to the sea.

They play through her head as she runs alongside Sundae, her boots pounding against the dull wood of the boardwalk. The crowd has mostly been cleared by the cops who are still shouting on megaphones somewhere behind them, which means that Sundae and Lia don't have to navigate the shoving, panicked throng anymore—but it also means that they're very, *very* visible.

A loud yelp rips from Sundae's mouth.

She stumbles on her heels, rolling her ankle and collapsing to the ground with a dull thud.

"Shit, Sundae, are you okay?" Lia says, crouching down in front of her. Sundae groans, her legs sprawled like a rag doll, her hand reaching for her twisted ankle.

"Fuck," Sundae whines. "I just lost, like, fifty slut points for falling in my Pleasers."

"Jesus christ." Lia laughs, hooking her arm around Sundae's chest to start pulling her up.

But she freezes when she hears something below them, in the black void underneath the boardwalk.

At first, it sounds like a stone ball rolling across concrete. Then it gets deeper and louder, so loud that Lia can feel it rumbling through the wood, vibrating her boots. It's an animal sound that seems to strike some instinctive, primeval fear hardwired into her DNA, and she yanks on Sundae, dragging her up off the ground.

"What is that?" Sundae hisses, gaze searching the worn planks beneath her.

"I don't know. Something big," Lia whispers. She's looking down too, eyes straining at the cracks between the boards. Whatever it is, it's massive, with fur that glints gold in the little slices of light slipping between the gaps. "Come on, let's get the fuck out of here," Lia says.

But Sundae's limping on her sore ankle, flinching with every step. She definitely can't run anymore. Lia glances around, evaluating their surroundings. If they can't *run*, they at least need to find some shelter before *whatever it is* underneath the boardwalk decides to come up for them.

A gaping mouth catches Lia's eye, rows of pointed teeth blue in the moonlight.

Her heart drops into her gut, and her fingers curl reflexively against Sundae's ribs. But her knee-jerk horror gives way as soon as she realizes what she's *actually* seeing. A giant fiberglass shark hangs beneath a sign shaped like a cresting wave, where a single word glows in sharp teal: AQUARIUM.

And below the toothy grinning great white, a set of doors promises some protection from the growing list of horrors hunting them.

"Come on, over here," Lia grunts, helping Sundae over to the entrance. She tries not to shiver as they pass beneath the fake shark's bared fiberglass teeth and slip inside the aquarium.

They step into a dark hallway, and through the glass walls, swimming fish glow beneath indigo lights. Lia stops to lock the door behind them, though she knows a deadbolt is probably no match for any of the things that might be coming for them now.

"Oh. I pet a stingray in here once," Sundae whispers as she hobbles along, leaning against Lia's side. "I wonder if he remembers me."

"I bet he does. Who could forget you?" Lia says, adjusting her grip on Sundae to help her walk.

They turn the corner, stepping into a maze of deep blue tanks. Fish flit around them, and the only sounds Lia hears are bubbling water and humming filters. She sets Sundae down on a bench and kneels in front of her, gently lifting Sundae's leg to set her foot on Lia's thigh. Carefully, Lia unhooks the strap of Sundae's heel.

"Sundae . . ." Lia says, meeting her eyes as she slides Sundae's shoe off her foot. "We need to figure out what's going on now, but first, can you please tell me what happened? Seven years ago, when you survived him the first time?"

Sundae winces as Lia rubs her sore ankle. She bites her lip and flexes her toes, keeping her eyes on Lia's hands, seeming to deliberately avoid her face. Finally, she begins.

"I was eleven. My mom and me came to live at the Coral Cove Motel to get away from my dad. . . ."

Sundae tells Lia about the man she met at the bottom of the pool, and the story she was told by a bartender named Tony about the doo-wop singer who drowned himself there. She says that the next time she saw him, he offered her three wishes. Lia feels her dread growing thicker, festering like an algae bloom.

"Did you make any wishes?" Lia asks, hushed in the quiet of the cold blue aquarium.

"Yes," Sundae answers, closing her eyes.

"What did you wish for?"

"You have to promise not to hate me when I tell you," Sundae whispers.

"Of course. I promise," Lia says, and then she holds up a hand, pinkie out, just like she did in the diner. She nudges Sundae's knee with the heel of her palm, and Sundae opens her eyes, stares at Lia's hand for a moment, then lifts her own and hooks her pinkie with Lia's.

Sundae's gaze finally meets Lia's, for the first time since she started telling her story. "I wished for my hair to turn pink in the sun."

She says it with the air of a terrible confession, but Lia doesn't see what the big deal is. It's exactly the sort of thing an eleven-year-old Sundae *would* wish for, and it explains why Sundae's hair went from blond to pink seemingly overnight, why it seems to shine like tinsel in the light.

"Why would that make me hate you?" Lia asks with a scoff.

"Because . . . after I made my wish, he killed Tony," Sundae admits.

Lia's brows shoot up her forehead and her stomach feels like it's full of icy needles as understanding settles over her. Is *that* how it works? Does someone have to die for every wish?

Did someone die for *Lia's* wish?

Suddenly, Lia feels a realization coming on. Like when she's writing a new song and the chord progression begins to emerge out of the noise, it's coming to her in pieces. But there are still gaps. She leans in, pinkie tugging on Sundae's as she asks urgently, "Did you make any other wishes?"

"Yeah. One more. I wished . . . that I could have whatever I want, and never have to pay for anything. Because I wanted a hermit crab."

Lia can't afford to think about how cute and kind of heartbreaking that is right now. So she narrows her eyes and presses, "Did someone else die when you made that wish?"

"No. That's the one he says I stole. He came to kill my mom, but it was like he *couldn't*. And then he couldn't kill me either," Sundae says.

Lia nods her head a couple times, the clues dropping into place like Tetris pieces in her mind. Then she mumbles, *"One, for a path I crossed. Two, for my love I lost."* Sundae's body tenses at the lyrics to the song, her foot digging into Lia's thigh, and Lia rushes to explain. "Sundae, the song—it's about the wishes. About what they cost. For the first wish, he kills someone you know. *One, for a path I crossed.*"

Sundae's lips part on a ragged exhale. Her eyes widen, glossy with tears that start to flood her lash line. "Oh," she whispers. "*Oh*. Oh my god, I didn't get it. . . ."

"You were just a kid, and there was a fucking monster after you," Lia says, leaning forward, her hands coming to rest on the bench on either side of Sundae's hips.

"*Two, for my love . . .* That's why he came for my mom. For the second wish, he kills someone you love," Sundae says.

"Right. But he couldn't kill her, because of the wish you made. *That's* why he thinks you stole from him," Lia says. "And 'three, and you will come for me' means that after the third wish, he can kill *you*."

"But I didn't make the third wish," Sundae says. "I never did. So why the hell can he kill me *now*?"

Maybe because Sundae's not the only one making wishes now.

Lia made a wish of her own.

And isn't Sundae someone that Lia knows? Wouldn't killing her settle the cost of Lia's first wish?

But maybe it's *not* Lia's fault. There are still so many unanswered questions. Like, *why* does he kill the wishers at the end? Does he *do* something with them after they die, or does he kill for the sake of killing?

Has he done this before, or are they the only ones?

Is he really the ghost of a doo-wop singer, or is he something else?

What about the man with the harpoon? Or the version of Holly Jolly wrapped in chains? Or the growling beast they heard beneath the boardwalk?

Or the guy standing at the end of the hall, holding a long black pickax, who captures their attention with a loud, keening whistle.

Lia jumps to her feet, immediately sweeping her arm around Sundae to help her back up. The strange man's clothes are dirty and old-fashioned, marsh muck caking his tall boots and a flat cap on his head. His fists grip the handle of his pickax tightly, like he's ready to swing. He takes a step toward them, and Lia looks down at Sundae's leg, wondering how fast they'll be able to run.

"I'm guessing you don't know this guy, either," Lia murmurs, and Sundae shakes her head.

"I bet you regret asking me to be your prom date now," Sundae says through gritted teeth as they start to back away down the corridor.

A stab of guilt skewers Lia's chest, because the truth is, she *didn't* ask Sundae to be her prom date. And if she had, she wouldn't regret it—but she most definitely regrets what she *did* do.

"Sundae, I—" she starts to say, but her confession ends on a strangled gasp as the man launches toward them, swinging his pickax.

Sundae screams, and Lia whips them both to the side, their backs smacking against a tank as they dodge the point of the pickax. The man lets out a cry like the blast of a train horn, and he drives the butt of the handle forward, plowing it into Lia's stomach.

Lia chokes as the impact punches the breath from her ribs. She hears Sundae call her name through the ringing in her ears as she falls, hitting the concrete floor hard enough to make her vision swim. Feeling like her guts have been knocked into her lungs, she looks up helplessly from the ground as the man swings his pickax toward Sundae's face.

But Sundae sinks down, pulling the knife from the sheath on her thigh as the tip of his weapon cracks into the tank instead. The glass spiderwebs around it, a trickle of water slipping through as he yanks angrily on the handle.

Before he can free his weapon, Sundae slams her blade into his chest.

She stabs him once, then wrenches the knife back out. A spurt of thick, rotten blood splashes her face, and she lets out a furious yell as she plunges the knife in again, burying the blade in his neck.

His hands slide off the handle of the pickax, and he slumps to the floor, the gouge in his neck making a sucking wet sound as Sundae tears her knife back out.

Sundae stands over him, holding her gore-slicked knife, splashed with blood that smells like decaying seaweed. Lia finally manages to swallow a full breath, her hand pressed to her ribs as she feels her lungs expand.

"Are you okay?" Sundae's whisper is nearly lost under the glug of the tanks around them. Lia stands, facing Sundae, the handle of the pickax still stuck in the glass jutting in between them.

"Yeah. Are you?"

Sundae shakes her head a little, looking down at the knife in her bloody fist. "I've never killed . . . *anything* before."

Lia reaches over the pickax to press her hand to Sundae's cheek, lifting her face away from the knife. Sundae's gaze is blue and wet as the tanks around them.

"He would have killed *us*." Lia says, insistent. "You did what you had to do to survive. And besides, I don't think . . . that he was totally *alive* to begin with."

To demonstrate her point, Lia taps her boot against the spill of blood oozing from the man's split-open neck. It's more sludge than liquid, and thick muck-black ropes stretch between the bottom of Lia's shoe and the floor as she lifts her foot. The stink of rot wafts up, and Sundae wrinkles her freckled nose.

"God, it smells like the time Francesca threw up a Filet-O-Fish in Times Square," Sundae says. "I don't feel bad about it. Killing him, I mean. That's the weird part. I just feel like . . . he should have stayed the fuck away from you if he didn't want to get stabbed in the throat."

A surprised laugh chokes out of Lia. "Good," she murmurs, swiping her thumb across Sundae's cheek. "I'd have done the same, if he didn't almost knock me out with that goddamn pickax."

At this, Lia glances at the dead man's weapon still embedded in the glass, handle protruding between their chests. A detail catches her attention, and her hand drops away from Sundae's cheek to skim along the words burned into the old wood of the handle.

"Hold on. Look," Lia says. "*Property of the West Jersey Railroad Company.*"

But as she lifts her eyes from the handle and looks across it at Sundae, darkness seems to gather at the corner of her vision.

They both turn to face the tank.

A colossal form moves through the murky water toward them, skin gleaming like sharpened steel. A dorsal fin cuts the water like a razor. As it approaches the glass, its mouth gapes open wide, showing rows of black teeth.

Sundae and Lia both scream, jumping away from those jaws.

Lia loops her arm around Sundae. And as they rush for the exit and stumble out onto the boardwalk, Sundae looks to Lia and says, "I think I know that shark."

TWENTY

NOW

Sundae gets that it's prom weekend, but when she and Lia burst through the gates of the motel, it's like no one's concerned *at all* about why the cops shut the boardwalk down.

If anything, the party at the motel has taken on a delirious kind of fervor since they left. Everyone is yelling, having reached the point of drunkenness where it's impossible to speak without shouting. Crumpled Solo cups float in the packed pool, red as blood spatters as they lash through the water. Broken glass litters the ground, winking like glitter under the courtyard lights. As she and Lia fight through a rave of writhing bodies, they have to scream to hear each other over the deafening beat of the music playing from the balcony.

"Hey! *Desert Hearts*! Way to leave us alone at the ranch!"

Sundae looks up toward the voice, spotting Lia's friend Dallas leaning over the balcony. With his black hair a mess and his silk shirt wrinkled, he looks harried, though not as bad as Edison, who gawks at them with bugged-out brown eyes, sweat soaking his T-shirt.

"The ranch is on fire!" he yells.

"Is anyone dead?" Lia asks.

"Not yet, but if somebody puts on another Imagine Dragons song, I'm jumping off this balcony," Dallas says.

"Is that *blood?*" Edison suddenly demands, his voice going a little shrill.

"Don't worry, it isn't mine!" Sundae says, but when she shrugs she feels the gash on her arm strain against the movement, and she corrects herself. "Most of it, anyway. Have you guys seen my friends?"

"Uh, I think they're in the suite," Edison says, pointing to the balcony on the opposite side of the courtyard.

"Meet us there," Lia tells them, then starts helping Sundae to the stairs. Sundae's ankle still throbs with every step, but if that keeps Lia's arms around her all night, she might not mind so much.

When they reach the second floor, there's a group of boys playing beer pong on the suite's balcony, partially blocking the open door to the room Harper booked for himself. Sundae and Lia dodge swinging elbows and splashing beer to enter the suite.

It's immediately clear why Harper chose this room.

A heart-shaped tub takes up half of the room, positioned in a corner framed by mirrors. Purple lights turn the bubbly water vibrant amethyst as the cheerleaders lounge in it, and Sundae is not at all surprised to find that Harper picked a room with a feature he knew the girls wouldn't be able to resist.

Hell, seeing all her friends lazing in the candy-scented bubble bath, Sundae wishes she could climb in with them. But she doesn't get to bask in a big tub with her friends. She doesn't get to wear all the cute bikinis she brought or get drunk on champagne or win the Slut Cup. She doesn't get to *enjoy* prom weekend.

Instead, she has to try to *survive* prom weekend.

"Her majesty, the queen!" Jackie coos in an awful fake British accent, announcing Sundae's arrival.

Neeli, who had been in the middle of giving herself a bubble beard, whips her head around to look at Sundae and Lia. She immediately rises to her feet, nearly whacking her head on the beaded purple chandelier that hangs over the tub.

"Oh my god, Sunny!" Neeli gasps, rushing to Sundae's other side and helping Lia bring her over to the edge of the heart-shaped platform.

"I'm okay, I'm okay," Sundae says, but she winces as she sits on the cold tile, stretching out her wounded leg.

"What's going on? Why are you covered in *blood*?" Neeli asks, sitting down beside Sundae and gently sweeping her hair away from her shoulder as she looks her over.

Dallas and Edison wander in at that moment, looking unsure about intruding on a roomful of bikini-clad cheerleaders in a bubble bath until Lia turns and waves them forward.

"Don't worry," Dallas says sarcastically. "Hardly any of it is hers!"

"What the hell does that mean?" Neeli snaps, narrowing her eyes at the gore splashed on Sundae's dress. "Whose is it, then?"

Sundae twists, looking to the girls in the tub behind her. Her friends, who just a moment ago were luxuriating in drunken bliss, have sobered up instantly. She wishes she didn't have to rob them of their fun. The whole reason she came on this huge mistake of a trip in the first place was to avoid fucking up their weekend, and now she's here to tell them that a demonic doo-wop singer might be coming to kill them all.

Sundae wouldn't blame them if they can't forgive her. She just hopes they believe her.

"I'm going to tell you guys what's going on, but I need you to promise me you'll listen to what I say, even if you think it's bullshit," Sundae says to her friends.

"You are the prom queen, and we, your loyal subjects," Tasha says, giving a soapy little salute.

"Yeah. And I believed you when you said you found your Vivienne Westwood heels at the thrift store, even though everyone else secretly thinks you got them on Depop," Jackie says.

"Oh my god, Jack, shut *up*," Francesca says, flicking the water on her fingers at Jackie. She gives Sundae an apologetic look. "All I said was, it's kind of funny how you always seem to find designer stuff in your size at the thrift store, but every time *I* go there, it's just mothball muumuus and grandpa sweaters."

"Fresca, be so for real right now, have you actually set foot in a thrift store? I thought you didn't like used stuff," Amber says.

"When I said that, I was talking about your ex-boyfriend," Francesca shoots back.

"Guys, shut up and listen to Sunny," Tasha snaps.

Sundae gives Tasha a thankful half smile. Then she takes a deep breath. And she starts telling them everything.

She makes it as quick as she can, because there's really no way to know when Holly Jolly—or any of the creatures they encountered tonight—might show up. But she knows it's important to tell them *everything*, because they all need to know what to look out for if she's going to keep them safe.

Plus, it's kind of a relief to finally tell her closest friends the whole story. Especially Neeli, who listens attentively, her long emerald nails combing through Sundae's hair.

When she finishes recounting everything that happened seven years ago in Wildwood, she pauses, giving the girls a chance to process.

"Sundae, that is . . . like, holy shit, that's literal nightmare fuel," Amber says.

"Why didn't you tell anyone about this?" Francesca asks, and she's unable to keep the accusatory tone out of her voice.

"Fresca," Neeli snaps, but Sundae shakes her head, squeezing Neeli's knee.

"I *tried,*" Sundae says. "The cops asked me over and over again to tell them what happened, and I *did,* but they wouldn't believe me. And then they brought in this psychologist who told me it was all some kind of delusion my brain made up to process what had happened to me. So I was like, uh, if you're all just gonna sit here and mansplain my trauma to me, I'm not gonna talk about it anymore."

"You could have told *us,*" Francesca says. "I didn't even *want* to come here. Maybe if you mentioned that there's an actual *killer demon* in Wildwood, everyone would have listened to me about going to Seaside instead."

"I'm sorry," Sundae says, closing her eyes as guilt twists tighter around her heart. "I thought he couldn't hurt anyone. I thought he was trapped. I thought it would be okay. I just wanted it to be *okay.*"

"It is. It is okay," Neeli says, rubbing a hand across Sundae's back while she shoots a glare at Francesca. "What matters is, what do we have to do to keep you safe from this thing?"

Sundae can only feel guilt at Neeli's rush to defend her. She glances at Lia, hoping to find some comfort there—but Lia's eyes, usually warm and sticky as hot lava, are flat obsidian when Sundae meets them. Sundae has to look away, and she stares up into the beaded chandelier instead as she goes on.

"Um. This is where it gets complicated, I guess," Sundae says.

"No offense, Barbarella, but it already seems pretty complicated," Dallas says.

"Yeah, I was gonna say this seems super Wes Craven at first, but it ended up pretty Clive Barker," Edison says.

"It's the whole pocket-dimension thing, with the ride under the motel pool," Dallas agrees. Then he seems to remember that he's interrupting, and he waves for Sundae to continue.

She leans into Neeli a little and tries to tell them the rest.

Holly Jolly attacking her and Lia on the Ferris wheel. The fact that he suddenly seems able to kill her, even though she never made her final wish. The cop who questioned her as a kid trying to arrest her and Lia, only to be harpooned by a guy with coins for eyes. The weird chain-wrapped version of Holly Jolly, the thunderous growl of some unseen beast beneath the boardwalk, the guy with the pickax in the aquarium, the enormous silver shark that appeared in the tank.

Suddenly, Neeli interrupts her to say, "Sunny, that's the ride."

"That's what I was about to say: I saw that shark on the ride, the one he brought me to through the bottom of the pool," Sundae says, wondering how Neeli could know that.

"No, I mean *that's the ride on the pier*! The one you wouldn't go on last night!" Neeli says.

"Neeli's right," Tasha says. "That Haunted Forest ride was super weird. It had all these fucked-up scenes, and in some of them there were wax figures and stuff, but all of them had—I mean, I thought they were actors or something, because they looked so real, but there was no way they could have had a real shark in there. . . ."

Sundae shudders when Tasha mentions the wax figures, recalling the paste-faced model of Tony lying on the ground in the replica Coral Cabana, ribbons of red spooling out from his neck. "What did the last scene look like?" Sundae asks, her voice a reedy whisper.

"It was a pink motel with a tiki bar," Amber says. She leans over the edge of the tub, her soapy hand squeezing Sundae's shoulder before she continues. "And a dead guy lying on the floor."

Sundae groans, gore-sticky hands wringing between her knees as she curls in on herself. It's still there, just the way it was seven years ago—the fake Coral Cabana, the fake Tony, the fake pool she managed to escape through. . . .

"But he brought me there through the motel pool, I *left* through the motel pool, and now the pool is gone. The whole *motel* is gone. And when I told the cops about the ride, they said they looked for it and couldn't find anything like it on the boardwalk," Sundae says.

Jackie coughs papaya vape-smoke as she huffs out a laugh. "Sunny, the cops also didn't find the blunt we hid in your Starbucks cup when they searched us in the mall parking lot, even though it stayed lit the whole time and you were literally holding a smoking cup."

"Maybe they didn't look. Or maybe . . . it's not *always* there," Sundae says.

"Maybe it's back because *you're* back," Dallas suggests. "You *are* the common denominator here, right? What else has been consistent about him showing up besides . . . ?"

Sundae ticks through all the times she's seen him, and a pattern *does* emerge.

"I think he only comes out at night," Sundae murmurs, winded by the realization. "When I made my first wish, he killed Tony right away. But when I made the second, he didn't come for my mom until nighttime. And when I escaped, it was sunrise, and he totally flipped when the light hit him. He tried to get away, but it was like the portal we came through was closed, and then he just went *poof*."

"Shit, so he's like a vampire?" Dallas says, turning to Edison. "Clive Barker does a Buffy reboot, but he wants it to be more Murnau than Whedon."

Francesca snaps her fingers in Lia's direction. "Can you get a grip on your boy-friends? They keep speaking out of turn," she commands, and Jackie giggles out more fruity fog.

Lia has been standing so still, but when Francesca addresses her, she seems to startle, her chin jolting up. For an instant, her eyes track from the spot on the carpet she had been staring at to Sundae, but she looks away just as fast.

Why won't she look at me?

"Shut up, dorkwads," Lia mutters at Edison and Dallas. Her dark hair brushes her jaw, and she tucks it behind her ear, purple light catching on her silver rings. Sundae wraps her hand around the bracelet circling her wrist, pressing the shells into her palm as she aches with the memory of Lia's fingers on her skin.

"Did anyone see what else is on the ride?" Jackie asks.

"I had my eyes closed. Raleigh was doing a little downstairs DJ," Francesca says, placing her two fingers like they're on a turntable and biting her lip.

"I had my eyes closed most of the time, too," Sundae admits. "I only saw the shark and the motel at the end."

"So let's go look for it," Dallas says, pointing his thumb in the direction of the boardwalk. "If we can find it, maybe we'll be able to figure all of this out."

"Yeah. We gotta know what else we're dealing with," Neeli agrees, nodding at Dallas.

"Hold on. Before we go anywhere, Sundae needs to clean out that wound," Lia says, though she's speaking to Neelima, not to Sundae.

Sundae can't bear this anguished uncertainty one moment longer.

She holds out her hand to Lia, arching her eyebrows expectantly. "Okay. Take me to the bathroom. I'm pulling the glass out of your shoulder, too." Sundae waits, afraid Lia will refuse to take it, but after a pause, Lia steps forward and hooks her hand around Sundae's. Sundae lets Lia haul her up to her feet.

As Lia helps her across the room, Sundae grabs a bottle of vodka off Harper's nightstand. She looks to Neeli and says, "Lock the room and don't let anyone in. We'll be right back."

Then she steps into the bathroom with Lia and closes the door, because no matter where Holly Jolly and his beasts might be, Sundae doesn't think she can face them until she knows if Lia still likes her or not.

TWENTY-ONE

NOW

Guilt has rows of serrated teeth, and it's eating Lia alive.

She's trying to distract herself by pulling apart the lines of Holly Jolly's song, searching for more clues in the words he croons. As she helps Sundae over to the baby-blue bathroom counter, she tries to puzzle out what the first verse might mean.

"Lia?" Sundae says in her silk slip of a voice, her back resting against the edge of the counter, her hand sliding up from Lia's wrist to hook behind her elbow. "Are you, like, mad at me?"

"What?" Lia startles, her eyes snapping to Sundae's face. Sundae's pale eyebrows are crumpled, her sunburned skin washed out under the fluorescent lights, dried blood splattered on her cheeks like black freckles. She looks afraid, but not in the way she was when Holly Jolly found her, or any of the other monsters that have come after them tonight.

And yet, just like everything else that scares her, Sundae confronts it head-on, meeting Lia's gaze with her wide blue eyes as she waits for an answer.

With shame chewing a hole in her chest, Lia says, "No, god, *no*,

I'm not mad at you. I'm just . . . I'm just trying to figure it out. *Why* he does it. The three wishes, the three sacrifices, it seems like a ritual, right? There's got to be something else in the song."

Lia says it all quickly, like she's hooking a hard U-turn, because she is. Driving the conversation away from the question she keeps asking herself about what her wish might have cost.

"Right. Sorry, I just— It's so weird, telling the whole story. I keep thinking everyone's gonna hate me."

"Why should they? It isn't your fault," Lia says. "You were a *child*."

I should tell her, Lia thinks, but then Sundae's body is uncoiling like a knot cut loose, a long breath escaping her, and Lia can't bear to rob her of her moment of relief.

Gently, she grips Sundae's waist and lifts her up to sit on the bathroom counter. "Is that why you never told any of them? Were you scared they'd blame you?"

She almost hopes Sundae will say yes. Then she might understand why Lia kept *her* wish a secret. But as Sundae unwinds the sheath strapped to her thigh and sets it aside on the counter, she shakes her head. "No. I just didn't think they'd believe me. I'm surprised they believe me *now*. I mean, would you, if you hadn't seen him for yourself?"

"I might have." Lia shrugs, reaching for a clean towel while Sundae unscrews the cap on the bottle of vodka. Her even tone belies the anxious shame still snarling under her skin, but she can tell that Sundae is buying it. Already, she seems less tense than when they entered the bathroom, so Lia does her best to appear unruffled. "I think Bigfoot is an interdimensional traveler from an alternate timeline where humans evolved psychically instead of physically, so I've believed crazier things."

Sundae almost chokes on a swig of vodka. She lowers the bottle, pressing her wrist to her lips as she swallows. "You *what*?"

"I also think that Mothman was just a faery who was super concerned about infrastructure," Lia says, taking the bottle from Sundae to pour vodka onto the towel.

"Oh my god," Sundae laughs, and her giggle sounds like a cascade of bubbles. She throws her bloodstained hair over her shoulder and watches as Lia gently starts to dab at the wound on her upper arm. "When this is over, I hope you'll go on another date with me. One where we're *not* running for our lives, so you can tell me all your weird theories."

Lia looks up from Sundae's wound, meeting her eyes. Her gaze is syrupy blue, like a melted sno-cone, and Lia finds herself in awe of Sundae's ability to shed her fears long enough to giggle and flirt like this. Staring at Sundae, it seems impossible not to meet her there, not to surrender to this moment too. As Lia's muscles begin to unwind, she says, "Well, just in case we don't get to have that date, I want you to know that if this is my last night on earth, I'm glad I got to spend it with you."

Sundae's lips part, her lashes lowering, shading her gaze. And then her mouth is on Lia's, her kiss tasting like blood and vodka and coconut lip gloss.

Lia's fingers push into Sundae's hair, dragging against the back of her scalp, pink strands soft as spider's silk. Sundae's arms slide around Lia's waist, tugging her closer so her knees squeeze either side of Lia's hips. Lia drops a hand to Sundae's thigh as she presses close between Sundae's legs, guitar-rough fingers trailing over glitter and flecks of dried blood.

Sundae moans against her lips as Lia's thumb grazes the inside of her thigh. "If you don't stop now, I'm gonna beg you not to stop at all," she whispers.

"Fuck," Lia hisses. Her other hand hooks into the strap of Sundae's dress, knuckles tracing down. A little spark of guilt manages to reach her through the haze, and she draws her mouth from Sundae's to say, "Maybe we shouldn't do this."

"Sure, *but* . . ." Sundae ducks her head against Lia's throat. Her lips brush Lia's pulse, dragging up to her ear. She lets out a breathy sigh as Lia's thumb slides up the hem of her skirt. Against Lia's ear, she purrs, "If this is my last night on earth, I'll be glad I got to fuck you."

And that just about destroys any chance Lia had of coming to her senses.

Sundae pulls the straps of Lia's dress off her shoulders, careful not to snag the glass still caught in her skin. One of Lia's hands trails up from Sundae's leg, tracing the curve of her hip to the dip of her waist, all the way to where the tissue-thin fabric of her tight dress stretches across her breast. Sundae shudders, throwing her head back as Lia's thumb brushes her nipple.

Like sparks crawling up a lit fuse, like the feeling when her hands first strike a chord onstage, there's no stopping it once Lia starts. She presses her fingers between Sundae's legs, drawing moans from her lips that Lia swallows greedily with kisses. Sundae pulls away just long enough to peel Lia's dress off, letting it slip down her back to pool around Lia's boots, and then they're locked together again, Sundae's legs winding around Lia's hips.

Sometimes, Lia is focused only on Sundae, on the way she hums and sighs with every movement of Lia's fingers. She trails her lips across Sundae's cheek, kissing the glitter off her skin, listening to the hitches in Sundae's breath against her ear. She looks over Sundae's shoulder in the mirror, watching them together, Sundae's long hair skimming the small of her back as they rock against each other.

Then, sometimes, she's focused on what Sundae's hands are doing, the way they claw and caress, the slow building way she finds just the right rhythm to leave Lia shuddering in her arms.

In the aftermath, Sundae's cheeks are as pink as her hair, her lips parted on pleasured gasps. She looks at Lia through the thick strip of lashes glued to her eyelids, a smile tucked in the corners of her mouth.

"Thanks for coming," Lia says, and Sundae bursts into breathless laughter.

"Not for the last time, I hope," she purrs, echoing her words from earlier.

Suddenly, shouting voices filter through the closed bathroom door.

"Shit," Lia hisses, drawing away from Sundae.

Lia steps back into her dress, pulling it on in such a hurry one of the straps rips a shard of glass from her shoulder. Sundae jumps off the counter, grabbing her thong from the floor and drawing it up her legs. As she tugs the hem of her dress back down, Lia swings the bathroom door open.

The cheerleaders are huddled together—they've dried off and put their prom dresses back on—while Edison is peeking through the cracked door to the balcony, where someone is shouting. The door abruptly swings open, nearly knocking Edison off his feet with its force. Dallas catches him before he falls, pulling him away as a bulky shadow steps inside.

When the light falls on him, Lia realizes who it is.

"Jesus christ, Harper," Neeli snaps.

"Where the fuck is Luke?" Harper demands, looking right at Sundae.

"What? How should I know?" Sundae asks, her voice soft and her eyes wide.

"Because the last time I saw him, he was leaving the motel with *you*, and he hasn't been back since," Harper says. "What the hell did you do to him?"

"I didn't do anything to him," Sundae says. "Can you—can you please close the door?"

"You know, I've been trying to warn him about you for *months*, but he refuses to listen," Harper says.

"Close the door," Sundae desperately repeats.

"He planned this whole trip for you," Harper says. "He thought it would help you. But I was like, man, that's like trying to fix a stretched-out sock. You can put it in the dryer, but it'll still be loose."

"Shut the *fuck* up," Lia snaps, stepping in front of Sundae. But now that she's found the guts to actually stand up to him, she doesn't get the chance. Something barrels into Harper's back, and he falls forward, face colliding with the carpet, which muffles the sound of his scream as savage fangs tear into the back of his neck.

A lion crouches on Harper's back, claws embedded in his shoulders, teeth crunching on his spine. A deep snarl, just like the one Lia heard under the boardwalk after Sundae twisted her ankle, rattles through the room as the lion rips through skin and sinew. Blood sprays from Harper's throat. He spasms on the floor, trying to grip his neck.

He pushes out a gurgling scream as the lion's jaws clamp down on the back of his neck again and the beast starts to drag him toward the door. Harper tries to dig his fingers into the carpet, but it's no use. Sundae bursts from behind Lia, limping on her injured leg as she rushes to grab hold of one of his arms.

"Let him go!" Sundae shrieks at the lion. She struggles to keep her grip on Harper's wrist, and his other hand grabs for her dress, snagging on to the hem of her skirt.

The lion huffs out an angry growl and yanks, hard.

Sundae slips in the puddle of blood pooling on the coarse carpet and crashes to the floor. Still holding on to Harper, she screams as the lion drags them both.

"Sundae!" Lia shouts, charging for the door. Neeli meets her there, and the two of them pry Sundae loose from Harper.

The lion drags its prey out onto the balcony, though Sundae tries to rip herself from Lia and Neeli's grasp. But as she claws toward him, a set of wet penny loafers steps into the doorway, blocking their view of Harper and the lion hauling him away.

Sundae looks up into the smiling shark mouth of Holly Jolly, and her screams drown out Harper's dying gurgles.

TWENTY-TWO

NOW

Sundae's heart is kicking against her rib cage, making her chest so tight she can hardly breathe. She's limp as a rag doll as Lia and Neeli drag her backward across the carpet.

Holly Jolly strides through the door, tracking salty wet footprints through the blood slicking the floor. There's a hungry smile on his toothy mouth as his silver eyes sweep the room like an ax swinging on a pendulum.

With a long-fingered flourish, he tucks his hand inside his brown suit jacket, reaching for his saw.

This is not the version of him that Sundae and Lia saw on the boardwalk, wrapped in chains outside the T-shirt shop. Now that she's looking at him in the light of the motel room, she can see all the ways they are different. The Holly Jolly who stands before her looks like the doo-wop singer in the same way that her knock-off Betsey Johnson bag looks like a real Betsey Johnson bag until you notice that the heart-shaped clasp says *Betty Jason* instead.

Whatever they saw on the boardwalk, Sundae thinks it was more like the lion, or the man with the flat cap and pickax, or even the guy with coins on his eyes who shot the harpoon through Detective Morton's head.

And whatever *he* is, he's something different. *This* is the Holly Jolly she remembers meeting in the dark of the deep end when she was eleven. The Holly Jolly who pressed a taffy into her palm 156 feet in the air. There's a slight limp in his walk—Sundae wonders if it's from the fall off the Ferris wheel—but otherwise, he's just as he looked when she first saw him.

She can smell him when he gets close. That seaweed, sour berry, rotten meat stink. Sundae wedges herself against Neeli and Lia, who are both crouched at her back, their grasping arms like anchors around her.

"Foolish fish," he says as he looks down at her. "Will you finally make your wish?"

"What does it matter, if you can kill me either way?" Sundae snaps.

"Because it will be so much better for me if you do," he answers with a dreamy little sigh. "And you owe it to me, for all you've put me through."

"But it doesn't make sense," she declares. "You said you can kill me now. *How,* if I haven't made my last wish?"

"Because someone you *know* has wished," he says. "And I can take you as payment, if I must. But I would so much rather you pay for your own wishes instead."

Cold engulfs her like icy water as his words settle over her. Sundae feels Lia's fingers press into her arm, her guitar-string calluses bruising Sundae's flesh.

A laugh lilts from Holly Jolly's lips, and his silver eyes track over Sundae's shoulder, where she knows Lia is crouched behind her back.

"Have you not told her?" he says in a sandy purr. "Perhaps you should have. Since your wish was to *have* her."

Sundae twists, casting her watery eyes behind her, hooking Lia's gaze. Everything's hazy through her tears, but she can still see Lia's molten dark eyes, shot through with gold embers. Her wild brown hair, the anguish stitching her brow. And Sundae knows what she's about to hear will rip her heart in two.

"Lia," she whispers, her voice thready and weak. "What did you do?"

"I didn't . . . I didn't know any of this would happen," Lia protests. She whips her face to Holly Jolly, glaring up at him. "I was high. I didn't even think you were *real*. You didn't tell me someone would die!"

"The both of you, believing you can have all you wish, for *free*." Holly Jolly snickers. "What a perfect match you are. Both so hungry and so vain."

"Fuck you," Lia snaps. "I thought I was tripping balls. That wasn't even a real wish."

"You got it, didn't you?" Holly Jolly's hand unfurls, long crab-leg fingers gesturing toward Sundae. "You did get what you wished for."

Sundae is shivering, her jaw clenched against the mixture of horror and hurt that's almost overwhelming her. Lia's hands are still on her arm, and she wants to scream and rip them off, but she also wants them to hold her tighter, wants to cling cling cling and beg Lia to tell her none of this is happening.

But it is.

"What did you wish for?" Sundae asks her softly. "Oh god, Lia, what did you wish for?"

"I . . . I wished . . ." Lia blinks, and two tears slip through her spidery lashes to race down her cheeks. "I wished I'd been brave enough to ask you out."

"But . . . but you did ask me out," Sundae says. "You asked me last night to be your prom date."

"No. I remember *wanting* to ask you. But I didn't do it, Sundae. I only wished for it."

"Dude, Lia, what the fuck," Dallas murmurs from somewhere behind them, and Sundae wonders if he *also* remembers it happening the way she does.

Sundae's heart feels like a fish washed up on the beach, flopping in agony, slowly suffocating on the burning sand. The memory she has of Lia asking her to be her prom date seems just as real as all her other memories—except now, when she thinks of it, she tastes blood in the back of her throat.

He put that memory there, in her mind.

Because Lia wished for him to.

"Why?" Sundae asks, the word hitched on a sob. "Why didn't you just ask me?"

Lia bows her head, dropping her gaze from Sundae's, then drags her face back up. Meeting her eyes only makes it all hurt worse.

Because even when she's breaking Sundae's heart, she looks beautiful. Like an explosion, dazzling as it rips her to shreds.

"Because I'm a coward," Lia says. "I pretended, for a little while tonight, that I was brave. But it was only *you*, making me brave. I'm really just a fucking coward."

Suddenly, the monster's long shadow sinks to a crouch at the edge of Sundae's vision.

She twists, and Holly Jolly's sharp smile is just an inch from her face, his saw blade against the side of her neck. His breath smacks her nose, reeking of sea-scum rot and old blood. Sundae recoils against the girls behind her, Neeli trying to tow her farther away from him, and Lia . . . Lia, there too, solid as a knife against Sundae's back.

"How many more will need to die before you pay your debt?" Holly Jolly snarls.

"Are they all you?" Sundae asks through chattering teeth. "The lion, the guys with pickaxes and harpoons, all these things that are killing people—are they *you*?"

Holly Jolly's smile creeps wider. His head tilts, thorny crown gleaming, his long saw grazing Sundae's collarbone. "Just as much as they are you," he says.

Sundae hears Amber shout *"Go!"* and all the cheerleaders dive forward at once.

In perfect, choreographed unison, they collide with Holly Jolly. They sweep him like a tidal wave, plowing him backward and out the door. His kicking legs drag through the pool of Harper's blood, smearing it across the balcony as the girls keep pushing.

They maintain their momentum, all the way to the railing.

With a collective shriek, they haul him up and over the top rail. He roars like the lion as he tips and falls headfirst, dropping toward the courtyard, landing with a meaty thunk.

Neeli and Lia are moving before he even hits the ground, pulling Sundae to her feet. Her legs are streaked with Harper's blood, too, still sticky and warm. She wishes she could peel off her skin, but instead she peels Lia's hands off her arm.

"Get away from me," she says.

"Guys, come on!" Jackie calls from the balcony with an insistent wave.

"Let's get out of here!" Tasha agrees, stomping her feet, ready to run.

"Sundae," Lia whispers, a shaky plea. Her beautiful hands are poised to reach for Sundae again, all the scratches on her worn silver rings shining like little sparks in the light, her dark eyes sludgy with shame. "Sundae, please, I'm so sorry—"

"Leave me alone," Sundae hisses, grasping Neeli's hand as she backs toward the door with her. "Just stay away from me, Lia."

"Sundae, he *tricked me*—"

"You made a wish that planted *fake memories* in my head, and then you didn't even tell me about it. I had to learn the truth from *him*!" Sundae shouts, ragged and furious.

"I'm sorry," Lia says again. "Sundae, I'm going to figure out how to stop him, I swear—"

"Bullshit," Sundae snaps. "You couldn't even figure out how to ask a girl on a date."

"Sunny, *come on*," Neeli says, pulling her through the doorway.

The wind on the balcony blows Sundae's sweaty, blood-streaked hair off her shoulders. The other girls surround her, herding her away, but Sundae pauses just long enough to look back into the motel room.

Beyond the spill of blood on the floor, Lia is standing there, tears clumping her spiky lashes. Just as beautiful as she looked when she asked Sundae to be her date—in a memory that never actually happened.

And as much as Sundae hates Holly Jolly, in that moment, she thinks she hates Lia even more.

TWENTY-THREE

NOW

Lia feels like a spent mortar, blasted-open and empty inside.

"Lia," Edison says into the quiet of the motel room, vacant now except for a pool of blood and them. "Are you okay?"

Lia finally breaks from her devastated stupor to turn her tear-soaked gaze on her best friends. They look shell-shocked too, but likely because this has hit them all at once, and Lia's sure it's been *a lot* for two boys who have spent most of their life watching weird movies and playing punk music in Edison's basement. Before this, the most harrowing situation they've encountered was the time they got lost on their way to a house show way out in Sussex County and had no cell service.

Now here they are. Standing in a blood-soaked room, hunted by a monster and, apparently, his freaky army.

"No. I'm not okay," Lia says, but then she starts to walk toward the door. "I have to go find that ride. You guys should stay here."

"Like fuck we are," Dallas scoffs, kicking into motion and charging onto the balcony with her.

Lia stops at the railing, leaning over to peer at the spot where Holly Jolly fell. Aside from a splatter of seawater, there's nothing there. A chill skitters down Lia's spine, and she looks at her friends.

"I'm serious," Lia says. "If we're right about all of this, then he can't kill me yet, because I've only made one wish."

"What about the lion, though? And the harpoon man? And whatever the fuck else might be out there? You don't know *they* can't kill you," Edison says.

Lia glances at the cheerleaders, making their way down the staircase closest to the parking lot. She turns the opposite direction, and the boys follow her as she takes the other set of stairs into the courtyard. It's empty; all the kids who had been partying around the pool must have scattered after the lion attacked Harper. Lia's not sure if they evacuated or if they're holed up in their rooms, but she's not concerned about that right now.

There's just one thing she has to check before she goes.

As she strides up to the room next to the lobby, she says, "Maybe they *can* kill me. Which is why I really need to get to that ride, so I know what else is out there."

"Well, we're coming with you," Edison says. He looks over at Dallas, pushing his long curls off his face. "Right?"

"Of course we are." Dallas nods.

Lia leans against the window to the room, peering through the crack in the curtain. Aunt Violet and Theo said that the only way they survive prom weekend every year is with Ambien and earplugs, and sure enough, through the sliver between the celestial-patterned curtains, Lia can see them both sleeping soundly, Theo's arm tossed over Aunt Violet, neither one disturbed by the violent animal attack that just took place at their motel.

Lia pulls away from the window, sighing with relief.

"You two stay here," she says again. "You can watch out for Aunt Vi and Theo. I need to go do this."

"Lia! You *cannot* be making the rookie-level mistake of *splitting up* right now!" Edison snaps.

Lia rolls her eyes, spinning on her heel and marching across the motel courtyard. She stops at the edge of the boardwalk, looking toward the parking lot, where Sundae and her friends were headed.

She sees them there, all crowded around a silver Corolla. Briefly, Lia entertains the fantasy that Sundae is about to leave with them, but Lia knows better. She can tell by Sundae's rigid stance, her heels planted on the pavement, that she's not leaving Wildwood tonight. Not until this is over.

The only way to keep her safe is to figure out how to kill this monster.

As she marches onto the boardwalk, Lia says to Edison and Dallas, "This isn't a horror movie. Do you understand that? Do you *get* that this is real life?"

"Bro. We just watched a lion take the term *meathead* super literally. We get that this is really happening," Dallas says, sticking close to her side.

"Point still stands," Edison says, trotting over to bookend Lia. "Splitting up is stupid. You can't break up the band."

"Yeah, you're not going solo, you can't Stevie Nicks us," Dallas agrees.

"That's crazy, because last night, you threatened to kick me out of the band," Lia says.

"What? No, I did not," Dallas says with a scoff.

"You did, actually," Lia says. "After we got back from hanging out with Sundae, you guys were teasing me for not asking her out, and it turned into this big fight about the Spaced show, and you threatened to kick me out of the band. Only you don't remember, because in this timeline or whatever, I *did* ask her out."

"Whoa," Dallas says, rubbing his head, leaving shocks of his blue-black hair sticking straight up. "Damn, this is like some *Rashomon* shit."

"No, *Rashomon* is about a bunch of people remembering the same thing differently. This is more of a *Butterfly Effect* situation," Edison says. "Except Lia can still remember the unaltered timeline, which creates a kind of quantum decoherence—"

"Oh my god," Lia snaps, abruptly spinning around to face them both. "All right. Do you fucking nerds have weapons?"

"Weapons?" Edison repeats, and he puffs out an incredulous laugh when Lia sticks her leg out through the slit in her dress to show the knife strapped to her thigh. "Dude, I can't even use a can opener without cutting myself."

Lia sighs, looking around at the nearby game stands. She strides over to the frog launch game, hopping onto the counter to grab two big wooden mallets. Holding them out to the boys, she says, "Here. You can't cut yourself on these."

"Yo, this is so Annie Wilkes." Dallas laughs as he takes one of the mallets. He swings it playfully, imitating Kathy Bates as he crows, "'He didn't get out of the cock-a-doodie car!'"

"Can you keep it the fuck down?" Lia rolls her eyes and starts walking again.

"We're looking for the ride still, right?" Edison asks, keeping his voice low. "Do you think it's that one?"

Lia's eyes follow his pointing hand down the pier. There, between the Gravitron and the Balloon Race, looms a ride that isn't like the others.

It's not just the fact that there's no gate surrounding it, no sign of a booth for an attendant or ride operator. It's the way the green light that stripes up the facade makes the holly trees painted on it seem to rustle and sway, the way the edges of the structure look fuzzy against the backdrop of the moonlit sky, the way the lantern that hangs from the front of the train waiting on the platform flickers to life when Lia looks at it, like it's somehow aware of her presence.

It's the way, the longer Lia stares, the more the taste of blood and salt water seems to fill her mouth.

"Yeah. I'd say that's it," Lia murmurs.

She's more cautious as they approach the platform, her steps as slow and silent as she can make them on the creaky boardwalk. There's no way of knowing what's waiting for them inside, but Lia hopes she'll at least find some answers.

Looking back at her friends at the bottom of the stairs, the Haunted Forest sign dousing them in red, Lia asks, "Are you guys sure you want to do this?"

Holding up his mallet, Dallas says, "Yeah, let's get *in* that cock-a-doodie car."

"Jesus christ," Lia sighs, rolling her eyes again as she turns and climbs the stairs to the waiting train car.

Lia gets in the first car, with Dallas and Edison squeezing into the bench behind her. She braces her hands against the sides as the train jerks into motion and starts to roll down the tracks.

"I'm pretty sure Annie Wilkes has a sledgehammer," Edison whispers.

"Huh?" Dallas grunts.

"These are mallets, dude."

"Oh. Who uses mallets, then?"

"Uh. I think Leatherface does, a couple times," Edison says.

Lia ignores them, leaning forward to peek around the corner as the ride pulls out of a dark tunnel, trundling up to the first scene.

Like set decoration for a school play, the walls are lined with wrinkled blue foil, and paper cutouts of fish dangle from above. The sea creatures look bizarrely alien, like they might be ancient, from some time and place beyond Lia's understanding. At the bottom, there's a painted wooden sign, red brush-stroked letters reading,

FIRST I WAS THE SHARK WHICH ATE OF THE SEA.
THIS IS HOW I GREW MY TEETH.

"Okay, yikes," Lia says, thinking of the monstrous black jaws behind the cracked glass in the aquarium. She grips the sides of the ride a little tighter, wondering if the shark will come lunging out like Sundae described, but the train starts moving on to the next scene.

They pull up to a forest full of trees constructed from painted paper with cutout leaves of spiky holly pasted to their branches. Behind them, a mural of a pastel sky, and the sun setting over a bright white beach. Lia can hear the lap of the waves and the trill of seabirds, and at the center of the forest of fake trees, there's one that looks vibrantly real.

The bark is rough and rugged and full of knots. The twisted branches bear waxy green holly leaves and ruby-red berries, gleaming in the flickering light from the lantern on the train car.

Where the tree's roots sprawl along the ground, there are piles of bones. Some strange and animal. Some appearing almost human. The painted sign in front of this scene reads,

**WHEN I WASHED ASHORE, MY BONES FED THE TREES.
THIS IS HOW I GREW MY CROWN.**

The train jerks forward again, chugging down the tracks to the next scene. A rocky coastline, a wrecked ship. Wax figures of dead men are strewn about the beach, silver coins laid over their dead eyes, just like the silver coins covering the eyes of the man with the harpoon who attacked the cop car.

The painted sign in front of this scene reads,

**THE MEN CAME IN SHIPS HUNTING FOR THE FAT OF BEASTS.
THIS IS HOW I GREW MY TONGUE AND LEARNED TO SPEAK.**

The next scene is in another forest of paper holly trees, only now there are stumps where some of the trees were, and the sound of soft waves and chirping birds has been replaced by the cracks of blades chopping through wood. Wax men stand around the trees, frozen with their tools in hand. Some have small hatchets, some axes, and some even have long saws, just like the one that Holly Jolly carries.

**THEN THEY CAME TO CUT ME DOWN WITH THEIR BLADES.
THIS IS HOW I GREW MY LEGS.**

And as their train car stops in the middle, all the wax men around the trees suddenly split in half, ribbons of red silk gushing from their guts like blood as their torsos strike the ground. Dallas lets out a high-pitched scream, and Edison claps a hand over his mouth.

"Let's not shout on the demon ride," Edison hisses.

The train chugs ahead, rounding a turn to lurch through a marshy wetland, tall grass reaching into the car. A large sign rises from the grass, and this one says,

THEY BUILT ROADS INTO ALL THE WILD PLACES.
THIS IS HOW I GREW MY FACE.

The train starts to stall, then bucks abruptly to the side. Lia nearly falls, but she grabs hold of the sides of the cart, the glass still embedded in her shoulder needling as she anchors herself.

"Lia!" Dallas gasps, diving to grab her wrist.

But as he helps haul Lia back into the train car, she notices something painted on its side.

THE WEST JERSEY RAILROAD COMPANY

A chill creeps over Lia as she recalls those same words inscribed on the pickax carried by the man who attacked her and Sundae in the aquarium. As she settles back down on the bench, she looks at Edison and Dallas and says, "Do either of you have your phone?"

"Yeah, of course," Edison says, drawing it out of his pocket.

"Can I use it for a sec?" Lia asks, but she's already snatching it out of Edison's hand and typing in his passcode, which is his dog's birthday.

"Why don't you have *your* phone?" Edison gripes.

"Because I'm wearing a dress, shitbrain," Lia says, and when she glances up and sees Edison and Dallas both looking at her bemusedly, she clarifies, "I have no pockets."

The train starts moving again as Lia pulls up the browser on Edison's phone. She searches *West Jersey Railroad Company Wildwood,* and the first result is an article titled "The Mysterious *Mud Hen* Disappearance." It's from *Weird NJ*—Lia is familiar with the magazine, sold at gas station checkout counters across the Garden State and filled with write-ups about haunted places and bizarre local lore. Lia clicks on the link to the article to scan the lede, which reads, *In September of 1900, a West Jersey Railroad train known as the* Mud Hen *derailed while crossing the Grassy Sound of Wildwood. When rescue teams were able to access the crash site, none of the riders or crew could be located. In all, 73 people were missing from the derailed train. They were presumed lost in a rogue tide, but the Mud Hen Massacre is one of many deadly disasters in Wildwood's history.*

As Lia is reading, the train's engine cuts out. There's a long beat of silence. And then the sound of screams fills the air—this scene must be a depiction of the derailment from the article Lia is reading.

It's also the scene where she suspects the man with the pickax would be, if Sundae hadn't killed him already.

Scrolling down farther, Lia sees that the article's author has compiled a list of *Deadly Disasters of Wildwood,* in chronological order. With her heart pounding in her ears, she begins to read through the list.

May 1845. The whaling ship Pontus *wrecked off the shore of the island and sank into the Atlantic. The wreck was blamed on everything from sea serpents to scurvy, and of all the 24 men aboard, there were no survivors, despite the fact that the ship was equipped with lifeboats and sank close to shore.*

July 1890. Twelve loggers working for the Holly Beach Improvement Company were murdered by Joseph Cook, who became delirious after consuming poison berries from the holly trees the men were cutting. We'll never know what compelled this killer to chow down on the forbidden fruit, because after the massacre, Cook himself died of poisoning.

The train starts moving again and rolls into the next scene, but Lia keeps reading.

June 1917. An amusement industry engineer named Baron Louff debuted a wooden roller-coaster ride on the Wildwood boardwalk called the Haunted Forest. It proved to be the ultimate thrill ride, because on its opening day, the ride derailed, killing 8 children and 3 adults.

May 1926. Walter Kintzel, a confectioner with a popular candy shop, passed out hundreds of saltwater taffies that were laced with arsenic. 10 adults and 19 children died as a result of arsenic poisoning, and many others were hospitalized. Kintzel was found dead by apparent suicide.

August 1938. A stunt rider who trained her lion, Tuffy, to ride in the sidecar of her motorcycle was mauled to death by the lion, who then went on to attack other riders performing inside of the boardwalk attraction known as the Motordome Wall of Death. Eleven people were killed before the lion was shot, making the name of the attraction all too literal.

She looks up at the scene in front of her, a re-creation of the boardwalk with the gateway to a roller coaster that disappears into the ceiling, the awning of a candy shop that advertises SALTWATER TAFFY, and a wooden construction labeled THE WALL OF DEATH where wax bodies lie mangled atop spills of red satin, crashed cutouts of motorcycles tossed about the scene. Here, the painted sign says,

I FOUND THE MEN WHO WERE AS HUNGRY AS ME.
THIS IS HOW I GREW MY GREED.

There's only one more disaster on the list in *Weird NJ*, and Lia has a feeling she knows what it is. As the ride pulls into the next scene and the air is filled with the scent of acrid smoke, she scrolls down to read.

July 1961. A fire at the Riptide Club killed 68 people. Strangely, the fire marshal noted that no one in the club tried to escape their fiery fate, burning alive on the dance floor. The cause of the fire has never

been conclusively determined, and there was only one survivor, who went on to drown himself the same night at a nearby motel.

The train pulls into an old-fashioned club with an empty stage, all the wax figures in the crowd smiling and on fire.

"Hey, Lia . . ." Dallas says, his voice laced with concern. "Um, what's going on? What are you reading?"

"At the end, you don't just die," Lia says, in barely more than a whisper.

"Huh?" Edison grunts.

"At the end of the three wishes. He doesn't just kill someone you know, someone you love, and then you. He kills so many more, and then he *keeps you here. . . .*"

The ride rolls into the final scene.

Unlike the others, this one looks to still be under construction. It's a patchwork of pink and blue, caught somewhere in between the Coral Cove Motel and the Blue Velvet Inn, like it could end up being either. The tiki bar, where a wax figure of the bartender lies dead on the floor, is halfway redone in cool chrome with starry pendant lights. The pool is half pink and half blue, the doors mismatched, some of the palm trees turned into moons and stars.

This scene is being set for Lia, too.

"Godammit," Lia hisses, twisting in her seat to look at Edison and Dallas. "We have to get out of here. We have to find Sundae."

"Watch out!" Edison shouts, and Lia turns back around in time to see a hatchet swinging toward her face.

Throwing herself to the side, Lia narrowly dodges the edge of the blade, tumbling out of the train car with her momentum. She shouts as her back collides with the edge of the track, driving glass deeper into her shoulder.

Edison and Dallas call her name as they launch out of the ride after her. Lia looks up as a figure prowls closer to them, clutching a hatchet like the woodcutters in one of the first scenes.

As he steps into the light, Lia can see his face. His eyes are bloodshot and his pupils blown wide, and all around his mouth are bloody red stains like mashed berry guts. Bile-green foam bubbles from his lips as he bares his teeth, charging at Lia again with his hatchet held high.

Edison cracks his mallet into the man's leg with a primal yell.

The woodcutter falls, his hatchet flying out of his hand as he slams into the tracks in front of Lia. Foamy spittle sprays from his berry-stained mouth, landing on Lia's bare leg. It burns like acid, and Lia shrieks, scrambling away from the man.

"'Almost done. Just one more!'" Dallas says, doing his Kathy Bates impression again as he smashes his mallet into the man's other leg.

Edison lifts his mallet up like he's ready to bring it down on the man's head, but Lia holds up her hand. "Wait!" she cries.

Despite the scorching pain where his spit landed on her leg, Lia scrambles to her feet. She stands over the woodcutter, looking down at him. His eyes roll in his head, seeds and ruby gore caked between his chomping teeth.

"Joseph Cook?" Lia asks.

She watches as the man's eyes jerk to her, a delirious scream leaving his throat in answer. It's a grim confirmation of what Lia already suspected was true.

Lia grabs the mallet from Edison's hand and lifts it up high, driving it down into Joseph Cook's skull. It splits with a sickening crack, like a stomped-on berry, and spills sour red jam out onto the train tracks.

Lia hopes that if she turns into something like this, someone will do the same for her.

TWENTY-FOUR

NOW

Sundae can't stop thinking about what Lia did.

It's not the fact that she made a wish—Sundae made wishes too, and she wouldn't be able to blame Lia for being tempted by Holly Jolly's sales pitch. It's *what* she wished for. It's the fact that she never told Sundae the truth. Sundae had to hear it from *him*.

Sundae wants to scream, but she keeps her jaw clenched against it. There's no time for screaming right now. She needs to get her friends out of here before something happens to *them,* too.

Sundae glances back once to see Lia and her bandmates going the opposite way before she leads her friends down the balcony in the direction of the parking lot. The party music is still playing in the courtyard, but everyone's gone. There's a trail of blood down the balcony where the lion dragged him, and before the first step of the staircase, Sundae has to hop over Harper's gnawed-off arm.

"Ew," Jackie huffs.

"Serves him right," Amber says.

"Amber," Francesca hisses, shooting a glare at her.

"What? How many times has that hand touched a girl without her permission?" Amber shrugs.

"She has a point. Does kind of seem like poetic justice," Tasha says.

At the bottom of the stairs, Sundae looks across the desolate courtyard. Briefly, her eyes wander to the diner, the balloon arch over the door shining like a string of pearls in the moonlight. She reminds herself that the memory she has of Lia promising her that balloon arch is fake.

Sundae's thumb rubs across the bracelet on her wrist, tracing the floral patterns made by beaded seashells. She hooks her fingers under the bracelet, ready to rip it off.

But her heart writhes at the thought, and her hand drops away, leaving Lia's gift on her wrist.

So she turns her focus to the parking lot. She can see Jackie's silver Corolla under the yellow beam of a streetlamp, just a few spaces away from the motel entrance.

She couldn't save Harper or Detective Morton, or even Tony all those years ago. But at least she's about to save her friends.

"Jack, you have the keys, right?" Amber says as they all rush into the parking lot.

"Shit. No, I don't, and I'm just mentioning that now," Jackie responds dryly.

"Right, because you've never been a space case before, Jackie," Tasha says. Francesca is clinging to her arm like she's ready to use Tasha as a human shield.

They get to the Corolla, and Jackie unlocks the door. As the girls all load in, Sundae stays standing under the streetlight, crossing her arms around herself to fight off the chill from the ocean breeze blowing through the lot.

Neeli freezes. "Sunny, what are you doing, *get in the car,*" she snaps.

"You guys are safer if I'm nowhere near you," Sundae says with a shake of her head.

"No way," Jackie says, popping back up from the driver's seat. She leans over the top of the car, jabbing a bedazzled nail against the roof. "Get in this fucking car right now, bitch. We're not leaving you here."

"Yes, you are," Sundae says. "Please. I can't let him hurt any of you. *Please.*"

"I mean, you don't have to beg me," Francesca says, planted in the back seat. "I'm actually fine with not sticking around, waiting to get eaten by a lion."

"Maybe we shouldn't go," Amber says. "Like, we can't take everyone in Wildwood with us, which seems kind of fucked up. Do they all deserve to get eaten by a lion?"

"Should we try calling the cops or something?" Tasha asks.

"Remember the part where a cop got his skull harpooned? The police can't help us," Sundae says. She takes a step back, away from the Corolla, trying to seem steady on her feet even as her sore ankle sends shock waves of pain up her leg. "Please. Just go."

"Sunny's right," Neelima says, looking at the other girls, who are frozen around the car (save for Francesca, who still sits stubbornly in the back seat, ready to go). "She survived this thing once, and she can do it again, but you bitches barely even made it through Regionals. You need to leave Wildwood."

"Oh my god, Neeli, you literally almost *passed away* because you flunked one AP Bio test. *You* shouldn't stay either," Francesca snaps.

"This discussion is over," Neeli says, whipping her finger in a loop as she puts on her team captain voice. "You guys are getting in this car and *leaving*. Right fucking now."

But Neelima is backing away from the car too, moving closer to Sundae's side.

"Neeli—" Sundae starts to say, but her best friend shakes her head and turns her severe brown eyes on Sundae.

"Don't you dare tell me to leave," Neeli says, and Sundae knows she means business.

"God, you're such a bitch," Sundae sighs.

The other girls are slowly, reluctantly settling into the Corolla. Jackie twists her key in the ignition, starting up the car.

"Please don't die," Tasha says as she climbs into the back seat. "They'll make us have one of those depressing assemblies like they did when Mark Sheldon OD'd."

"Ugh. Principal Rennals is such an ugly crier," Francesca says.

Amber is still lingering at the passenger side. She pushes her seat into place after Tasha gets in, her warm coffee eyes on Sundae and Neeli. "Keep our queen safe, all right?" she says to Neeli, who responds with a solemn nod.

Amber slumps into the Corolla and reaches to close the door.

But before her hand touches it, the door swings shut. So does the one on the driver's side, slamming so hard that Francesca yelps. Through the windows, Sundae can see them looking at each other, confusion on their faces. Their voices are muffled, but Sundae can read the movements of their mouths as they ask each other, "Did you close the door?"

"No, did you?"

"What's going on?"

Terror wraps cold hands around Sundae's throat. Every thud of her heart seems strained, pounding in her ears. Like shock has driven her out of her own body and she's observing from somewhere outside herself, Sundae watches as Amber reaches for the door again, tugging on the handle.

"It's locked!" she shouts to the other girls. She swivels in her seat, facing Jackie, saying something to her that Sundae can't hear.

But Sundae *does* hear the radio when it switches on with a static buzz that blasts through the speakers. In the quiet of the parking lot, his voice croons through the glass and metal enclosing her friends.

"The wanting hearts of dreamers here,
Will find only nightmares when you appear . . ."

"No" is all Sundae can manage to say, raw as a prayer from the viselike squeeze of her chest. *Please, no, not them, don't do this—*

Finally, she gasps in a full breath and throws herself against the side of the car, clawing at the door handle. Something caught between a scream and a sob rips from between her teeth as she tries to pry the door open.

Through the windows, she sees their fearful faces as they try to open the doors themselves. Jackie is pounding on the lock button. Francesca is yelling to be let out. Tasha is crawling around the back seat like she's looking for some other way out. Amber is kicking at the door panel, her eyes locked on Sundae's through the glass.

A metallic clank echoes across the parking lot.

"Sundae," Neeli snaps from behind her, her hand hooking Sundae's elbow to twist her around. "Look!"

At the end of the lot, a man in a top hat stands next to a lever that has sprouted out of the asphalt.

He's grinning wide, his long nose pointed over his curled lip, his round face as white as the moon. As he hunches over with his hand on the lever, the brim of his top hat carves a shadow over his eyes, hiding them from view.

This one, Sundae recognizes, though not from when she rode the Haunted Forest seven years ago. No, she remembers him from last night, the silhouette behind the train car her friends were all climbing into—the one who pulled the lever to send them rolling down the track.

Rage punches her in the gut, and she jerks out of Neeli's hold, flinging herself at the Corolla again. She drives her fist against the glass, desperate to break it, to free them, to keep this from happening—

But there's no way to stop the ride.

"Sundae, watch out!" Neeli shouts.

She grabs Sundae's arm, dragging her away as the man cranks the lever. As soon as he does it, Jackie's car bucks into motion, dragged forward like it's on a track. Jackie's hands are gripping the wheel, twisting it back and forth, but she's not in control of the car. It's on its own path, driven by the thrust of the lever in the hand of the top hat man. Tasha wraps her arms around Francesca in the back seat, holding her tight as the Corolla careens away.

Sundae tears out of Neeli's grip and runs across the lot, chasing the car as it jumps the curb, swerving out onto the road. Pain shoots up her leg with every step on her busted ankle, but she doesn't stop running.

She can hear the tires squealing, the engine screaming, the car speeding way, way too fast. . . .

"No, no, no," she begs on panting breaths.

A deafening crash shakes the ground, so loud it throbs inside Sundae's skull. A flare of orange light bursts up toward the sky.

Sundae's legs give out as she reaches the street. She collapses, her knees scraping the pavement, a scream tearing from her throat. In the distance, she can see the roaring inferno, the Corolla crushed like a beer can against the side of a chain hotel that towers over Ocean Ave. Cracked concrete spiderwebs up the wall of the building, destroyed by the impact of the car.

Smoke and flames plume out of the mangled wreckage.

Sobs rake through Sundae's body, her teeth chattering as she doubles over, shuddering. Neeli collides with her back as she slumps to the ground too, her arms winding around Sundae to squeeze her tight.

"We have to—" Sundae starts, but when she looks back at Neeli with tear-blurred eyes, she doesn't finish. They both know there's no saving their friends from the ruins of the flaming Corolla—no one could have survived the crash, or the explosion that followed it.

Shock and anguish overwhelm them both as they sit in the middle of the road, the blazing Corolla burning behind them. Sundae's clingy hands tug at Neeli, like the only thing holding her together is the knowledge that Neelima is *here,* crying and alive in her arms.

Then, out of the despair blooms the rage.

They both twist toward the parking lot. Toward the man in the top hat.

The mask of shadow over his eyes from the brim of his hat carves right, then left, as he watches them.

"That guy was part of the ride, too," Neeli says, her voice warbly but her eyes hard.

"I know," Sundae says. "I saw him last night."

"Let's get him," Neeli says. She springs to her feet, leaving Sundae behind as she marches toward the top hat man.

Sundae struggles to get up and follow her, her ankle feeling like a worn-out hair tie ready to snap. "Neeli!" she cries, trotting to catch up to her.

"You creep-ass fucking *piece of shit*!" Neeli screams as she makes a fist and slams her knuckles into his face. He stumbles back, and Neeli drives her strappy heel into his thigh, kicking his leg out from under him. He falls to the ground, his black coat flying open to reveal a ruffled shirt and sparkly cummerbund. The cry he lets out sounds like the churn of rusty machinery. When the parking lot lights flood his face, Sundae sees that his eyes are blood red and waxy, like two poison berries set in his skull.

He reaches for the lever next to him. In the cracks where it sprang up through the pavement, little roots coil like snakes into the ground.

Before he can grab it, Neeli plants her feet on either side of the lever and wraps her hands around it. Her strong arms flex as she pulls, ripping it up out of the ground like a fledgling tree. With a tear-choked scream, she swings it down into the man's round white face.

His head splits and sparks shoot out of the sides of his top hat. Neeli drives the lever down again and again, beating the thick seaweed-scented blood out of the man, until all that's left of his head is oozing black gore, sparks sizzling here and there like he's made up of mangled machinery, gray fumes billowing from his crumpled top hat like a smokestack.

Finally Sundae grabs Neeli's arm, and Neeli drops the lever to the pavement with a hollow clatter.

"He killed them," Neeli says on a raw sob. "Oh my god, he killed them all."

"No," Sundae replies, closing her eyes. "I did."

"Sunny—"

But Sundae doesn't want to hear Neeli's protest. She doesn't want to hear Neelima tell her that this isn't her fault. It *is* her fault.

All her life, Sundae has known monsters.

Maybe that's how she ended up becoming one.

How could she have come back to Wildwood, even though a part of her knew he might still be waiting for her? No matter how many times she tries to tell herself she didn't want it to ruin anyone else's prom weekend, she knows that, really, she didn't want it to ruin *her* prom weekend.

Now all her friends are dead.

And it *is* her fault.

Sundae rips away from Neeli and starts running. She dashes across the parking lot, her ankle feeling like it's made of shards of broken glass as she reaches the boardwalk. But even if she was uninjured, Sundae wouldn't be able to outrun Neelima, and her best friend doesn't let her get far.

"I swear to god, Sundae, if you try to turn yourself over to that *thing*—"

"I can't let anyone else die because of me!" Sundae says. "I can end this if I just let him have me!"

"No," Neeli snaps, grabbing hold of Sundae's arm and spinning her around so they're facing each other. "You're not giving up. I'm not losing my best friend to some parasitic evil genie, or whatever the fuck this thing is. It tricked you as a kid and it killed our friends and now it has to *fucking pay.*"

Neeli's deep brown eyes are fierce as a hurricane, and Sundae knows she believes what she's saying completely. Unfortunately, that doesn't make it true. Maybe Holly Jolly *did* trick Sundae when she was eleven and in Wildwood for the first time. But nobody tricked her into coming back here at eighteen.

She did that all on her own.

"No, Neeli. Now *I* have to pay," Sundae says.

She wrenches her arm out of Neeli's grip and turns to run toward the pier.

"Sunny!" Neeli screams.

Sundae pulls the piece of wax-wrapped black taffy out from under the strap of her dress. Black swirls into red as she unravels the wrapper and pushes the candy into her mouth. Neeli is closing the space between them, and Sundae knows that if she's going to do this, she needs to go where Neelima can't follow.

A bitter laugh escapes her as she remembers the first conversation she had with Holly Jolly, all those years ago. Sundae reaches the end of the pier, the railing slamming into her gut.

"I wish I could breathe underwater," she whispers.

And she bites down on the candy as she falls into the lashing black ocean.

TWENTY-FIVE

NOW

The moment her wish is made, he can smell it.

Like blood blooming in water, it tangs inside his nostrils, bright and sweet as candy crushed between his teeth. Salty sap wets his tongue, drool leaking between his rows of sharp black teeth.

For too many years, the space he made for her has stood empty. No one has ever taken so long to use all their wishes, and in the time he has waited, he has grown *so hungry*. He could have killed her at any time tonight. But it would have been a kill wasted.

Now that she's made her wish, he is so glad he waited.

It was the other wishers who drove her to it. They are so good at coaxing the reluctant ones. He does not have to tell them what to do—they know already, as ants obey their queen, as roots send water to the tree.

Unfortunately, it seems some of the roots have been sawed off him tonight.

He is limping as he makes his way to the pier, aching from the parts that have been carved away. One of his arms, which had been toned like a whip from swinging a pickax, is now soft as unmolded clay. His legs are unfit for walking, stiff as tree trunks. Luckily, the scent of her wish is drawing him to the water.

Of course, little fish. Of course she is waiting for him in the water.

He cuts into the icy current like a silver blade, the taste of her blood running between his teeth as he follows it down.

TWENTY-SIX

NOW

In the cold blue water, Sundae waits for Holly Jolly to come kill her.

It's almost peaceful, this surrender. To just float here and let the tide wash away her sins, after all the clawing and fighting and screaming and crying. Maybe this is what she should have done from the very beginning. But she was too greedy. She wanted to live, no matter the cost.

And look what she has to show for it.

Nothing but dead friends and a broken heart.

Her eyes open and she watches long tendrils of hair float around her like pink serpents. She still tastes salt and blood between her teeth from the sticky taffy.

There's a metallic shhhk in the water behind her, and she knows he's here, swimming toward her, just like he swam out of the dark of the deep end when she first saw him seven years ago.

This long, terrible nightmare is finally over.

Something slams hard into her shoulder.

The pain is sharp and immediate, ripping an agonized scream

from her throat. She kicks, her heels heavy against the tide, but still she's jerked backward, dragged fast through the dark water.

Her hand lifts, grasping at her shoulder. To the left of her collarbone, a sharp metal point juts out of her flesh, anchored in place by a brutal barb. There's a hard tug from the other end, and her eyes roll up to the surface as agony rockets through her body again.

But the surface is getting farther and farther away.

Sundae knows she's been impaled by the same harpoon that pierced straight through Detective Morton's skull in the cruiser earlier. It's not Holly Jolly who has her now, it's the man with the silver coins over his eyes. And he's dragging her down, deep into the ocean.

Despite the pain of her skewered shoulder, despite the way her pulse drums a frantic rhythm, a limpness takes hold of her, and she doesn't fight his pull. Why resist the death the harpoon is dragging her toward? It might be fast, like Detective Morton's. Or a little slower, like Harper McCall's. Either way, it won't be Holly Jolly who gets to deliver it to her.

But I don't want to die.

There's an acrid taste to the thought, a trickle of doubt seeping into her mind—a doubt that carries the faces of her friends, the terror in their eyes before the car sped away from her. The death-rattle gurgle of Harper, fangs tearing into his neck. The way Tony's face is forever burned on the backs of her eyelids, his mouth frozen open in a perpetual scream.

And his words, always echoing—*Sometimes, if something bad enough happens to somebody, they're never really gonna be okay again.*

But even if it means she has to live with these awful memories, and even though it seems selfish to want it when there's so much blood on her hands, *still* she feels the thought jolting through her, electrifying her limbs, sparking power back into her muscles.

I don't want to die.

A black spire juts into her vision.

A structure is rising out of the murky deep. She kicks her legs, her pink toenails flashing as she struggles weakly against the harpoon's pull. But the man with the coin eyes yanks hard on the rope, hauling her toward a shipwreck on the ocean floor. The mast is a javelin stabbing through the inky sea, and he follows it down to the deck, where seaweed ripples like waving fingers from the blackened wood.

I don't want to die, Sundae thinks again.

Then she grabs hold of the spear in her shoulder with one hand and uses it as an anchor as she swings herself in an arc to kick the coin-eyed man in the face.

The point of the harpoon digs deeper into her shoulder, but when Sundae's heel connects, the coin flies off the man's left eye, exposing a cloudy white orb underneath.

He jerks on the rope, swinging her down onto the deck of the sunken ship. Her hip thuds against the rotted planks, and she grits her teeth as he lands beside her and starts to drag her. Thick green seaweed brushes her legs as she kicks against his pull. Anything she tries to grab hold of is slick with algae, and her fingers slip right off. She reaches for her knife, then realizes it's still in its sheath on the bathroom counter back at the Blue Velvet.

He tows her to a hatch, and they drop down into the black hull of the ship.

Little fish glimmer like stars as they flit around the cabin. The room is shrouded in a dense veil of seaweed and barnacles, but Sundae can make out the shapes of furniture underneath, the broad surface of a captain's desk and a high-backed chair, obscured portraits hanging on the wall.

Not covered in overgrowth, however, are the tools laid out on the desk.

Sundae's stomach drops as the man wrenches her up through the water and loops the rope around a rack that hangs from the ceiling.

Then he slowly makes his way over to the desk, trailing his fingers along the rusty instruments arranged in front of him.

Again, her hands find the end of the harpoon jutting out above her collarbone. There's a savage barb that curves away from its point, keeping the hook from slipping back out the way it came. She reaches up, feeling along the shaft of the spear, hoping to at least free herself from the rack she's suspended from—but the rope is too taut to give her any leeway, and no matter how much she writhes and kicks, she can't wriggle free.

All she can do is watch as he selects his weapon.

His fingers skim over knives, some of them narrow and long, some of them hooked or arched or pointed like angry spikes. All of them meant for butchering, for carving away flesh and hacking through bone.

His fingers close around the handle of a knife with a blade that curves like a sharp claw, and he turns to her, his white eye rolling in his head like a loose marble.

Kicking and screaming and thrashing, Sundae struggles uselessly as he advances on her. There doesn't seem to be any bloodthirsty glee in his actions, no feral rage either. His motions are rote and cold, devoid of any sentiment at all. Like she is simply a slab of meat that must be carved, and he is only trying to get the job done.

Somehow, this stony brutality seems even more terrifying than all the frantic violence she's seen from the monsters so far.

Her legs pedal wildly as he comes toward her, but he grabs hold of her from the side and steadies her enough to place the blade against her waist. Slowly, he slicks the knife through her skin, drawing a line below her rib cage.

She screams from deep in her chest, but it comes out as a gurgle of bubbles.

I don't want to die.

Wrapping both hands around the shank of the harpoon piercing her shoulder, Sundae swings her legs up and throws herself at the ceiling of the cabin hard enough to rip the barbed hook right out of her flesh.

She feels it drag through muscle and sinew on its way out, and a gush of blood spills into the water.

Shoving her palms against the ceiling, Sundae somersaults over the man as he grabs for her. His hands miss her, but she lands hard on the desk. A pronged fork stabs into her leg and she shrieks, the sound a muffled screech in the deep dark water. She yanks the fork from her thigh and raises it just as the man jumps up to grab her.

The long prongs drive into his ribs, skewering his chest.

He hangs on the other end of the long wooden handle gripped in her fists, his milky eye wobbling, his long hair sweeping through the water. Sundae pushes off the desk, plunging the handle toward the floor, thrusting the ends of the prongs into the soft rotten wood.

Pinned to the planks beneath him, the man gives one final gasp before the other coin slides off his face, and he falls limp.

Sundae clutches the gash in her side as blood slips out from between her fingers. She closes her eyes for a moment to rally against the pain. There's still a long way to swim up to the surface.

The first thing she does is kick off her heels. It's a shame to watch them drift to the ship's floor, but they're *impossible* to swim in.

Floating to the hatch, Sundae slips back out onto the deck. She looks up and finds she's barely able to see the moonlight dancing off the top of the water.

She's still staring up when a dark shape descends from above, jaw open wide, rows of razor teeth ready to tear into her.

Adrenaline hits her like a punch to the gut, but she doesn't flee at the sight of him. Mostly because she's too stunned to move at all, frozen on the slimy deck as she blinks through the salt water burning her eyes, trying to make sense of what she's looking at.

It *is* him, body slithering, carrying him fast through the water. But his suit looks ragged, and some of his skin has sloughed away to reveal a mess of animal parts and thorny leaves. Shock locks Sundae in place until he gets close enough for her to see that the silver is gone from his eyes. Now one is a knot of gnarled bark, the other gold like a stalking cat's.

Like the coins that fell off the face of the man she just killed inside the ship's cabin, Holly Jolly's gaze has lost its knife-blade shine.

A flutter of excitement runs through her, raising goose bumps on her arms as her body finally springs into motion.

Sundae spins out of his path to avoid the snap of his teeth, pedaling away from him in a cloud of bubbles. He twists like a cracking whip and lunges through the water, open mouth surging toward her like he's ready to swallow her whole.

Sundae drops, falling back through the hatch into the hull of the ship.

She dives past the desk and grabs a weapon at random. Her fingers close on the handle of a long, razor-sharp spade, and she swims through the doorway of the cabin, deeper into the dark shipwreck.

Behind her, Holly Jolly blasts into the cabin, his twisting body crashing against the walls.

Swimming through the maze of cabins and holds in the depths of the ship, Sundae jumps at every flitting fish, every ripple of seaweed stretching out of the walls. She can hear him chasing her through the hull, and she twists back to spot him, his cat-eye reflective in the dark.

When Sundae swings her head forward again, she's staring into the mouth of a human skull.

She can't stop herself from plowing into it, scattering the bones into the water. Yelping, she recoils, but her back bumps into another skeleton, this one hanging from a harpoon on the wall just like the one that had pierced her shoulder.

They're everywhere in the hold. At least a dozen skeletons, strewn about with coins laid over their eyes, their bones stained green from the murky water. Their slack, open jaws, the sea creatures scuttling between the gaps in their ribs, the empty holes of their nostrils, the stillness of their bones spilled across the floor—it sends queasy horror twisting through her stomach as she stares at them for one hushed, horrified moment.

But there's no time to wonder who they were, or what their place was in all of this.

She can hear him coming closer, his thrashing movements knocking against the decaying wood of the shipwreck.

Sundae tears her eyes away from the skeleton horde and looks up, noticing another hatch above her head.

She kicks off the floor, her ankle throbbing as she shoots through the opening and onto the deck once more.

He explodes out after her, and his teeth snap down on her thigh. Suddenly, she's swinging through the water, shaken back and forth like a dog shakes a bone. She wails out a stream of bubbles as his teeth sink deep into the meat of her leg, sawing with every thrash of his head.

Clasping the handle of her spade, Sundae thrusts it down at him, jabbing it into his junk-pile face. His teeth unclench from her skin, and Sundae falls to the deck as he rolls in the water, trying to dislodge the blade from his cheek.

Sundae grabs the anchor rope spilled across the deck and darts up, swimming in a quick loop to spin the rope around his twisting body. As he keeps rolling, it winds tighter, slowing his momentum and binding him to the heavy anchor.

Pedaling her legs through the water, Sundae plunges to the anchor sitting on top of the transom. She tries to push it off, but it's too heavy for her to move, and the open water offers her no resistance. Dropping to the deck, she tries again, but her feet just slip against the algae-slick wood beneath them.

Then Holly Jolly swerves to the side, and the rope swings into her, sweeping her off her feet.

Slamming down on the planks, she looks up to see him sailing back toward her, using the snap of the rope to gain momentum. His jaws are open, bloody black teeth ready to rip into her again.

Sundae's feet find the stock of the anchor. Her hands reach up, bracing against the wood that frames the hatch.

And then she kicks with all her might, propelling the anchor off the side of the boat.

Like the snatch of a yo-yo, his velocity is reversed. He's flung out into the open water, then downward, falling past the edge of the shipwreck.

Sundae has no idea how long that rope might hold him, but she doesn't wait to find out.

Reeling up off the deck, she swims for the surface.

TWENTY-SEVEN

NOW

The boardwalk stretches for miles down the shoreline, which has never bothered Lia until now, when she is desperate to find Sundae before *he* does.

Immediately after leaving the Haunted Forest ride, she (and Dallas and Edison, still refusing to let her go it alone) had returned to the Blue Velvet. She wasn't sure what she hoped to find—maybe some sign that Sundae had escaped with her friends? But Lia knows Sundae was never planning on getting in the car with them.

Still, when she reached the parking lot of the Blue Velvet and saw that the Corolla was gone, Lia let herself hope that Sundae was gone, too. That she had fled Wildwood, and wherever she was headed, Holly Jolly's roots couldn't reach her.

Then Lia noticed the flashing lights throwing beams of red into the night-blue sky, and she heard the sounds of shouting voices and the thrum of idling trucks.

As she stepped out onto the street beyond the parking lot, she stared past the emergency vehicles into the blackened, twisted windows of the car Sundae was leading her friends to when Lia last saw her. Coiling terror crept through her chest as she thought of the promise Holly Jolly had made to Sundae atop the Ferris wheel—*Soon you may find yourself with nothing left but a wish for death.*

If all of Sundae's friends are gone, that might already be true.

The mangled Corolla was surrounded by cops, ambulances, and firefighters, so she couldn't get closer and risk being recognized. Still, Lia is certain Sundae wasn't in the car when it crashed.

Partly because of what she knows about Sundae. And partly because of what she has learned about *him.*

Now that she's processed everything she read and saw inside the ride, she's certain she understands why Holly Jolly hasn't killed Sundae yet. She's explaining it to Edison and Dallas as they hunt for Sundae through miles of abandoned rides and game stands. Even if the cops hadn't cleared out the boardwalk, it would probably be just as deserted at this hour—Lia isn't quite sure of the time, but it must be long past midnight by now.

"He needs her to make her last wish so he can collect her. So he can, like, use her for parts," Lia says, throaty and breathless as she sprints. "That's what he did with all the others. Now they're his minions, and he's made up of pieces of all of them."

"It's like . . . a ritual," Edison pants, clutching a stitch in his side. "Three wishes . . . three sacrifices."

"Right," Lia agrees. "Even though he *can* kill her, he doesn't *want* to until she completes the ritual. Otherwise, he doesn't get to use her."

"All right, but what *is* he?" Dallas asks. With his drummer endurance, he's the only one of them who seems unfazed by all the running. "Is this, like, a *The Thing* situation? Some kind of eldritch-abomination primordial-soup monster? Was he the shark first, or was that just the first thing in his collection? Can a shark even wish for things? Or a tree?"

"Seems . . . kind of unknowable . . ." Edison grunts and gasps. "More important question is . . . how can he be killed?"

"Do we have to kill him? I think we should just get your girl and get the fuck out of here," Dallas says.

"She's not my girl," Lia says, shame a whip lashing against her heart. "But we *do* have to kill him."

Lia told Sundae she'd find a way to stop this. And she has to.

For the both of them.

Otherwise, won't they just spend the rest of their days searching for silver eyes in the dark? How can they know for sure that his range is limited to Wildwood? Edison is right—too much about him *is* unknowable—and the only way to truly be safe is to kill him, once and for all.

Unfortunately, Lia hasn't the faintest idea how that can be done.

As if he's having the same thought, Edison says through his wheezing, "How do you kill . . . an eldritch-abomination . . . primordial . . . soup monster?"

"Look, I'm not married to that as a concept," Dallas says. "He could also be a forgotten pagan deity, and the three wishes are his rites of worship."

"Maybe . . . he's like . . . an ultraterrestrial . . ." Edison suggests.

"An interdimensional traveler! Very *Mothman Prophecies*, Eddie," Dallas says. "Perhaps we don't have to kill him at all. We can just show him the door back to his home dimension."

"No. We're killing him," Lia says.

A guttural roar shakes the boardwalk.

Lia spins, just in time to see a flash of gold before the lion collides with her, slamming her to the ground.

Long white teeth flash in her face, breath that smells like blood and popcorn filling her nostrils. The lion pins her to the sunburned planks of the boardwalk, golden eyes gleaming in the flashing lights of the nearby arcade sign.

She waits for the lion's jaws to close on her throat, for what is probably a fraction of a second but feels like a long frozen stretch of stillness. She stares up at the beast, breath knocked out of her, as it looms. And this close, she can see details she missed in the low light of the motel room. The shabby mane and mottled fur, sloughing off in patches like a tatty old stuffed animal, revealing raw pink skin underneath. The way its misshapen muzzle reminds her of seeing the musical *Cats* with her dad when she was six, how all the dancers with their feline prosthetic faces pranced across her nightmares for weeks afterward. How beneath the lion's hungry snarl, Lia can hear the echo of a revving motorcycle.

Of course the lion wasn't the one who made three wishes.

It was the stunt rider, the woman who forced the beast to be part of her act and was ripped apart by the lion when all her wishes were up. Now she's trapped in a replica of her own demise, just like the woodcutter forever gnawing on his poison berries, or the whaler wearing the coins over his eyes to pay the ferryman's toll, or the railway worker swinging his pickax into eternity.

The same thing will happen to Sundae, if she makes her final wish.

"'Long live the king!'" Dallas cries, crashing his mallet into the side of the lion's head.

The mallet snaps in half from the force, splintered wood raining down on Lia. It stuns the beast long enough for Lia to roll away. The lion recovers from its shock just as Lia scrambles to her feet, and it lets out a furious roar and swipes at the back of her leg, claws slicing into her skin.

Lia stumbles, nearly falling, but Edison grabs her by the arm and wrenches her upright just as the lion prepares to pounce again.

Already winded from all their running, the members of Morticia take off, trying to outrun a hungry lion-zombie-stunt-rider-woman.

"Ridiculous." Lia huffs, her teeth gritted against the pain in her claw-gouged leg. "This is so fucking ridiculous."

"Fuck . . . killing an . . . eldritch-abomination primordial-soup monster. . . . How the fuck . . . do we kill . . . a goddamn lion?"

"Anyone got a stampede of wildebeests handy?" Dallas says.

"That's your second . . . *Lion King* joke . . ." Edison says. "Way past . . . your allotted number . . . of *Lion King* jokes."

Lia's barely listening to them. There's a plan forming in her mind, and it might be a little more vindictive than necessary, but she's going to try it. She veers to the left, headed for one of the rides left unmanned when the boardwalk was evacuated.

"Listen . . . I'm gonna get it . . . to follow me on here," Lia says, panting just as much as Edison now. "You guys start the ride."

"What?" Edison squawks, looking up at the ride they're approaching.

The SpringShot is one of Lia's worst nightmares, as far as rides go. Even worse than the Ferris wheel, which at least moves slowly and has the slight consolation of enclosed carts, the SpringShot is just a set of flimsy chairs that gets flung two-hundred-some-odd feet into the air at supersonic speed.

Definitely enough force to throw someone to their death if they're not strapped in.

"Do I have . . . to repeat . . . the instructions?" Lia growls.

"No, we got it! Question, though," Dallas says. "You're gonna get off the ride before it goes up, right?"

"I sure fucking hope so," Lia says. Then she turns around, calling out, "Hey, ya undead animal abuser! Over here!"

And the lion-zombie-stunt-rider-woman dashes after her, straight toward the SpringShot.

Blood is pouring down the back of Lia's leg, slicking the inside of her boot as she runs up the stairs to the platform. She trips at the top, catching herself with her hands on the wooden planks. A massive paw swipes at her, claws tearing into the back of her dress, grazing her spine.

Lia's not sure what's going to piss Aunt Violet off more when she wakes up—the state of her motel, or the state of the dress she let Lia borrow for the night.

Either way, she'll probably make some sounds pretty similar to the lion currently roaring at Lia's back.

Edison and Dallas are arguing over the control panel at the bottom of the platform. Lia can only hope that they won't spend so much time comparing the situation to movies that they fail to get the ride moving. She leaps onto the seats, the lion not far behind. Realizing that the bench is definitely not big enough for her to avoid ripping claws and savage teeth, and not wanting to end up as Meow Mix before the boys figure out the controls, Lia grabs hold of one of the cables that will slingshot the ride into the sky, pulling herself up and out of the lion's reach.

The lion jumps into the suspended basket, its weight bouncing the cables Lia is clinging to. She yelps and squirms up a little higher, farther from the lion's swiping paws.

"We got it! You ready?" Dallas yells from the ground.

"Yup!" Lia chokes out as the lion lurches up, pawing at the bottom of her boot. Lia kicks, slipping down the cable a little, dangerously close to the lion.

She hears a thunk from the anchor point below the bench.

Right as the cart flies into the air, Lia lets go of the cable. But the bench is already hurtling upward, and its distance from the ground has increased significantly. Her shoulder slams into the wooden platform, the breath punched from her chest by the impact.

Rolling onto her back, she looks up toward the sky.

The lion is still on the bench, held in place by centrifugal force, until the cart reaches its apex. Like a giant slingshot, the lion is flung into the air, a golden blur of swinging paws and roaring jaws against the starry sky.

Vindictive, definitely. But Lia can't deny that it's kind of apropos to send the stuntwoman on one final ride.

With a crash so loud it makes Lia's jaw clench, the lion's body smashes into the metal roof of one of the stands farther up the boardwalk. Sitting up, Lia tries to roll her arm, but between the shattered glass driven deeper into her shoulder and the damage done by her impact with the ground, every movement sends starbursts of agony through her nerves. Holding her elbow against her side, she gingerly climbs to her feet.

The truth is, what Lia's always been afraid of is *nothing*.

She's been afraid of hypotheticals, afraid of possibilities, afraid of the unknown. Afraid of what she wants, afraid of what she'll lose, afraid of who she is.

But now, after facing down a host of monsters, she finally understands what true fear feels like.

Because of all the things that Lia has ever been afraid of, the fear that Sundae might turn into something like *that* is the worst of them all.

And if she doesn't find her soon, that fear just might come true.

TWENTY-EIGHT

NOW

When Sundae breaks through the surface of the water, Neeli is waiting for her.

"Sunny!" she screams, her eyes wide, her wet black hair falling forward as she leans over the rail. She's soaked, her emerald dress stained dark as a forest floor by the sea, like she jumped into the water after Sundae. "Holy shit, Sundae, I thought you were dead! You were down there so long—"

"We're killing him!" Sundae shouts, too excited to wait. "Neeli! We're fucking *killing him*!"

"What?" Neeli says.

Sundae pushes her hair back, wincing as the harpoon wound in her shoulder sends needles of pain down her arm. Bobbing closer to the edge of the pier, she grasps for the ladder, and Neeli rushes over to help her up.

"Holly Jolly. I saw him down there. And he looks *fucked up*," Sundae says.

"Baby, *you* look fucked up," Neeli says, her usually plum-blushed brown cheeks washed wan by shock and salt water as she assesses Sundae's bloody state. In the seawater running off Sundae's body there are blooms of blood, leaking in rivulets down her shoulder, her side, her thigh.

All of it hurts, but the adrenaline pumping through her veins is stronger than the pain.

Sundae swings her leg over the top of the rail and Neeli helps her down, wrapping an arm around her to keep her upright. "I'm serious, Neeli. He looks different. Like a jigsaw puzzle with missing pieces. I think that killing all his little *minions* is killing him, too."

Then she reaches up and pats the top of her head, pouting sullenly. "Oh no. I lost my crown."

"Jesus *fucking* christ, Sunny. You're bleeding from everywhere, who gives a shit about the crown? Are you okay?"

"I'm doing better than *he* is," Sundae says. "He doesn't even have his eyes anymore."

"We need to get you bandaged up," Neeli says, like she's only half listening.

"I'm fine. We have to find the rest of the—"

"Sunny," Neeli snaps, interrupting her. "You're, like, *really* hurt. We need to stop this bleeding, *right now*."

"Okay, okay," Sundae says, because when she looks down at her aqua prom dress, she has to admit it probably shouldn't be completely blood red.

The cold water has numbed Sundae's body, dulling the pain of all her wounds, but as Neeli starts to drag her up the boardwalk she can feel sharp pricks radiating from the shark-bite gouge in her thigh with every step. It makes her put more weight on her busted ankle, which hurts just as bad, to compensate.

"Sundae . . . how were you down there that long?" Neeli asks tensely, like she's afraid to hear the answer.

"I made a wish," Sundae admits. Neeli gathers her tighter, holding more of Sundae's weight as she veers toward the nearest building on the boardwalk. A candy shop lit in acrid green, the painted awning advertising SALTWATER TAFFY.

"Why would you do that? Isn't that what he *wanted* you to do?" Neeli snaps.

"I was having a moment, all right?" Sundae grunts.

They pass through the front door into the candy shop, and the bell thunks a sour note as it closes behind them. Just past the doorway, Sundae steps on a sticky peach ring with her bare foot, and she shakes it off with a little *"Euuugh!"*

"There's gotta be some towels or something in here . . ." Neeli murmurs.

They move to the back of the shop. Like the rest of the boardwalk, the place seems deserted, but as they enter the kitchen, Sundae notices a steady sound like a knife falling against a wooden block.

The only light in the room filters in through the windows, barely illuminating the bulky silhouette of a figure by the counter.

The smell of hot sugar and bitter almond fills the air.

The figure raises a cleaver up high, then drops it down, hacking off a chunk from something laid out on the counter.

"That . . . is another one of his minions, isn't it?" Neeli hisses near Sundae's ear.

Sundae nods, casting her eyes around for something to use as a weapon, wishing she'd kept one of the knives from inside the sunken ship.

"We have to kill it," Sundae whispers.

The candy maker freezes with his cleaver in the air.

Slowly, he starts to turn. The boardwalk light leaking through the windows finds his face, his thick white mustache, his round cheeks, his apron spattered with sticky wads of taffy like bloodstains.

A giggle creeps from his mouth, the sound like a grown man imitating a toddler's laughter.

Then he's striding toward them, the tile beneath Sundae's bare feet shaking with every step he takes.

Sundae and Neeli scamper around him, darting to the other end of the kitchen. He spins, bringing his cleaver up, peering through the hole in the corner of the blade at them. He giggles again, belly rolling with the sound of his childish laughter.

"He's so babygirl," Neeli says, dry as can be.

"I wish we had a flamethrower right now," Sundae mutters.

And then he charges with his cleaver swinging.

Sundae and Neeli scream, grabbing each other's arms as they drop and roll away, a move that comes to them instinctively from hours of cheer practice. He collides with the wall, a shelf full of candy jars collapsing under the impact. Glass and gumdrops rain to the tile, and the man lets out a furious roar.

The girls jump to their feet, and Sundae shrieks against the pain in her legs as she runs out of the kitchen and dives across the checkout counter. Neeli follows, but he comes barreling in, cleaver rushing toward her.

Neeli yells as the blade drags across her back. Sundae grabs her wrists, yanking her off the counter before his blade can dig any deeper.

"Shit! Are you okay?" Sundae gasps as she and Neeli land on the floor and crouch on the tile.

Then a massive arm reaches over the counter and folds around

Sundae's neck, lifting her off her feet. She thrashes against his pull as he hauls her back toward the kitchen, one elbow connecting with the metal cash register on the counter, and the drawer snaps open with a cheery cha-ching to reveal change wells filled with swirled pastel taffies.

Sundae's shriek is smothered by the powerful arm squeezing her neck. Her bare feet kick against the air as he bends her back over his broad belly. His mustache feels like sticky spun sugar against her cheek as he giggles by her ear.

Her breath is crushed from her throat.

She claws at his arm, scraping her glittery nails against the long leather gloves he wears.

Out of the corner of her eye, she can see the glint of his cleaver lifting high.

Then something collides with them, so hard he's plowed to the ground.

Sundae is thrown from his arms, and the back of her head smacks against the tile as she hits the floor. Squinting through the blare of pain in her skull, she looks over to see that Neeli's pushed a wheeled worktable into him, and she's standing over it now, gripping the edges of the table as blood pours down her back.

The candy man rises up again, grabbing hold of Neeli's arm.

Sundae jumps to her feet, ignoring the stab of agony from her shark-bitten leg. As the man brings his cleaver up again, Sundae leaps onto his back, digging her sharp pink nails into his eyes.

He roars, stumbling backward and smashing Sundae's spine against the wall beside the oven.

That's when she notices the vat of molten candy boiling on the stove.

Sundae grits her teeth and worms her fingers deeper into his eye sockets, blood pouring over her knuckles. A scream tears out of her when his elbow smashes against the gash on her side. She uses her grip inside his skull to steer him as she rides on his back until he tips forward, falling toward the candy vat.

Sundae rips her hands away from his face just as he goes headfirst into the boiling pot of sugar.

As he fights and flails, she presses down against his back, keeping his head submerged. The candy bubbles over his neck, blistering hot and viscous. Gradually, his thrashing slows, and he slumps into the pot, the hot sugar melting away his flesh.

Sundae drops from his back, yelping as she lands on her bad ankle again. She turns around to look across the dark kitchen at Neeli, who points at the candy man's hunched-over form and declares, "I won't sugarcoat it, you're gonna be sticking right there!"

Sundae releases a breathless cackle, then adds, "I'd say he really can-*died*!"

Neeli snorts loudly, and Sundae matches the peal of laughter that follows. Still giggling, Neeli circles the kitchen to find the light switch. She flips it on and greenish bulbs buzz overhead, flooding the kitchen with sickly light.

And as the table where the man had been working is illuminated, Sundae screams.

A body lies encased in gold butterscotch, several bite-sized chunks already hacked away from the arms and gathered in piles on the cutting board. Even coated in sticky yellow candy, Sundae recognizes his body immediately.

"Is that *Luke*?" Neeli says.

Sundae nods, pressing her fist against her lips as hot bile creeps up her throat. She looks away, but it's too late. The image of his mouth twisted open in a scream, frozen beneath a layer of hard candy, is burned into her mind.

"My therapist is gonna have to work overtime after this," Sundae grumbles into her fist. "Please, can we get out of here?"

"Yeah, let me just— I'm gonna grab some towels," Neeli says. She rushes around, snatching whatever she can use to dress their wounds, stuffing as many rags as she can under her elbow before she hooks her arm around Sundae to help her to the door.

As they step out onto the boardwalk, the cool air chilling Sundae's damp dress and dripping hair, someone screams, "Sundae!"

Even though her voice is in tatters, the sound sends a shiver down Sundae's spine, just like it did when she heard Lia singing onstage only a few hours before.

And even though Sundae is still angry, even though she still feels the sting of Lia's awful wish, her heart darts into a gallop when she spots Lia sprinting toward her and Neeli across the boardwalk.

"Fuck," she whispers to Neeli. "I'm down bad."

And then Lia is skidding to a stop in front of them, blurting out, "I know what happens when someone makes their last wish!"

Sundae lifts her chin a little, and as Edison and Dallas catch up to Lia, she makes her own announcement.

"Cool. I know how to kill him."

TWENTY-NINE

NOW

Sitting around a picnic table under the twinkling boardwalk lights with her bandmates, Sundae, and Neeli, just like they were yesterday, Lia can't help thinking about everything that has changed in the past twenty-four hours.

Yesterday, Lia was trying to work up the courage to play a show again. Yesterday, the scariest thing Lia could imagine herself doing was attempting to flirt with the weird, funny, super-hot girl she'd met on the beach. Yesterday, Lia had no idea monsters existed.

And yesterday, Lia had never seen someone die before.

The one thing that *isn't* different is that Lia still can't stop staring at Sundae.

For a multitude of reasons, it's hard not to. One is that Lia feared she would never see Sundae again, that she might have been inside that wrecked car after all, or that she'd already made her final wish and been turned into one of those undead things Holly Jolly keeps in his Haunted Forest ride, and she's so glad to find that Sundae is still alive and still *Sundae*. Another is that Sundae has so many injuries that it's difficult not to look on in worry as Neeli carefully wraps them in scraps of kitchen towels. But most of all, it's hard because even ocean-drenched, with seaweed caught in her hair and her little blue dress stained with gore and all her makeup washed down her face, Sundae is still the weirdest, funniest, hottest girl Lia has ever seen.

Let alone kissed.

Let alone totally fucking fumbled.

But that's not really the most pressing matter right now. Lia *actually* needs to be focusing on the plan to kill Holly Jolly.

Since he's already proven that he and his minions can find them wherever they try to hide, it seems pointless to hole up somewhere. Instead they've chosen to set up camp around a table that affords them a clear view of the long stretch of the boardwalk on either side, so no one—and no*thing*—can sneak up on them.

"We don't have much time," Sundae tells them, pausing to wince as Neeli tightens the rag she's tying around the gouge in Sundae's shoulder. Lia's fingers curl into a fist as she fights the urge to reach out and squeeze Sundae's hand. "I tied him up, but I don't know how long it'll hold him. He *is* pretty injured, so it might take him a second."

"How?" Dallas asks, seated on the corner of the table, swiveling around every so often to surveil the length of the boardwalk. "How did you injure him?"

"I bet it was the salt water," Edison says. "This guy totally has a Julian Sands, *Warlock* kind of vibe."

"Shit, you're right. *Another* horror movie villain undone by sodium," Dallas says.

Sundae sighs, her blue eyes rolling up toward the round opal moon. Judging by how low it hangs over the beach, Lia thinks it must be just an hour or two until dawn.

Sundae says, "If only it was that easy. But no. It's all his little guys. When we kill *them*, it's killing *him*."

"You mean the past wishers?" Edison says, and Lia clenches her jaw, because she knows this is news to Sundae—and she can tell by the way Sundae's gaze hardens and drops to Edison that it's going to hit her hard.

"Is that what they are?" Sundae whispers.

"It is," Lia says, sitting up a little straighter, though her glass-encrusted shoulder stings in protest. Sundae's eyes swing to Lia, and it steals her breath for a moment, but then she pushes on. "We figured it out. On the ride. The scenes are for everyone who made wishes before. He keeps them there, and they become, like, a *part* of him."

Sundae looks away, staring down the boardwalk, her face turned just enough that it's hard for Lia to see her expression. But Lia doesn't have to see it to know what Sundae is feeling. It's the same horror Lia feels when she thinks back on all the nightmare creatures she's seen tonight, knowing that their fate might be hers too, if Holly Jolly gets his way. It takes Sundae a moment to respond, and when she does, her voice is strained through the clench of her jaw.

"That makes sense, I guess," Sundae whispers. Finally, she turns her face toward the table again, blinking the shine from her eyes as she tells them, "When I saw him in the water, he was *missing parts*. I think if we kill them all, there won't be anything left of him."

"Well, how many more do we have?" Neeli asks.

"There were nine of them, before me and Sundae," Lia says.

Sundae pulls on her hair, dragging the sopping pink seaweed-streaked mop of it over her shoulder. Neeli hisses through her teeth in reprimand, quickly sweeping Sundae's hair away from the clean towel Neeli had wound around her shoulder.

"Sundae, gangrene is *so* not your color," Neeli says sternly. "Let's keep that wound clean."

"I love you, Neeli, but I had a rusty harpoon covered in cop brain shot through my shoulder. I think I'm already fucked," Sundae murmurs. Then the blue pools of her eyes find Lia's, and she presses, "Tell me about the others."

Doing her best not to drown in Sundae's gaze, Lia says, "First, there was the shark. Then a holly tree. Next, there was a whaler who killed all his crewmates when they shipwrecked here. Then a logger who was chopping down trees on the island hacked up a bunch of his coworkers and died from eating poison berries. Then a railroad worker, who was working on a train called the *Mud Hen*—it derailed, and everyone disappeared."

As Lia ticks through the previous wishers, Sundae's eyes fall away, sticking somewhere on the boardwalk planks while her fingers stray to the shell bracelet she's still wearing. Every time she twists it around her wrist, Lia feels it wring her heart, but she keeps going.

"A ride engineer who designed a wooden roller coaster that malfunctioned. A confectioner who sold poisoned candy. A stuntwoman who forced her pet lion to ride a motorcycle, and then, surprise, surprise, the lion went on a killing spree. A doo-wop singer who played a single show before the entire club went up in flames."

The blue of Sundae's eyes is almost entirely blotted out by the end, like storm clouds covering the sky. Her hand is coiled around the bracelet, pressing the shells into her flesh, her chest rising and falling with slow shallow breaths like she's trying to keep calm.

"So. That's all nine of them," Lia says. "And I know we're already down three. Sundae killed the railroad worker earlier, and we got the logger and the stuntwoman."

"Excuse me. We didn't kill any women," Dallas says, throwing his hands up. "We killed a lion. Well, we more like yeeted a lion into hyperspace. The point is, I'm no Ted Bundy, all right?"

"Got it. You're not Ted Bundy, just Scar," Neeli says with a nod.

Dallas looks to Edison, arching his brows and pointing his thumb at Neeli. "How many *Lion King* jokes is *she* allowed?"

"*Anyway,* we got the candy man, for sure," Neeli says, and she and Sundae shudder, exchanging a look. "And the deadly ride guy, he must have been the one who killed our friends. We wasted that *London After Midnight*–looking motherfucker."

"I got the whaler," Sundae says, her voice small as she sits tensely at the edge of her bench.

"So that leaves the shark, the tree, and the doo-wop singer," Edison says.

"Cool. I'll handle the tree; someone else can get the remaining apex predator, thanks," Dallas says.

"How big is this shark, exactly?" Edison asks.

"Big," Sundae and Lia say in unison, which stupidly makes Lia's heart flutter. Then Sundae goes on to say, "Like, if all the guys on Hinge whose profile pic is them holding up a really big fish were stacked on top of each other, this shark could probably swallow them whole."

"Is this a shark, or a fucking megalodon?" Edison scoffs. He looks around like he expects a laugh, but he deflates when he sees even Dallas doesn't get the joke. Like a puppy waiting for a ball to be tossed his way, he says to Dallas, "You know, the prehistoric shark?"

"Ohhh, like in *The Meg*!" Dallas declares, and Edison's nodding head somehow has the effect of a wagging tail. As if to bring everyone *else* up to speed, Dallas explains, "This movie where Jason Statham fistfights a giant turbo dino shark."

"Did you guys know sharks are older than trees?" Edison says.

"Bullshit," Dallas says.

"No, I'm serious. Sharks have been around for like, four hundred million years," Edison insists.

"Please tell me you didn't learn this from the Jason Statham movie," Neeli says.

"Look, we'll figure out a way to kill the shark, and the doo-wop singer, and then the tree will be easy. It can't exactly *go* anywhere. We can just cut it down," Lia says. She twists on the bench, careful not to let her knees bump into Sundae's as she faces her. "The most important thing is, Sundae, you can't make that last wish. Because if you do and he kills you, you'll turn into one of those *things*, too."

Sundae's misty eyes lash at Lia's heart like a hurricane as they meet her gaze. The longer Lia looks into them, the tighter dread seems to twist around her throat. *No, she didn't, she couldn't have,* Lia tries to tell herself, but the stormy resolve darkening the blue of Sundae's irises says differently.

"I already did," Sundae confirms in a whisper. Sundae stands and grabs one of the towels off the table, handing it to Lia without a glance her way. "Here. Wrap this around your leg, stop the bleeding."

Lia takes it, careful not to let their fingers brush as she does.

Sundae paces, her steps limping but steady. "I don't think we should just cut down the tree. I think we should destroy the entire ride. That way he'll have nowhere to hide when the sun rises."

"Okay, scorched earth, I like it," Dallas says, then holds up a finger. "Actually. We should blow it up."

"I bet that piercing place has way more fireworks in the back," Edison says. He laughs, turning to Lia. "Look, it's your time to shine. Instead of blowing up Sundae by accident, you can blow up the ride on purpose."

"Fuck off," Lia grumbles, pausing to elbow him before she

continues winding the towel around her bloody shin. "Everyone's avoiding the big question. What about the shark?"

"I'm going to go deal with the shark," Sundae says, already backing away from the picnic table. "You guys get the fireworks, and I'll meet you back here. All right?"

"The way you say you're gonna go *deal with the shark* genuinely makes me afraid of you," Edison says.

"Sunny, are you sure about this?" Neeli asks, standing and eyeing Sundae worriedly. "We can all come with you, you don't have to do it alone."

"Yeah, I'm sure," Sundae says. She gives them a little smirk and says, "Jason Statham has nothing on me."

Then she turns and starts walking toward the aquarium, barefoot and blood-soaked and all alone.

And Lia finds herself frozen in her seat, terrified to go after her.

It's not facing the shark that she's afraid of. Well, actually, she *is* afraid of that, but who could blame her? That's not what's *stopping* her. What keeps Lia stuck in place, her body locked up like a clenched fist, is the fear that if she goes after Sundae, it will be the wrong move. It'll be crossing a boundary, and she's clearly already on Sundae's shit list. It'll be an intrusion, a gross overstep, a terrible miscalculation on her part. She's terrified it will just make Sundae more furious with her. That if she goes after her, she'll be forcing Sundae to remind her that she told Lia to get away from her, and that meant for good.

But if she doesn't go . . .

If she doesn't go, she fears Sundae will fall victim to Holly Jolly, once and for all. And that's scary—much scarier than all the imagined scenarios where Sundae tells her to fuck off.

Worst of all, Lia is afraid letting Sundae walk away like this will make her think she *deserves* to go it alone.

And even though she's scared, Lia propels herself off the bench.

"Sorry. You guys do the fireworks. I'm going with her," Lia says to the others.

Then she takes off, jogging to catch up with Sundae.

THIRTY

NOW

The pain radiating through Sundae's entire body is nothing compared to the ache currently ripping her heart in two.

Which is why she's not glad to hear Lia coming up behind her. Lia can't make this better. Lia has no right to even *try* to make this better.

And yet somehow, the sound of her boots closing the gap between them *does* comfort Sundae, no matter how hard she tries to smother the thrill it gives her.

"Sundae, wait!" Lia calls, but Sundae doesn't slow her stride. Not that she's walking very fast on her injured legs, but still, she keeps marching.

"I told you to stay behind," Sundae says without turning around.

"I know, I—" Lia stumbles beside her, catching up and keeping pace. "I know you said that, but... Sundae, you don't have to do this alone."

Lia's words are a finger prodding the bruise that is Sundae's entire chest. Sundae bites down to keep it from overwhelming her, her jaw clenching so tight it feels like it might crack. Staring ahead, not daring to glance Lia's way, Sundae grinds out the words "Yes. I do."

"You *don't,*" Lia snaps, and her hand—her perfect, guitar-callused hand that just a few hours ago was making Sundae see stars in a motel bathroom—reaches out to wrap around Sundae's arm, pulling her to a stop, turning her to face Lia.

And, oh god, when she does, the sight of her burns like sparks in Sundae's eyes.

Tears glaze Sundae's vision, thankfully obscuring Lia's features, but she can still make out the shape of her. The sharp sweep of dark hair at her jaw, the tar-pit stare, the square set of her shoulders. Her focus is locked on Sundae, her hand on Sundae's arm gentle but firm, anchoring her as she looks into Sundae's eyes.

"Sundae. None of this is your fault. You know that, right?" she says—and her words cut right through the center of Sundae's anguish.

Sundae's lip trembles, and she bites down on it, trying to blink back the tears. "It is, though, isn't it?" she says. "All those others . . . they were bad people, Lia. Cutting down trees and hunting whales and killing things. Making a lion ride a *motorcycle*—"

At this, Lia snorts, but then she gets serious again. "Sundae. Come on. You're not like them."

"What if I am? What if that's why he picked me?" Sundae asks.

"Well, if you're a bad person, then so am I," Lia says, shrugging, "'cause he picked me, too."

"I am actually kind of worried you *are* a bad person," Sundae says. "Your wish was pretty fucked up, Lia."

"Look, I'm not trying to make excuses, but I didn't wish that you *would* go on a date with me. I just wished that I'd *asked*. I get that it, like, tore a hole in the space-time continuum or whatever, but you still had free will to say no," Lia says. Her hand slips off Sundae's arm, like she's finally certain Sundae won't run away. "It makes me pathetic, sure. But, arguably, not evil."

Sundae does find this detail somewhat reassuring. If Lia only wished she'd *asked,* then Sundae knows her enthusiastic acceptance wasn't coerced. There's no way these intense, heart-fluttering, belly-full-of-fireworks feelings could be artificial. The way it thrills her when she looks at Lia, when they touch, when they *kiss*—that all has to be real.

"Fine," Sundae says, wrapping her arms around herself, shivering in her wet dress without the heat of Lia's hand on her arm. "But maybe he only came to *you* to get to *me*. So I'm even more to blame than I thought."

"Stop," Lia says, stepping a little closer to Sundae. Not too close, though. Not as close as Sundae wants her to be. "How the fuck could you be to blame for this? He started this when you were just a *kid*."

"Yeah, and I was just as greedy, and vain, and stupid then as I am now," Sundae whispers.

"Sundae, no," Lia says, shaking her head. "You're not any of those things. You're kind, and adventurous, and gentle, and no matter how many times monsters mistake that gentleness for weakness, you're brave enough to stay soft in spite of them all."

Tears dash down Sundae's cheeks, salty as the sea. She closes her eyes; looking at Lia hurts too much. "Lia . . . Why couldn't you read me this well when you decided not to ask me out after I'd been flirting with you all night?"

"I think I could. I just didn't know how to be brave yet," Lia says.

Sundae lets her eyes open, and she looks at Lia, who's standing in front of her despite her trepidation. She notes the tense stitch in Lia's brow, the reluctance to get too close, the fear of overstepping Sundae's boundaries. Lia *is* afraid. She ran after Sundae, knowing she might be turned away, knowing that Sundae might not want to hear what she had to say. Sundae draws in a deep breath and whispers,

"Well, I hope we both make it out of this alive, so I get to see how brave you can become."

Then she steps away from Lia and passes underneath the fiberglass shark, with its open, toothy maw, into the aquarium.

THIRTY-ONE

NOW

Now that the hard part is out of the way, Lia is ready to kill a colossal prehistoric shark.

As they walk down the long hallway of tanks in the aquarium, Lia notices that all the water is strangely clouded, and there are no fish in any of the tanks, as if they've all disappeared—or have been eaten. Alien plants and bizarre coral formations have coated the bottoms of the tanks and are starting to sprout from the ground outside them, too, turning the floor slick and sludgy.

She also notices how the murky light that gleams through the tanks catches on the shimmery oil still lingering on Sundae's skin, making her glow in the blue-green dim.

"You never told me what you wished for," Lia says, keeping her voice low.

Sundae sighs, reaching out a hand to slide her fingers along the glass as they walk. "I wished that I could breathe underwater. It's funny, because when I was a kid, I wanted to be a mermaid."

"Well, look at you now. You can breathe underwater and you're being hunted by an evil sea monster you made a Faustian bargain with," Lia says.

A soft laugh escapes Sundae's lips, which Lia does her best not to read into. She knows it doesn't mean she's forgiven. They finally reach the stretch of hallway where the railway worker's corpse lies, his pickax still embedded in the glass of the tank. The floor is puddled with water that has poured through the cracked glass, and this area of the aquarium is even thicker with grotesque vegetation.

Sundae stops by the railway worker's body, and they both look down at it. The primordial plant life has started to cover him; a luminescent sea anemone sprouts out of his cheek. Suddenly, a glowing isopod comes scurrying out of the man's ear and dashes across the tops of Sundae's bare feet. She shrieks, flailing, and slips on the wet overgrowth. Lia reflexively puts her arms out to catch her, pulling her close as the creature vanishes into the seaweed.

"Euuugh," Sundae whines, her hand skimming up Lia's forearm before she catches herself. She pulls away with a shudder. "Let's do this and get out of here. This place is giving me the heebie-jeebies."

"Where *is* this thing?" Lia asks, slowly twisting to look around them. The water is thick and cloudy, as if it's been moldering in the tanks for decades. Sundae walks up to the glass, presses her palms to it, and leans close to peer into the misty water.

"It's in there," she says, sounding certain.

"And . . . how are we going to kill it, exactly?" Lia asks, dread rising up her spine, goose bumps pricking her skin.

Sundae wraps her fists around the handle of the pickax sticking out of the glass.

With two quick wrenches, she tugs it out, unplugging the hole it made.

Water starts to ooze from the uncorked crack, but with the size of the tank, it'll take hours, maybe *days* to drain completely. And Sundae clearly doesn't plan to wait that long. She lifts the pickax up to her shoulder like a baseball bat, then twists to look at Lia.

"You a good swimmer?" she asks.

"I mean, I'm no mermaid. But I'm all right," Lia says.

"Well. There's about to be a lot of water."

Sundae turns forward again, swinging the pickax into the glass with the motion. The crack widens, veining outward, little webs forming along the edges. Sundae pulls the pickax back and swings again, even harder this time.

Another hit, and the glass splits wider.

A shadow glides out of the murky depths, lurking near the bottom of the tank as it creeps closer to the glass. Its massive body sways slowly, tail swinging through the dark green water. Sundae keeps slamming the pickax into the glass, even as the beast waits, black eyes gleaming.

"It's fucking huge," Lia says, in horrified awe.

"Meh. I'm not much of a size queen," Sundae says as she smashes the pickax into the glass one last time.

Finally, the glass caves in, and the water comes in a flood.

It hits Lia so hard that she's thrown back against the opposite wall, her head thunking against the tank. She's swept up into the current as the deluge charges down the hall.

In the frantic moments when her head surfaces, she sees the silver blade of a dorsal fin darting through the rushing water.

But she doesn't see Sundae anywhere.

Giving up on swimming against the tide, Lia takes a deep breath and sinks down instead, opening her eyes underwater. The long skirt of her dress catches at her legs as she kicks and twists, peering into the dark.

And she does see something, but it isn't Sundae.

Jaws full of serrated teeth hurtling toward her, silver body slicing through the water.

Lia paddles for the surface, gasping for breath when she breaks through. The deluge is impossibly fast, and there's no way to escape the surging flood.

"Lia!"

Lia looks up to see Sundae—coasting on the back of the giant shark.

She has the pickax hooked into its neck, and she grips it like the pommel of a saddle as she rides the beast down the hall. Her other hand reaches out to Lia, who has an instant to grab on as the beast swipes past.

Lia's hand swings up, clasping Sundae's.

Sundae pulls, and Lia scrambles onto the back of the shark, its skin rough against her bare legs. She holds on to Sundae's waist to keep from sliding off, careful of the cut on her side. The shark is so huge, Lia is honestly not even sure it notices their weight or feels the point of the pickax embedded in its flesh.

"Is this more fun than the Ferris wheel?" Sundae asks her, laughing as they barrel through the water.

"Marginally," Lia says, gritting her teeth.

They're headed for the double glass doors at the front of the aquarium.

"Shit. Maybe we should have opened those," Sundae says, right before they crash through them.

The metal frame of one door catches Lia's leg, ripping her off the shark's back. She slams to the ground, falling on glass for the *second* time that night. Water pours over her and it sweeps her away from the doors.

Meanwhile, the shark shoots on its belly down the boardwalk, carried by the force of the flood pushing out the doors. Sundae slips off its back before the beast skids to a stop, flopping against murky puddles.

Lia gets up, glass crunching under her wet boots. Beached on the boardwalk, the shark twists against the planks, gills working uselessly as it writhes.

Sundae stands nearby, away from its thrashing tail, holding the pickax as she watches it flounder. Its unblinking eyes reflect the stars in the sea-black sky, the moonlight painting its silver skin blue as it squirms. Outside of the water, even the snapping of its rows of saw-edged teeth seems more agonized than aggressive. Sundae lifts her head, looking to Lia, brow furrowed and her pretty mouth pulled into a grimace.

The misery on her face reminds Lia of Sundae scraping through the sand on her hands and knees, tear-smudged and worried that a fish might choke on her lost rhinestone. Wordlessly, Lia holds out her hand for the pickax. Sundae places it in her palm, and Lia gives the twisting beast a wide berth as she paces up the length of its long body. She raises the handle up high and brings the chisel end of the blade down into the shark's head.

It takes a couple more strikes, but eventually the shark stops moving.

Lia heaves a sigh, dropping the pickax to the ground as she turns to Sundae.

"Thanks. For coming with me," Sundae says.

"Thanks for letting me," Lia says. "Now we finish this."

THIRTY-TWO

NOW

Sundae expects everyone to be jealous that she and Lia rode on the back of a monster shark, but when they return to the pier it's clear the others had their own fun raiding the stash at the back of the piercing shop.

"So here, we have a fine selection of Pyro Viagra," Dallas says, gesturing to one stack of boxes.

"Not to be confused with Pyro Propulsion, Pyro Boner, or Great Balls of Fire," Edison says, hands waving over the other boxes they've stacked up on the picnic table.

"And if you're looking for something with less toxic masculinity, fret not, we've got your Girl Power right here," Neeli says, leaning her elbow atop a pyramid of pink boxes.

"I can't believe none of you mentioned American Pyro," Lia says flatly, picking up a box adorned with American flags and blood splatters.

The cold pit in Sundae's stomach distracts her, turning their banter into white noise in her ears. Dawn is fast approaching, and the Haunted Forest ride looms behind them, green lights beaming into the streaky violet sky. As Dallas says something that makes Neelima giggle the way she only does when she thinks a boy is cute, Sundae abruptly interjects.

"Are these fireworks actually going to blow up this ride, or do they just have funny names?"

Lia taps her thumb against the bald eagle on the box in her hand. "Sundae, these are bombs covered in clip art. So unless the ride has some kind of magic armor on it, they'll blow it up."

"Well, we should do it, then," Sundae says, eyes on the horizon over the jagged wooden leaves crowning the Haunted Forest.

"What about the doo-wop singer?" Neeli frowns. "Don't we have to kill him, too?"

"We're not exactly hard to find out here," Sundae says, gesturing to the boardwalk that stretches out around them. "I'm guessing he'll come to us. But it'll be morning soon, so we need to get rid of this ride *now*."

"You really think this thing disappears when the sun comes up?" Edison asks, squinting at the glowing green facade.

"I'm pretty sure it just, like, appeared at sunset while I was listening to Luke embarrass himself earlier."

"Ouch. RIP," Neeli mutters.

"Sorry. Right," Sundae says, dryly making the sign of the cross across her body. "But if the sun hurts him, and this thing only appears at night, then this might be where he hides during the day. If we get rid of it . . ."

"Then at sunrise, he's toast," Dallas says, and does a dramatic rendition of getting cooked alive by the sun, sizzling sounds hissing through his teeth as he shakes and shivers.

"But like, what happens if we're still inside the ride when it portals out?" Edison says.

"Maybe we get trapped in the pocket dimension forever. Like in that episode of *Are You Afraid of the Dark?* with the mall inside the pinball machine," Dallas says.

"Yeah, or like *Cube 2: Hypercube,*" Edison says. "Though I never understood why the cubes are in another dimension in *Cube 2,* but not in any of the other Cube movies. Oh! What about Fulci's *The Beyond?*"

"Don't you mean Fulci's *E tu vivrai nel terrore! L'aldilà*? Please, have some respect," Dallas says.

Lia sighs heavily and shoots Neeli and Sundae a look. "The good thing is, if we *do* get stuck in a pocket dimension, we have a ready supply of virgin man meat to eat."

"I'm a vegetarian. But I guess eating men isn't really like eating animals, is it?" Neeli says. "I mean. One has complex emotional inner lives and the other is *men.*"

"Whoa, whoa, whoa," Edison says. "Is it just me, or is it getting a little *Cannibal Women in the Avocado Jungle of Death* out here?"

"Yeah, cool it, Piranha Women," Dallas says, hauling up a stack of fireworks. "Let's get a move on the pyrotechnics."

"One of us should keep a lookout, though. So if the real Holly Jolly or the primordial soup monster Holly Jolly shows up, someone will see them coming," Edison says.

"Cool. You should do it, since it was your idea," Lia says, slapping Edison on the shoulder. He groans, deflating like a pile of leaves scattered by the wind.

"But I wanna help blow shit up," he whines. Still, he dejectedly sticks his hands into the pockets of his patch-covered denim vest and kicks the leg of the picnic table, like he knows there's no use fighting his fate.

While Edison takes up his post atop the platform, where he'll have a better vantage point, Sundae and the others gather stacks of fireworks and carry them into the ride. Hiking barefoot down the rusty train tracks that wind into the dark belly of the Haunted Forest, an unwelcome sense of familiarity ripples through Sundae, quickening her pulse.

The smell of salt water and rot floods her nostrils. The tinny crackle of cresting waves and calling birds breezes in her ears, as if from unseen speakers. Underneath it all, the iron bite of blood, and muffled, distant screams.

Her breath catches in her closing throat.

"Sundae," Neeli says beside her, stepping close enough for Sundae to feel her warmth against her goose bump–covered arm. "You're not alone in here this time. We're with you. And we're going to absolutely *demolish* this fucking creep's interdimensional neckbeard nest."

"Hell yeah! Let's send this Pinhead wannabe back to the Cenobite realm!" Dallas crows, his voice echoing through the cavernous tunnel, louder than the whispering soundscape.

Edison calls out from his post by the entrance, "Hey! You better not be in there solving the Lament Configuration without me!"

And even though she has no idea what the hell they're talking about, Sundae feels the tension in her body unwinding. Neeli is right—she wasn't dragged here by a monster this time, and she isn't alone.

They're going to destroy this place.

And when the sun rises over the pier, he'll have nowhere to hide.

The walls wrapped in blue foil reflect the friends' movements as they start setting up fireworks in the underwater scene where the shark should be. Sundae hardly pays attention to the ridiculous packaging, focusing solely on the goal: achieving maximum damage.

Paper fish sway overhead. Sundae sticks a firework in the claw of a giant papier-mâché crab. Her eyes wander, watching as Lia crouches at the edge of the model ocean, her capable hands twisting the fuses of two fireworks together, stringing them out to the tracks for easy access. A shiver hums through Sundae, and she takes a second to congratulate herself. Even now, terrified and tense in this place that's haunted her nightmares, she can still find it in herself to be horny. Her libido is truly an indomitable force.

As they step out to trek to the next scene, Dallas turns to call up the tunnel, "Eddie? You good out there?"

"Aside from the FOMO?" Edison shouts back. "I'm kinda hungry. You guys wanna get breakfast after this?"

"Dallas is going to *be* our breakfast if we don't hurry this shit up!" Lia says, her powerful voice carrying easily along the tracks. She kicks at the backs of Dallas's legs, though her boot doesn't connect with him. "Move it, you do *not* want to get trapped in this pocket dimension with us."

"Yeah. I'd totally eat you up," Neeli says, her gaze sliding down Dallas's tall frame as she bites her lip. In his shock, Dallas trips over a tree root spilling out from the next scene, and Sundae giggles despite herself.

"You slut," Sundae coos fondly.

"A commendation from the Slut Cup Queen herself," Neeli says, laying a hand over her heart. "What an honor, truly."

Sundae gawks at Neeli as they enter the false forest that surrounds the craggy holly tree. "Wait. Did I really win?"

"I mean, you two *did* hook up in the bathroom earlier, didn't you?" Neeli says, glancing between Sundae and Lia. Lia's sharp cheekbones bloom scarlet, and she bows her head so that her dark hair falls forward, hiding her face as she busies herself with ripping open more fireworks.

Sundae breathes out a dreamy sigh, and Neeli's brows lift, her suspicions confirmed.

"Then you scored the highest," Neeli says.

"I don't think it's fair to call it." Sundae starts to open a box of fireworks, tiptoeing around tree roots that twitch and squirm on the sandy ground. "No one but us can really . . . compete anymore."

Neeli nods solemnly, working alongside Sundae to tuck explosives around the base of the tree. "I don't think they'd mind. Everyone knew you were going to win, anyway."

Sundae feels like oil and water, two disparate feelings bubbling inside her at once. Warm fondness for her friends simmers alongside anguished despair that they're gone. Fighting down the deluge of grief and love, Sundae blinks until the tears stop blurring her eyes. And then she steps out onto the tracks and moves to the next scene.

One by one, Sundae and the others fill each diorama of death with explosives. It's taking longer than she expected, so as they reach the eerie retro supper club full of wax figures on fire, cellophane flames fluttering with a soft crinkling sound, Sundae turns and points to Neeli and Dallas.

"You guys get this one," she instructs. She looks to Lia, nodding at the tunnel to the final scene. "We'll get the last one?"

Sundae almost cringes at the way her statement becomes a question when their eyes meet and the black tea of Lia's stare pours over her. Her voice betrays her, twisting up at the end, and she can tell Neeli notices by the way the corners of her lips twitch. While Lia nods and starts to walk farther down the tunnel, Sundae pauses to bat Neeli on the arm.

"Straight to horny jail," Neeli hisses at her.

"Nothing straight about it." Sundae smirks.

"I'm so done trauma-bonding with you, bitch," Neeli says as Sundae struts past her.

Sundae doesn't even realize there's a smile on her lips until she reaches the final scene and feels it fall away, her jaw clenching as she steps up beside Lia to take it in.

Much of it is exactly how she remembers it, not just from when she saw it seven years ago, but from all the times she's revisited this place in her nightmares. The Coral Cabana, like a dollhouse replica, strange and off-scale, chills her with its haunting familiarity. Tony's wax double is still splayed out on the floor, dust caked over his glassy eyes and red silk spilled around this throat. When Sundae looks into his sculpted face, she still sees the real thing.

But when her eyes travel past the replica tiki bar, out to the courtyard with its bright teal pool, she notices that the scene has also changed.

The pink motel has been repainted pastel blue, the palm trees and bamboo trim replaced with gilded stars and moons. The exterior of the bar has been redone with silvery chrome, half transformed into the diner where, just hours ago, Lia stood onstage captivating Sundae with her fierce voice and raucous music.

And when Sundae notices the balloon arch framing the entrance, her legs feel like melted ice cream, soft and wobbly beneath her.

"Holy shit," Sundae gasps through the shock that constricts her chest. "He set this up for *both* of us."

She turns her face away from the patchwork motel and finds Lia beside her. Lia's eyes have turned to volcanic rock, hard and black as they observe Sundae's reaction. Furious resolve has burned away any fearfulness in her, and Lia keeps hold of Sundae's gaze as she steps off the tracks, boots creaking on the foam pavers as she enters the scene Holly Jolly made for them.

Lia sets down the stack of fireworks she'd brought. As she starts to unwrap them, Sundae follows her in, horrified shivers still scratching down her spine at the surreality of this half-finished nightmare.

"How's that for a second date?" Lia mutters. "Getting trapped together for an eternity in some sick demon's freaky snow-globe universe."

"I was hoping we could do something a little bit more low-key. Dinner and a movie, maybe," Sundae says.

Lia sighs as she plants an explosive at the base of the balloon arch. "That would've been nice."

"Maybe you should try asking me sometime. I might say yes," Sundae says, ripping open a box of Girl Power.

Wandering away from Lia, Sundae walks on unsteady legs into the Coral Cabana. Her ribs squeeze tight around her lungs, and she can feel her heartbeat on her tongue, throbbing so fast she could choke on it. The urge to scream winds stronger with every step she takes toward the dummy Tony, until she's standing over him. Looking into his wide glass eyes, she sees instead the unblinking, lifeless stare of *Tony*, the kind but ill-mannered bartender who would pour her Shirley Temples and tell her stories children shouldn't hear, whose last words to her were a promise not to rat on her for sneaking out, as long as she let him escort her safely back to her room.

Tony, who was the first to die because of her greedy wishes—but most definitely not the last.

Sundae drops into a crouch, shark bite stinging beneath the towel wound tight around her thigh. She blows a sigh from her vise-crushed chest and slams the pink cardboard tube in her hand down into the crook of dummy-Tony's elbow.

"You were right," she whispers to him, unwinding the firework's fuse. "I'm not okay, and maybe I never will be. But at least I'm alive."

Sundae stands, knees wobbly as she backs away from the wax body, stringing the fuse out as far as it will go so it will be easy to light when they're ready.

Stepping back out onto the train tracks, with the cool breeze from the entrance behind her rustling her hair, Sundae looks to Lia. She's braiding red fuses together, explosives set around the powder-blue courtyard, surrounding the sapphire pool that shimmers in the false moonlight.

Sundae opens her mouth, ready to call to Neeli and Dallas, to ask if they're finished so they can finally blow up this nest of nightmares. But before she can speak, a scream rips through the cavernous tunnel, and Sundae spins to face the doorway to the platform just in time to witness Edison hit the tracks, before he's dragged away down the tunnel by something Sundae can't see past the glare of the lightening sky from the entrance.

Dallas jumps out onto the tracks behind the final scene, his eyes wide in the murky gloom. "Eddie?" he shouts.

"Something's got him!" Sundae exclaims, as all four of them take off running, following the sounds of Edison's shrill, desperate screams.

THIRTY-THREE

NOW

Every time Edison screams, Lia calls back to him, her cries loud enough to shake salt water drips down from the black ceiling that fall like rain on her head as she runs.

"Edison!" she shrieks, rounding the bend past the shark's underwater scene. That's when she spots him, his limbs flailing as he's being dragged along the tracks. At first, she can't figure out what's gotten ahold of him, but then she hears the snapping creaks of shifting wood, and she looks down just in time to jump over a tree root whipping toward her feet.

They're everywhere along the tracks—vining roots, writhing out of the sand that covers the floor of the ride. A thick, gnarled root is coiled around Edison's leg, hauling him into the scene with the captive holly tree as he shouts out for help.

"Eddie!" Dallas is about to plow past Lia, but she stops him, throwing her weight against his side to push him out of the way of a striking root.

"Watch out!" Lia says, not just to Dallas, but Sundae and Neeli, too, as they stumble closer, Neeli's arm hitched around Sundae's waist to support her. "The roots, they're—"

But another screechy, panicked scream from Edison cuts her off, and Lia grabs Dallas by the wrist, rushing forward despite the roots snapping at their feet.

"Holy shit, holy shit, please help!" Edison is pleading as Lia and Dallas leap from the tracks, crashing into the forest scene where only one tree looks real—trunk curved like a spiral staircase, bark craggy as coral, branches heavy with spiked green leaves and poison red berries.

And its roots, squirming like tentacles as more of them twist around Edison.

Dallas flings himself to the forest floor, ripping at the slithering ropes that bind Edison. "Eddie! No, no, no . . ."

Edison's copper eyes are bulging, wide with fear in his ashen face. His hands claw weakly for Dallas, but another root bursts out of the ground, circling Edison's chest to yank him down, lashing him against the base of the tree.

"Please! Don't let it Audrey II me!" Edison howls, and the anguished strain in his voice is a punch to Lia's heart.

"Let him go, let him go!" Dallas is screaming as he beats his fists against the tree, but the sound fades behind Lia as she leaps over a vine and tears across the tracks. Rage flames through her veins, and she burns with furious motion, moving down the tunnel like a flash-bang.

"Where are you going?" Sundae demands as Lia flies past her and Neeli.

"I'm getting a *fucking ax*," Lia says through gritted teeth.

She hears footsteps rushing behind her, fast enough that she knows it's Neeli, not Sundae, following. Lia doesn't pause to acknowledge

Neeli as they both jump into the scene where the butchered loggers lie strewn around wooden cutouts of holly trees. Sweeping an arm down, Lia pries an ax from the hands of one of the figures, wax fingers snapping as she wrenches it free.

Edison's screams grow weaker, more strangled, and terror flings Lia forward, sending her flying back down the tracks. Roots snag at her boots, but she stomps right through them, fists gripping the ax tight as she returns to the tree.

Dallas ducks out of her way, sobbing, "Lia, please, it's killing him!"

The roots have wound their way around Edison's torso, constricting, his body contorted by their pull. Blood oozes from his mouth, slicking his teeth red as he gasps for breath. His eyes roll up in his bruise-blue face.

Lia drives the blade of the ax down into the roots. A feral cry rips out of her as she swings again, wood splintering around her blade.

Dallas grabs hold of the root she split, wrenching it away from Edison's chest, but more worm their way out of the sand, zipping around him. There's a loud, wet crack, the sound of snapping bone, and Edison coughs out a spray of blood.

"No! No, please, Eddie, *please,*" Dallas yowls, scratching at the ragged bark.

Lia brings her ax down again and again, chopping faster as she sobs and shrieks. Neeli joins in, using a hatchet to help loosen the tree's grip, and Sundae fights barefoot through the snatching roots to drop to her knees alongside Dallas, their clawing hands tearing at the cut wooden cords until Edison is freed.

Freed, but not okay.

His chest looks collapsed, blood streaked across his shirt and vest, a mangled mess of gore. Every breath sounds flooded, and his glazed eyes stare up at the branches over his head, blinking blankly, absent any sign of *Edison* at all.

And more writhing roots are coming, rupturing the floor to race toward them.

"Get him up, get him up!" Lia barks, dropping the ax to grab hold of Edison. Dallas comes in on the other side, their arms crossing behind Edison's back, and they haul him up as gently as they can. Still, he mewls in agony, the cry bubbling out with a gush of blood from his pallid lips.

Neeli keeps hold of her hatchet, using it to lop off any roots that snatch at Lia and Dallas as they carry Edison out to the tunnel. His groans grow weaker, drowned by the fluid in his lungs, his head lolling against Lia's shoulder.

"Please, Eddie, don't die," Dallas whispers.

Ocean wind hits them as they approach the entrance of the ride, the sky outside milky lavender over the boardwalk. Just before the platform, Lia stops, looking to Dallas, then to Neeli.

"You two take him," she says. "Take him, and get help."

"Lia—" Dallas starts to say, but Lia shakes her head. Her gaze shifts to Sundae, and she recognizes the same sharpened fury in Sundae's eyes, the blue of her irises glacier-cold in her rage.

"We have to finish this," Lia says. She turns again to Dallas and Neeli, quietly commanding. "No one else is dying tonight. Take him and go."

Neeli nods, dropping her hatchet before sliding her arm under Lia's to take over her hold of Edison. His long hair sticks to the sweat on Lia's skin as she steps away, clinging for a moment after the contact is broken.

"Wait," Dallas gasps, one arm releasing Edison long enough to dig into his pocket. He holds out two lighters, thrusting them at

Lia. "Blow this fucking place back to whatever hell dimension it came from."

Lia nods, closing her fist around the lighters as she steps back from Dallas. She passes her knuckles across Edison's forehead, watching the fluttering of his half-closed eyes, and she hopes it won't be the last time she sees him alive.

"Sunny, just remember—if you die, I become the de facto Slut Cup winner," Neeli says as she crosses through the threshold with Dallas, Edison held carefully in her arms.

"I'll never let that happen," Sundae declares. "You couldn't handle the weight of my crown."

Then she turns to Lia, holding out her hand. The hazy glow filtered through the entrance to the tunnel catches on the tinsel sparks in her pink hair, and her fingers close on Lia's when she places the lighter in her palm.

"We have to do this fast. The fuses won't last long," Lia says.

"Are you okay?" Sundae asks, her soft voice like a cool cloth dabbed against Lia's clammy neck.

"No," Lia answers honestly, dropping her eyes to their joined hands. "But I'll feel a lot better when this motherfucker is dead."

"Same," Sundae murmurs. She draws away, thumb flicking the lighter in her fist, making it flare in the dusky tunnel. "Let's do this, then. We'll start with our scene."

It's weird that Lia feels her heart spark like the flame in Sundae's hand when she says it like that—*our scene*—but Sundae has a way of making even the most fraught moments feel a little romantic, somehow. It's dizzying, the fluttery thrill mingling with the worry and terror and anger all swirling inside Lia right now, but there it is anyhow, warming her blood as they turn away from the entrance to backtrack to the final scene on the ride's loop.

There are roots crawling slugglishly along the tracks, and Lia doesn't know when the tree might attack again. Perhaps, like the lion that disappeared for a time after killing Harper, or the whaler who paused after shooting his harpoon through Detective Morton's skull, the tree has been sated by Edison's blood and will rest long enough for Lia and Sundae to light the fuses and get out of the ride. Still, Lia considers doubling back to grab the ax she dropped, just in case, but when Sundae stumbles over a vine and cries out as she catches herself on her twisted ankle, Lia winds an arm around her instead.

When they reach the melded scene, half the Blue Velvet and half the motel where Sundae was staying when she first met Holly Jolly, Lia can feel the tenseness that stiffens Sundae's spine. She goes rigid in the fold of Lia's arm, goose bumps alighting on her skin as they step into the tiki bar, where the body of the bartender lies on the floor.

Sundae slips away from Lia and hobbles forward, thumb striking the flint of her lighter. As she reaches down and touches her flame to the first fuse, the one connected to a pink rocket tucked against the wax dummy, she says, "What a travesty. Tony had a *way* better hairline than this."

The fuse catches, and then they're on the move.

They only have to light a few fuses, really—the fireworks are placed close enough that they'll set each other off, and the fire that will ignite should take care of the rest. Scene by scene, they hurry down the track, lighting the fuses that are most accessible and then running on to the next.

Lia's heart is pounding like a ticking clock in her ears. She can practically feel the rising sun, scorching the horizon as it climbs over the ocean. With every lit fuse, she wonders what will happen if they get to the end and dawn's already arrived, if all these explosives start to fire and there's no way out of this ride.

As she puts an arm behind Sundae's back to help her climb up into the boardwalk scene, the sound of static buzzes against Lia's ears. She narrows her eyes, glaring past the wooden roller coaster that rises into the ceiling, searching for speakers in the dark.

But they aren't there, because the sound is like smoke on the air around them, a beat like cresting waves tapping against their eardrums.

"This *fucking song,*" Sundae hisses angrily. She jerks away from Lia's grip, limping across the boardwalk planks to light the braided fuses of a cluster of fireworks pointed at the Wall of Death.

Over their heads, he's singing,

"One, for a path I crossed.
Two, for my love I lost.
Three, and you will come for me,
Like the tide pulls the sand back to the sea. . . ."

Lia kneels down to light the other fuses, arranged near the facade of the candy shop and the roller-coaster gate. His voice seems to echo inside her skull, just like it did when she heard it the first time, crooning from the glowing green jukebox in the lobby.

A fuse blows little sparks as she lights it. She moves on to the next.

Her brow furrowed and her head bowed, she's distracted as she skips a few fuses to light one by the roller coaster. Maybe that's why she doesn't notice the shadow falling over her until it's too late.

"Lia!" Sundae cries, right as cold metal loops around Lia's neck.

She gags as she's jerked backward, her spine hitting the planks beneath her. Her fingers scratch at the chain wound around her throat, so tight she can barely breathe. Looking up, she sees the drippy, ash-streaked version of Holly Jolly—the *real* doo-wop singer, not the piecemeal shark-mouthed beast who has hunted them all night but the dapperly dressed ghost of a drowned man wrapped in chains.

Chains that are currently dragging Lia onto the tracks.

Lia wheezes as her hip hits the rail, pain rocketing through her body. She tries to dig her heels against the sand, and her hands grasp for anything that might slow her momentum. Sundae scrambles after her, shouting her name, but her leg gives out when she hits the drop off the boardwalk, her ankle rolling again as she falls to the ground.

"Lia!" Sundae shrieks, disappearing from sight as Lia is pulled around the bend, into the section of the ride full of burning lit fuses, snaking toward inevitable explosions.

And as Holly Jolly hauls Lia, he sings his song.

"All along, I knew the cost.
But I always thought I could stop.
That I would dig just one grave.
That my love could be saved."

He pulls her to his scene, the one right before the very end, deep in the belly of the Haunted Forest. The cellophane flames flicker on the dancing figures as he draws Lia into the center of them, their wax faces half-melted to reveal grinning skulls underneath. Lia's strangled breath catches in horror, and her body is limp when he reaches down and unwinds the chain from her neck.

Lia gasps for breath, tasting smoke in the air. His hands wrap around her arms, lifting her up to her feet in the crowd of burning dancers. With his sad eyes staring into hers, he sings the next verse.

"But now that I've paid the price,
I'll wish to forget what I've sacrificed."

His hand, ice-cold and slick, grabs hold of Lia's. He spins her on the dance floor, swirling her away from him. Releasing her, he points to the painted sign propped at the front of his scene.

She hadn't noticed this one when she went through the ride earlier. She'd been too distracted, reading about all the deaths and beginning to understand the wishers' fates. But she sees it now, the words painted bright candy red.

YOU WISHED FOR ME TO LIE TO YOU.
THIS IS HOW I GREW DECEITFUL.

One by one, she traces the clues like a roadmap in her mind. She's not sure where it's leading her, but she thinks again about the other times she's heard his song, and the way its words helped her unravel the cost of each wish.

And then he sings the next line, as if to confirm what she already suspects.

"So let this song be a warning
For the next one you come haunting.
The wanting hearts of dreamers here
Will find only nightmares when you appear."

Lia turns to face him again. Around them, the tinkling guitar and swaying beat of his song mingles with the sizzle of sparking fuses and the sound of Sundae stumbling down the tracks toward them. Watching the water drip from his brushed-back hair, Lia asks, "Did he tell you what the wishes cost before you made them?"

The real Holly Jolly nods, swaying slightly in beat with his tune.

"And he told all the others too?"

He nods again.

"But you didn't want to know. So you wished you didn't." Lia twists, craning around the burning dancers to peer at the sign in front of his ride again. THIS IS HOW I GREW DECEITFUL.

Like the other signs, which seem to allude to lessons the beast learned from each of his kills, Lia thinks this one means the singer's wish taught the monster how to lie about the cost of his wishes. That's why he didn't tell Sundae or Lia what would happen if they accepted his bargain. Why he never implied that it was a *bargain* at all.

Did the singer write the song before he made his wish? Did he record it hoping that it would serve as a warning for the monster's next victim?

Rage spikes Lia's pulse. She looks into the singer's pouty, mournful face, his chains clinking softly as he undulates to the beat of his own music. "You know, if you couldn't handle the consequences of your own actions, that's on you. But because of *your* wish, no one else gets to know the cost either."

All he does is sing back, *"Here in the Wildwoods, where you once stood, all clothed in green . . ."*

"It's a fucking riddle. You left behind a fucking riddle, in a jukebox that doesn't play," Lia growls.

"Now my love is gone, and before the dawn, you will be clothed in me. . . ."

Chills rake through her as she stares at him, the line running over and over through her mind. He wasn't wrong when he wrote it—the monster *does* wear his likeness now, or at least it *did,* the last time Lia saw him.

What will it wear once Lia kills the singer?

Lia lunges forward, plowing the singer against the stage. It hits the backs of his legs, throwing him off his feet, and Lia uses his momentum against him, grabbing the chain that wraps him and swinging it around his neck.

She plants a boot against his chest, driving the small of his back into the stage, and pulls hard on the chain.

"Lia!" Sundae shouts as she hobbles around the corner. In spite of her limp, she blasts into the scene so hard that she knocks several of the dancing wax figures into each other.

"I'm here, Sundae," Lia pants, strained as she presses her boot down harder on his chest. The singer thrashes as the chain chokes him, the music faltering, cutting in and out like a bad radio signal.

A blue guitar warbles, then dies. The drums slow, falling out of rhythm.

Sundae reaches Lia, crinkling plastic flames licking her elbows as she pushes through the frozen crowd. While the singer's squirming ceases under her foot, Lia turns to look at Sundae. In the glow of the stage lights, she could count every freckle dusting Sundae's nose, trace lines between them like constellations.

Lia gives one last hard yank on the chain as she tells Sundae, "It was him. He's the reason why you're different from the rest. All the others *knew* the cost of the wishes. *He* taught it to lie."

The doo-wop singer gives a final gasp and the music stops.

The only sounds are the sizzling fuses and their panting breaths.

"Really?" Sundae whispers. Raw and small and hopeful.

Lia nods.

Then the first firework detonates, a flare of light illuminating the dark tracks beyond the singer's scene. An explosive bang rattles the walls.

And in that brief flash of light, Lia sees something standing on the tracks.

At first, it looks like an oil slick in the air, or like a spiderweb drifting in the wind.

Then there's another flash, and this time, it's closer.

It's rough and misshapen, just an outline of thorny leaves and sharp branches, but there's no mistaking the shape it's trying to take.

The only person left who has made all three wishes. *Sundae.*

"Fuck, fuck, fuck, let's get out of here, come on—" Lia says, grabbing Sundae's hand.

They jump down from the stage and run out onto the tracks. Skull-rattling explosions shake the ground under their feet, and though the shortest way out would be past the last scene, the flames pouring into the tunnel from the Coral-Cove-turned-Blue-Velvet block their path. Colorful sparks chase them as they charge the other way along the tracks, trying to outrun the catching fuses. Their palms are locked together, hands squeezed tight.

They make it all the way around the loop, and as they pass the shark's blue-foiled ocean, Lia can see the violet glow of dawn reaching in through the open doorway. Salty air blasts against her face as she flies out onto the platform, below the feebly blinking THE HAUNTED FOREST sign—and then suddenly, Sundae's hand is torn from hers.

She whirls around, only to collide with a wall of vining roots that block the exit like the bars of a jail cell. On the other side, Sundae is picking up the hatchet Neeli dropped by the doorway, screaming as she swings it, blade slicing through the root wound around her leg that pulled her away from Lia.

"Sundae!" Lia cries, scrambling at the gnarled bars, ripping and punching desperately. "No, no, no—"

Sundae rushes toward the barricade, lifting the hatchet to chop herself free—but a thin, thready root whips out of the dark, wrapping around the head of the hatchet to rip it out of Sundae's hands.

"No!" Lia screams again, throwing herself against the branches between them. Sundae collides with them, too, pummeling uselessly with her empty fists before casting a glance over her shoulder at the flames and smoke racing toward her from the tunnel.

She swings back around to face Lia, her breath shaky, her eyes shining in the purple light streaming through the entrance. Sundae's hands clasp at Lia's, clawing her closer. She drags Lia against the rough branches and winds her arms around Lia's waist.

Their noses brush between the branches. Sundae's lashes are low, her eyes drawing a smoldering path between Lia's eyes and her parted lips.

"Just so you know, this doesn't mean I forgive you," Sundae whispers.

And then she crushes her lips to Lia's.

Lia's arms snake through the bars, fingers scraping into Sundae's hair, tangled with salt water and seaweed. Every movement of her mouth is charged. She thought she'd never get to do this again. And with the blaze closing in on Sundae's back and the sunrise at Lia's, they kiss like it might really be their last time. Fraught and desperate and tasting like tears.

Until Sundae rips herself back and begins to retreat down the flaming corridor.

"Run," she says, soft at first. Then, louder than the explosions, she yells, "RUN!"

And she turns away—from Lia, and from the bars that separate them—and disappears into the depths of the Haunted Forest.

THIRTY-FOUR

NOW

Sundae has to make it to the final scene.

The one he made for her, all those years ago. The one he planned to trap Lia in, too.

The one with the pool that is a door.

Sundae has no idea if it's still a way out. Maybe it will take her nowhere, or to the concrete foundation of the Dave & Buster's where the Coral Cove Motel used to be. But it's the only hope she has now, and she's running for it.

Unfortunately, the last scene also happens to have been the *first* one to explode, and the blaze has entirely engulfed this half of the ride. As she rounds the tunnel and stumbles into the conjoined motel scene, the smoldering ground sears her bare feet and flames whip at her legs.

And also, she's not alone in here.

Whatever *it* is, it doesn't look like the doo-wop singer anymore. Now that the fire filling the ride has probably begun to eat at the trunk of the tree, it doesn't even look like a mass of spiky leaves and gnarled bark.

It might be shapeless as a breath on a cold winter day, but she quickly learns it can still hurt her. It smashes into her, and when her back slams against the burning-hot tracks, she finds herself looking up at a cobweb glimmer in the air. As the smoke steals the breath from her lungs, that shimmery nothing starts to look more and more like *her.* Only wrong. All the right features are there, but there's something off in the way they're arranged—her eyes just a little too far apart, her jaw too slack, her pink hair stiff as marsh grass.

"God, you're such a poser," Sundae hisses, her words strangled by the hot air scorching her lungs. And then she jolts upward, head-butting her would-be double in the face.

Sundae rolls away from it and claws her way up from the tracks. She spots the steam rising off the replica of the motel pool, light from the crackling fire dancing across its surface. On her hands and knees, she crawls across the burning ground. She can't breathe. She's choking and scorched and she can feel herself dying, alone in the Haunted Forest, just like she should have seven years ago.

Hot cinders sting her palms. Her fingers dip over the edge of the foam pavers and cold envelops her hand, relieving the sting of her singed skin. A stifled cough huffs from her dry throat as she plunges her other hand into the cool water.

Desperately, she pulls herself to the pool and thrusts her face beneath the surface.

She takes a deep, watery breath, clearing her lungs.

Breathing underwater.

And then something wraps around her ankles, dragging her away from the water.

Her jaw slams against the ground and she bites her tongue. Blood fills her mouth as she twists onto her back. It's above her now, holding her down as the smoke strangles her again.

She closes her eyes and tries to think of things that comfort her, like Neeli's arms clamped around her in the back seat of Jackie's car, or how her mom still curls her hair for her before every cheer competition, or the lemon cake Francesca made for Sundae's eighteenth birthday, or her kiss with Lia on the Ferris wheel right before this nightmare began again, or the way champagne always tastes better when one of her friends pours it for her. But none of it works to ease her pain.

So she opens her eyes and thinks of things that piss her off instead.

Like her whole prom weekend being ruined.

Or how he—*it*—tricked her when she was just a child.

Or how it tried to blame her, just like everyone else who's ever hurt her and said *Look what you made me do.*

Staring up at it, watching as it tries so hard to steal her face, she asks in a croak, "Why? Why do you do this?"

"Because it is my nature," it answers, in a voice that's like *her* voice, but also like rustling leaves and waves sifting against sand.

"That's not true," Sundae says. "You're just as much the tree as you were the shark."

"Trees are cut down. It is better to be the saw," it says.

"Well. You can be whatever you want to be, but you can't be *me*."

Sundae channels all her rage into her toned arms as she shoves it off her. When she sits up, the fire burns even hotter, but she dives forward, throwing herself into the cold blue pool.

The water engulfs her, soothing the burning of her skin, and when she coughs, a cloud of ash puffs into the water. For a second, she just floats, catching her breath.

Then she twists to face the bottom, and she starts to swim.

THIRTY-FIVE

NOW

The dawn is here, and the Haunted Forest is gone.

One second, it was a conflagration of licking flames and sparking explosions, and the next, it was *gone*.

From where she landed after despair knocked her off her feet outside the ride, Lia never looked away from it, the smoke burning her eyes as she stared. She watched the painted trees on the facade twist and crumble, the green lights beneath them flickering out. As the rising sun spread a tangerine stain across the horizon, Lia's battered heart thrummed hard in her chest, but she felt certain that any second, Sundae would burst out of the entrance, pink hair swinging triumphantly. After all she's watched Sundae do tonight, how could Lia *not* expect her to find some miraculous way out of the burning hell ride?

But Sundae never emerged.

And now the ride is gone. Lia can only guess that Sundae is gone, too.

In the moments after it disappears, Lia feels frozen to the boardwalk. She squints at the spot where it stood, trying to convince herself that she can see a ghostly outline of the red-lit sign. But it's just the flames burned into her eyes, and the longer she looks, the more it fades. There's only a smattering of ash, steadily dissipating in the breeze that gusts off the ocean.

The fight has been pressed out of her. Lia feels like a squashed bug, her heart twitching its death throes in her chest. There are pins and needles in her limbs, and her lips are cold. The shock is numbing, icing her into a chilly calm.

Slowly, her muscles weak as frayed rope, she gets to her feet.

She doesn't want to walk away from the pier, from the place where the Haunted Forest was, but she knows she has to. Even if the pain of losing Sundae is trying to strangle her, she can't forget Edison. She needs to find Dallas and Neeli; she needs to know if they were able to save him.

And if they weren't, then she needs to be with Dallas now.

Lia drags herself down the boardwalk, miserable beneath the pink sunrise. She passes the aquarium, where a puddle of black ooze is dripping between the wooden planks outside, the massive shark melted to sludge. When she sees the mangled remains of a funnel-cake stand dripping with the same substance, she has to assume it's where the lion landed, the roof caved in like a crumpled beer can from the force.

She tries not to wonder if Sundae turned to the same inky ooze in the burning ride. Lia can't imagine a less fitting fate for someone so vividly sparkling and searingly bright than to be reduced to nothing but black slime, drippy and dull.

No. That can't be how it ends for her.

The Blue Velvet is buzzing with cops and kids and paramedics when Lia gets there. There must be a dozen scenes like this around the boardwalk, everywhere tourists are waking up to discover last night's carnage, and Lia doesn't know if they were already here on account of the crashed car full of cheerleaders or the uneaten body parts of Harper McCall scattered around the motel, or if they came because of Edison.

She stumbles into the courtyard, and her aching heart hitches when she sees Dallas standing there.

There's blood on his silk shirt, drying to dark brown splotches in the hazy morning light. He looks rattled, but not agonized, and the relief that overtakes his face when he sees Lia tells her that the worst hasn't happened—that Edison didn't die in Dallas's arms, that he must still be alive. Otherwise, Lia is certain, *nothing* could bring Dallas any joy at all.

Neeli is at his side, her prom dress stained and torn, her wide dark eyes watching as Lia trudges in off the boardwalk without Sundae. Lia recognizes the opposite of her experience on Neeli's face as she searches the space behind Lia, like she's struggling to believe Sundae isn't coming back.

"Is Eddie alive?" Lia rasps when she reaches them, ash still burning inside her throat.

"I think—I hope so. They took him to the hospital," Dallas answers.

"Is Sundae—" Neeli starts to ask, but before she can finish the question, Lia shakes her head.

"She got stuck in the ride, and . . . it's gone now, just like she said it would be," Lia murmurs.

"So she's just . . . *gone*?" Neeli says, shaky and tear choked, her arms crossing over herself as she takes a step back from Lia. Her eyes flood, and every tear that darts down her cheeks is a twist to the knife in Lia's chest.

"I don't know. I don't . . ."

"Is *it* dead, at least?" Dallas growls.

Lia glances toward the lobby, where the door stands open, the lamp on the desk tossing gold light on the jukebox in the corner. Even as it stands in the dark, shaded by a plastic palm, it has lost the look of a crouching beast, the dead lights no longer gleaming beneath the haze of dust. Whatever energy Lia felt humming off it when she first saw it is gone now.

Eyes watching the jukebox, she murmurs, "I think so. . . ."

"Holy *fucking* shit, Magnolia!"

Lia's gaze jolts to Aunt Violet. She's standing outside the lobby with Theo, the both of them still in pajamas as they talk to a cop, Theo with her curlers wrapped in a silk scarf, little tufts of spice-cake hair poking out. As soon as Lia spots them, Aunt Violet tears into motion, charging across the courtyard toward her.

Lia winces when her aunt collides with her, wrapping her in a tight hug. The glass shards in her shoulder grind uncomfortably. A smoky cough squeezes out of her. "Aunt Vi," she wheezes in protest, but then her body's betraying her and she's clinging to her aunt.

Lia shakes, sobs finally spilling out of her, and once she starts, it feels like she might never stop crying. Aunt Violet clutches Lia to her chest, and Theo comes in behind her, smoothing Lia's hair with her hand.

"Lia, Lia, baby, what happened?" Aunt Violet asks.

"Was it that piece-of-shit shape-shifter?" Theo says, almost too casually.

"What?" Lia gasps out, wrenching her face away from Aunt Violet's chest to glare at Theo. "You *know* about that thing?"

"I told your aunt it was a bad idea to keep that jukebox," Theo says with a sigh.

There's a loud splash from the pool behind her, but Lia barely registers it. She's too busy gawking at Theo, who is crossing her arms and turning an *I told you so* glare on Aunt Violet. Lia opens her mouth, ready to demand Theo explain herself, but then she hears Neeli cry out.

"Oh my god, Sunny!"

Lia chokes on her questions, soot coating her tongue as her jaw clamps shut. Her fingers tighten on Aunt Violet's shirt, curling to fists as she listens to the thrashing in the water. Blinking through tear-blurred eyes, she turns, just in time to see a head of pink hair rising out of the aqua blue.

For one frozen, horrified moment, Lia questions if it's even really *her.* What if the *shape-shifter*—as Theo called it—took Sundae's form when he killed her, just like he took the doo-wop singer's and parts of all the other wishers who came before? How could this *really* be Sundae floating in the pool like a cherry in bubbling soda, still weird and funny and super hot and *alive,* not oozing black sludge or burned to ash or bodysnatched by a patchwork beast?

But then Sundae twists in the water, and Lia sees her face, and she *knows.* She knows by the way she smiles when the sunlight hits her cheeks and how her eyes seem even more blue than the water that surrounds her, lit from within by a glow that no one could possibly imitate, let alone some ancient monster who trades wishes for skin. It's *her,* she's *here,* she's *alive.*

"Sundae!" she yells, and then she's running for the edge of the pool.

THIRTY-SIX

NOW

At first, when Sundae breaks through the surface, it feels like she's reliving the nightmare of her last escape, when she emerged in a courtyard surrounded by cops and spent the next seven years grappling with memories of a monster no one would believe her about. Now, just like then, there are cops all around, with their loud feet and clanging belts, and the sun is a yellow yolk in the marbled sky. Fear pulses through her, but then she hears Neeli call out to her.

She swings her arms through the water, spinning in the pool. Her eyes lock on Neeli, and warmth blooms in her chest, spreading through her as a smile curves her lips. If she were trapped forever in a snow-globe re-creation of the worst moments of her life, Neeli wouldn't be here. Sundae would be all alone, waiting to be tugged back down into the depths, always afraid it was about to start again.

But it's over this time.

She survived.

Lia shouts her name, and then she's there, hanging over the edge of the pool. Reaching out her hand, her *beautiful* hand, for Sundae to take. Sundae's heart jolts explosively, even more proof that she is most definitely *alive*.

Sundae paddles closer and slips her hand into Lia's, the locking fit of their palms and the feeling of Lia's rings against her skin firing sparks through her veins as Lia drags her to the edge.

Sundae releases Lia's hand and reaches up, hooking an elbow behind Lia's neck. Lia loops one arm behind her back, and as Sundae draws her legs up, she slides the other beneath her knees to drag Sundae out of the water. Sundae knows it must hurt her aching shoulder, but she does it anyway. In her arms, Sundae feels like melted ice cream poured against Lia's chest.

"You made it," Lia says, soft with awe.

"Of course I did," Sundae says, her voice a hoarse gasp.

Lia laughs, brushing Sundae's wet hair back, thumb dragging against her cheek. "Is it too soon to ask you out on that date now?"

"Don't get the wrong idea," Sundae says. "Just 'cause I kissed you when I thought I was about to die."

"What idea was that *supposed* to give me?" Lia asks.

"That if I was about to die, the last thing I'd want to do is kiss you, doofus," Sundae says, rolling her eyes.

There's a little smirk on Sundae's mouth. Her eyes draw a path from Lia's molten stare to her lips, with their perfectly carved cupid's bow. *Kiss me, kiss me*, she thinks.

And then something grabs hold of her leg, and she's nearly torn from Lia's arms.

Sundae screams, looking down at the cobweb threads that spin around her leg and wrench, hard. But Lia's arms are locked around her, refusing to let go, and she pulls Sundae away from the edge of the pool and drags *it* out into the light.

And, like shiny gossamer held up to a candle flame, there's a puff of smoke, and then it's gone.

So much for being the saw.

Now it's nothing at all.

Sundae looks into Lia's eyes again. Her hand cups Lia's jaw, her nails curling behind Lia's ear. "Thanks for holding on to me," she murmurs.

Lia's head bows closer. "I did what I had to do so I could do *this* again."

She leans in, fitting her lips to Sundae's.

The sun climbs in the sky, warming the water drying on Sundae's skin. Sinking into the pink of her hair. Sundae takes a breath and holds it in her lungs and smiles against Lia's lips.

She's *here*, and alive, and just as greedy as ever.

ACKNOWLEDGMENTS

First, I want to thank Catherine Caswell, who had an incredible talent for appearing in the lives of people just when they needed her help the most. So much of this book is born from the spirit of 55 Atlantic, which was itself so imbued with your energy that I believe the sunlight seemed to glow a little more gold through the windows there. I think a little bit of my ghost will always haunt it, and I hope it meets you there.

Many wise authors warned me that the second book is the hardest you'll ever write, but I thought they were all exaggerating. They were not. So I have to thank my editor, Rachel Stark, who read *many* drafts of this book. Rachel, thank you for repeatedly rescuing me from creative quicksand, and for THE CRITTERS. In the end, this book feels just as much yours as it is mine, like some kind of shark-tree hybrid creature bearing both of our faces! How cute!

I also have to thank Kim and Mike Hill at Nocturne, for tolerating me the past two years while I repeatedly wrote at work, or asked for weeks off to write, or sat in a catatonic state behind the counter because I was so burned-out from writing. You supported me in every way I needed to keep chasing my dream. I love you guys, and I love the home you've made for all the silly creative weirdos of Salem and beyond.

This book also couldn't have happened without my husband, Michal Drozd. Thank you for listening to everything I tell you about publishing, though no human should be forced to bear witness to such horrors, and for being my partner in everything, including the occasional alien abduction.

And all my friends who are still my friends even though I vanish into a pocket dimension every now and then, I'm sorry for all the unanswered texts and canceled plans. Endless love to Kelly Kapow, Courtney Brooke, Karl Diener, Freddie Kölsch, Alex Russell, Gabe Hernandez, Luis Hernandez, Mandy Ness, and Dylan Marie-Dosch. One haglike shriek for all the authors who listened to me bitch, gave me guidance, or helped boost my books: Skyla Arndt, Clare Edge, Dhonielle Clayton, Jen Calonita, Angela Montoya, Alys Arden, Natalie C. Parker, Cat Scully, and Lauren Carter Reilly.

To my agent, Larissa Melo Pienkowski, thank you for the deal that brought us this book, for helping me survive the eldritch abomination that is publishing, and for handling my anxious emails with kindness and unending patience.

Thanks to Courtney Brooke for the absolutely bimbo-fied author photo, and to Mandy and John from the Salem Witch Board Museum for lending us your tiki bar! On that note, I could not be more grateful for this book's killer cover. Thank you to Romain Billaud for illustrating all that knife-sharp chrome and candy-red blood! Thank you to Zareen Johnson for your incredible vision for the design of this book. You found the perfect blend of bubblegum and gore!

Thank you to Candice Snow, who read alongside Rachel and offered a fresh perspective when we needed it most. Thank you to Sara Liebling, Guy Cunningham, and Jerry Gonzalez in managing editorial and production, and especially Meredith Jones, whose close read and insightful feedback helped untangle the final knots in this book. And gratitude to those who will help carry this book into the world: In publicity, Kelly Forsythe, Crystal McCoy, and especially Daniela Escobar. In sales, Monique Diman, Vicki Korlishin, LeBria Casher, and the Penguin Random House sales team. In marketing, Daneen Goodwin, Scott Myles, and Kelly Clair. Special thanks to Matt Schweitzer, marketing director, and to Maddie Hughes in school & library marketing (every author dreams of their book being in a library or classroom for kids who need to find themselves in a story)!

Finally, I have to thank *Weird NJ*, for making me this way. You gave me a Garden State that is an eerie, strange, magical place full of abandoned mansions and discarded bodies, where every road has a ghost story and the urban legends all have a mind of their own. I owe it all to you, and a little article about a dismembered body in a Newark parking lot.